What others say about Hank Quense's fiction:

<u>Tales From Gundarland:</u>
"I loved these stories. They are filled with humor and some satire and all different".
Penelope Rivers: 5 stars

". . . is a marvelous book, and I quickly felt at home there. You NEED your own copy for those days the sun won't shine and you need some artificial warmth around you."
Mari Sloan

". . . is one of those books that could easily become a cult phenomenon".
Sherry Ficklin for Mind Fog Reviews

<u>Zaftan Entrepreneurs</u>:
". . . is an extremely funny and highly entertaining science fantasy novel by Hank Quense. This book has everything: humor, adventure, magic, war, aliens, fantasy creatures and humans. Spiced up with a hilarious political satire and a healthy dose of romance, it's a delightful fast-paced and engaging read, that will leave you craving for more. I can promise you that it's nothing like you've ever read before!" Ji-Ye: Goodreads

"Sam is a wonderful character, funny and clever. Slash 9 is an equally compelling character (or computer) whose love and lust for Sam is hilarious. Equally funny is Dot 38. I really enjoyed the banter between all the characters. The fact that Zaftan

females have three wombs and can go berserk was humorous in itself. Hank Quense has a vivid, wild imagination and obviously I had a lot of fun with these characters. This is a good read for Science fiction fans!"
Tamera L. for Readers Favorite

Zaftan Miscreants:
"Reminded me a lot of the Hitchhikers trilogy, in that we have a similar whacky `evil' alien race. The humor is also a little like Adam's, rather satirical in a over-the top fashion.This is a work of fiction. Names, characters, places and incidents are the product of the author's imagination or are used fictitiously".
Wulfstan "wulfstan"

"The story line itself was not just one cut and dried road, it had a lot of little twists and side-stories and I don't want to give away too much but a lot of the goings-ons could really be paralleled to things happening here and now. Life, love, government, deception, lies, hope, despair, it's all in there wrapped up with some of the best satirical humor I've ever read. Just like a good spaghetti sauce IT'S IN THERE."
Angela Hupp

ZAFTAN ENTREPRENEURS

By Hank Quense

Book 1 of the Zaftan Trilogy

First Publication

ISBN 978-0985006327

Published in the United States of America
Published by Strange Worlds Publishing
http://strangeworldsonline.com

For my grandchildren: Anna, Tom, William, Jenni and
Sean

ACKNOWLEDGEMENTS:
A number of people helped me out with this novel, by
critiquing it and advising me. Others read it and offered
more advice. Included in this group are Jan Clark, Doc
Finch, Jim Cue, Tracy Byford, and Shea Yoven. Without
their help, this novel would still be in the reworking stage.
Lynn Coyle read the novel and pointed out hundreds of ty-
pos.

The cover artwork was done by Gary V. Tenuta. He can
be contacted through his website:
http://www.bookcoversandvideos.webs.com/

Zaftan Entrepreneurs 6

PART ONE:

CONTACT

PROLOGUE

The solar system flaunted unpretentiousness. It existed in a shabby neighborhood at the raggedy end of an unremarkable galaxy and had a common yellow dwarf at its core with five planets in orbit.

Beyond the solar system, space expanded outward with nothing to see except the pinpoints of light coming from distant suns, a portrait of tiny jewels set on a black velvet cloth. The solar system centered a huge sphere of nothingness.

For eons, the system's peaceful vista existed undisturbed, unblemished and unvisited except for an occasional meteor or comet.

The only source of color came from the second planet. It sparkled in the light from the sun: blues from the oceans, greens from vegetation, reds, blacks and browns from mountains, whites from the clouds. They all combined to form a pleasant scene, especially when viewed against the blackness of space.

Near the solar system's outer edge, a gravity ripple appeared and broke the smoothness of space. When the ripple grew into a wave it broke apart and a space ship appeared to shatter the serenity of the panorama.

The ship could charitably be described as ugly, but that failed to account for the unsymmetrical and repulsive sight. The paint had peeled away in many areas showing bare skin in various stages of decay. Parts of the ship appeared cylindrical, other parts spherical, suggesting the ship had been made by cannibalizing a number of other ships and melding various parts together without a master blueprint. Grafted onto the exterior skin, these additions had different sizes, shapes and metals. They resembled burn blisters on skin. Antennae sprouted everywhere. It was as if the designers couldn't make up their minds about when to stop modifying the ship. As a result, it looked like a traveling junk yard.

The ship rolled, pitched and yawed in an uncontrolled manner while it plowed through the distant reaches of the solar system. Gradually, the gyrations slowed and stopped, leaving the ship motionless in space, as if deciding how to further besmirch the prettiness of the scene.

A legend on the side of the ship, in large blood-red letters, read *Black Carrion Flower*. Additional smaller lettering read, *Furshtanker Inc, Zaftan 31B*.

Inside the ship, Captain Yunta groaned on her reclining couch in the small flight deck. Another pair of couches, two control consoles and view screens filled the front. Electronic gear took up the left side and read-out devices were everywhere, even hanging from the ceiling. The flight engineer and the navigational shaman sat at the front consoles while the captain's couch occupied the space behind them and to the right. Like all zaftans, these three were seven feet tall and weighed over four hundred pounds. Their grayish-black, rubber-like skin oozed green slime. On the top of the body, over a cruel beak a pair of eye stalks protruded and held black eyeballs with red irises. Eight tentacles served as arms or legs. None of the zaftans wore clothes because the slime made most cloth material smolder and catch fire. The surfaces of their couches were treated with fireproofing chemicals to prevent a shipboard catastrophe.

Rank medallions hung from their necks; steel for the engineer, bronze for the shaman and gold for the captain. The engineer also wore earphones that covered the holes zaftans used as audio receptors.

Yunta, like all zaftan females, had three wombs and right now she suffered from triple menstruation. Chemicals and hormones waged war in her bloodstream producing three headaches. The first one settled in the area behind her eye stalks, the second near her right audio receptor and the third at the base of her head where it joined the main body.

Once the ship became motionless, Yunta looked at the forward view screen. Among other objects, it showed a small planet with definite bluish tint. Yunta tried to recall if she had ever seen another planet with that unusual color. She couldn't. "Drek," she said addressing the navigational shaman. "Where are we?"

"Drek is still in his coma, Captain," the engineer replied.

"Nonsense. If he was in a navigational coma, he would not be snoring. Wake him up."

The engineer reached over with a tentacle and shook the shaman. The navigator's eye stalks bobbed as he snorted and pushed himself up slightly.

"Where are we, Drek?" Yunta asked again.

Drek looked at a monitor on the console in front of him. After a brief interval, he replied, "I have no idea."

"How can you not know where we are?" Yunta snapped. She now regretted hiring a second-rate shaman to shave a bit off the ship's expense account and thus increase the profit margins.

"My farsight spotted an unknown worm hole and I drove the ship into it. Part of our mission is to explore new galactic areas, is it not?" Zaftan navigators put themselves into a shamanistic coma and let their minds roam far away from the ship seeking the safest course while piloting the ship with mental commands.

Drek's voice had an edge that Yunta found offensive. On the other hand, she found everything offensive these days. "Well, find some known stars and calculate our position."

"Captain," the engineer said, "this planet looks interesting."

"In what way?" Yunta rotated her eye stalks from the shaman to the back of the engineer's torso.

"It appears to have a varied geographical makeup. Using the long range scanner, I can make out mountains, rivers, marshes and forests. This could be a good place to explore."

"Drek. Put us into a stable orbit so we can get a better analysis of the surface." She called up a mental picture of the voyage's abysmal profit and loss chart. If this planet didn't yield the minerals they sought, the voyage was doomed to show a loss that meant the end of her career aspirations. She thought of herself as a corporate tree struggling in a forest of sap-sucking corporate bureaucrats. Profits would fertilize her tree allowing it to grow bigger and stronger. Losses would lead to infestation of bugs and diseases. For the first time in her career, Yunta faced failure. She would be hard pressed to eradicate a negative performance assessment from this voyage.

She massaged the slime by her aching audio receptor. It didn't lessen the pain. Again, she looked at the planet in the forward view screen. Perhaps her luck was about to change. She and the ship were certainly overdue for a break.

CHAPTER ONE

On the planet's surface, MacDrakin Gemfinder knelt in mine shaft number one. The tunnel was cramped even for a dwarf. On aching knees, he swung a small pickax one more time, sending a handful of dirt and rock tumbling to the ground. The heat in the tunnel was almost unbearable and sweat poured down his face in rivulets. He wore only leather breeches and a thick layer of dirt. MacDrakin dropped the ax, picked up a shovel and loaded the material into two leather sacks. In a muscle-straining crouch, he hauled them to the surface. He dropped the sacks and stretched to loosen up his back and shoulders. He lifted his arms to allow the slight breeze and the midday summer sun to play over his compact, muscular body. It felt wonderful to be out of the gloomy mine shaft and in the sunlight.

Once his muscles relaxed, he hefted the sacks and carried them to the sluice on the side of the mountain. He poured the sacks into a trough constructed out of wood and stiff netting and then opened a sluice gate. Water from an underground spring cascaded over the dirt and washed it through the netting. When only rocks and pebbles remained, MacDrakin shut off the water. He picked through the debris and tossed most over the side of the mountain leaving a dozen stones behind. He took each remaining one and rubbed it between his fingers. All but two he threw away. The last two showed a bit of green under a patina of stubborn dirt. After some more cleaning, he held two fine emeralds in his palm. Not a bad haul for a half-day's work.

He carried the gems to the small hut he called home. Along the way, he passed mine shafts two and three. Two wasn't as deep as number one, but had already disgorged a few emeralds. Number three wasn't deep at all and showed no promise of gems. All he had found so far in the shaft was a thick seam of coal.

His land, in the family for years, sat on a level patch and covered an acre or so of rocky ground in front of the face of the mountain that soared a thousand feet above MacDrakin's head. In the opposite direction, a path led to the base of the mountain five hundred feet below.

The hut, ten foot by ten foot, was furnished in typical bachelor fashion. Two chairs huddled under a wobbly table and an unmade cot lay opposite the fireplace used for cooking and heating. Clothes hung from hooks on one wall. A battle ax hung over the fireplace and several storage chests were piled haphazardly in a corner. Shelves held a few food items including a bag of coffee and an almost empty sack of flour. A single window, without shades or curtains, overlooked the road leading down the mountain. The view from the window showed smoke from cooking fires rising into the sky. The smoke came from Skensfirth, the closest town, three miles away.

MacDrakin pulled back a small rug to expose a trap door and removed a metal strongbox. He pawed through the loose dirt at the bottom of the hole and uncovered a leather pouch. He took it to the table and spilled the contents. The dozens of emeralds that rolled around the table made him smile. It would soon be time to take a trip to the capital, Dun Hythe, to sell the gems. This time, he would take the train from Ashton. On a newly opened extension of the main line, it reached Dun Hythe in a day. On his last trip to the capital, his pony took a week each way.

Meanwhile, he was out of supplies as well as cash. He selected a small and inferior green stone and set it aside. He reburied the pouch and covered it with the strongbox. To satisfy any thieves, the box contained four badly flawed emeralds.

After scribbling a list of needed supplies on a scrap of paper, he took a towel and a bar of soap and walked back to the sluice. In a few minutes he had rerouted the spring from the sluice to an overhead spray he used as a shower.

Back in the hut, he sat at the table and trimmed his beard using a hand mirror and a knife, then worked it into the traditional three braids beloved by dwarfdom. Each braid ended in a bit of ribbon. He dressed in a clean wool kilt, a leather vest and ankle-high boots. The kilt and beard braid ribbons displayed his clan colors: red, green and black.

He paused for a moment to gaze in reverence at the gleaming battle ax over the fireplace. It was ancient and originally belonged to the legendary dwarf hero, Drakin, who had founded the clan and after whom he was named. Family tradition called for the first-born son in each generation to carry the hero's name. He was the thirteenth MacDrakin in a line that went back hundreds of years. Another tradition concerned the coming of age of a new MacDrakin; he was given the hero's weapon by the older MacDrakin. So far, none of his relatives had spawned a new MacDrakin so the ax would remain his for many years.

He had inherited the land and the mines from his father and he carried on the gem mining tradition that gave the family the name 'Gemfinder.' He found mining more than a bit boring, but he had nothing else to do. What he yearned to do was to take the battle ax and go on an adventure. He sighed. The days of adventuring were long gone, a thing of the past.

He took down the ax, strapped it into a harness and settled the harness on his back. The weapon's handle extended over his shoulder where he could readily grab it. Not that he expected to use the ax, not on the ride to Skensfirth. The weapon was simply too valuable to leave in the hut unattended. After he saddled and mounted his pony, he smiled in anticipation. He hadn't gone to town in ten days. Living on the side of a mountain was lonely and he looked forward to companionship, a few ales and the latest gossip.

# # #

Leslie Higginbottom walked down the main street in Skensfirth. It was dirt and called High Street even though it was no higher than the other dirt streets in the town. She had a short sword on her left hip and a baton on her right. The weapons were badges of office; she was the town's entire constabulary staff. She wore a blue denim shirt, tan wool breeches and a blue, hard-billed constabulary cap. The proudest day in her life was the one when she took over as constable in Skensfirth. That was a month ago, two weeks after the previous constable, her father, died suddenly. She had worked the last three years in Ashton, the regional center, as assistant constable and had been promoted to replace her father.

She stared to the south with a worried look on her face. The Yukland border was only ten miles away and she feared that someday she would be called on to protect the town from yuk marauders. To prepare for that event, she planned to recruit some help. Her original idea to use the Skensfirth militia hadn't worked out. The militia was next to useless; a group of out-of-shape, old fogies who spent their drill-time drinking ale and swapping lies. She needed a few good fighters to stand in a battle line with her.

The town's business district ran the length of High Street and contained shops, a church, the town hall and a combination boarding house and tavern. At the north end of High Street, she walked around the market square where the farmers from the surrounding area came to sell their fresh produce. She smiled and joked with the folks in the square.

An hour later, she saw MacDrakin ride into town and decided to talk with him. Since he wasn't in town very often, they had exchanged only a few words since she had taken over the constabulary. This could be an opportunity to change that. Getting him to help defend the town would be an excellent way to start on her plan. What with the gleaming battle ax strapped to his back, he'd scare away yuks without doing anything other than waving it over his head. MacDrakin was handsome in a rugged, dwarfish way. His three-foot tall frame carried a great deal of muscle and his dark brown eyes, hair and beard curls exuded a certain sexiness. Sitting astride his pony, he radiated confidence unlike the other dwarfs in town. He owned land with gem mines, was rich and descended from a legendary hero. Everything considered, MacDrakin was the most impressive dwarf in the region. He was also unmarried, like herself.

MacDrakin pulled up his pony and greeted her with a smile and a nod. "Constable. How are you?"

"I'm fine." She returned the smile and patted the pony on the neck. "It's nice to see you in town again. How are things on the mountain?"

"Lonely."

Higginbottom's attention perked up at the word, 'lonely,' and her heart skipped a beat. "Listen. I want to ask you something. You know yuks have raided Skensfirth in the past. I'm sure they'll do it again someday. Can I count on you to help defend the town if that happens?"

MacDrakin pulled a face and didn't answer for a few seconds while he pondered the question. Finally, he asked, "You want me to join the militia?"

"No." Higginbottom shook her head causing her beard braids to bounce around. "The militia is an old-boys club and pretty useless. Will you stand with me to defend the town? I want to recruit a few other doughty warriors besides yourself just in case of a raid."

"Are the yuks getting feisty?" MacDrakin scratched his chin, puzzled by the request. "Is that why you're asking?"

"No. I haven't heard of any yuks crossing the border and everyone tells me not to worry. But I don't want to wait until Skensfirth is in trouble before I do something. It's my job to protect the town and that's what I intend to do."

"I don't know about any yuk troubles," MacDrakin said. "They've minded their manners recently. If you go looking for trouble, you'll end up finding trouble."

"Hogswaddle!" Higginbottom frowned at MacDrakin and spun on her heel. "Thanks for your time," she called over her shoulder as she stomped off.

He wondered why the constable seemed so touchy. As for Higginbottom's request, he didn't fancy coming into town to attend drills and maneuvers. He shrugged and rode to the general store.

CHAPTER TWO

Outside the store, MacDrakin dodged the open barrels of cheese, nails and stacks of cookware to get into the store where more goods covered every horizontal surface or hung in nets suspended from the ceiling.

"MacDrakin! It's good to see you again," Geno Aterrano said. The elfin shopkeeper was tall and angular with deep grooves in his cheeks like rain-gouged gullies.

"Hello, Geno. I need supplies, but I'm out of cash." MacDrakin smiled. "Again! Are you up for a bit of bartering?"

"I'm always open to trading for your emeralds." Geno waved a hand. "Come over to the counter and we'll do business."

MacDrakin followed Geno to the counter in the rear of the store. He took a list from his vest pocket and handed it to Geno. The shopkeeper slanted it towards a window to read it, but little light came through the dusty glass. Geno muttered a few words and a flame burst from his fingertip. MacDrakin grinned. Every elf he knew had a bit of magic to show off with.

"Looks like the usual supplies," Geno said, extinguishing the flame. "I believe I have everything on this list. Hmm, you want fodder for your pony. That's bulky so I expect you'll want this sent up the mountain. My delivery boy can take care of it this afternoon. I'll tell him to drop the supplies outside your house if you're not around." He gave MacDrakin an expectant look.

MacDrakin reached into the vest pocket again and took out the emerald. He handed it to Geno who screwed a loupe into his right eye. He held the gem in his fingers and turned it to examine it from several angles. After a few minutes, he took the loupe out of his eye and said, "A fine gem. I'll take it. I figure it's worth much more than the supplies on this list. Let me get your stuff and figure out what they cost. Then I can calculate how much money I owe you."

MacDrakin nodded. If he took the gem to Dun Hythe, he would get much more than what Geno offered, but he needed the supplies now, not in a few weeks. Besides, Geno was honest and would give him the best offer he was likely to get outside of Dun Hythe.

MacDrakin noticed a female dwarf batting her eyes at him. She had a disheveled, uncurled beard, cheap frock dress which was more than a bit ragged and no shoes. She worked for Geno cleaning the store and loading shelves. Like all the dwarf females in town, she came from humble stock and could barely read and write. When it came time to marry, he would have to go to another town to find a suitable mate because none of the females in Skensfirth were acceptable to him.

"Can I get ya a cup of water, Mister MacDrakin?" she asked.

"No, thank you."

"Oh, by the way," Geno said. "I just got a shipment of prime pipeweed. You want some?"

"All right. I'll take a pound." Pipeweed was a mild hallucinogenic narcotic and he enjoyed smoking a pipe of it at the end of the day. It soothed his muscles, often sore after a shift in the tunnels.

"How about a two pound brick of cheese? It's packed in wax to last a long time."

Drakin nodded.

Geno dropped a few items and the cheese on the counter.

MacDrakin noticed the Army insignia stamped into the wax. Army surplus, he thought.

"I saw you talking to the constable," Geno said. "Doing a fine job, I think. Just like the father."

"That's true." MacDrakin decided to talk some more to Higginbottom about the yuk problem. Maybe he was too abrupt with the constable. He needed a break from mucking about in a hole in the ground. Maybe the two of them could go scouting. A ride in fresh air would do him good.

MacDrakin suddenly realized Geno had said something to him. "Sorry. What?"

"Daydreaming, you were, MacDrakin. Wondering what to do with all your gems?

MacDrakin half-smiled.

Geno handed him a scrap of paper with numbers on it. "I have everything on the list and I've added up the prices. According to my calculations, I owe you twenty silver pennies. Is that acceptable?"

"That's fine." MacDrakin scooped up the coins as Geno counted them out and dropped them into his purse.

"Listen," Geno said,"if you're ever caught short of cash and don't want to barter a gem, my cousin can get you a loan. He offers good interest rates."

"Thanks, I'll keep that in mind." He didn't want to explore Geno's offer. Elves seemed to have a monopoly on under-the-counter loans; if folks couldn't get a bank loan, they went to the elves. Every elf clan had a few loan-sharks.

He waved goodbye to Geno and left the shop. Outside, he looked around to see if Higginbottom was still about.

# # #

Albert Webley, the President of The People's Federal Republican Government of Gundarland, sat behind a huge desk in his office in Dun Hythe. Since he liked things neat, orderly and simple, the only item on the desk was his appointment calendar. The huge room appeared unfurnished with only Webley's desk and chair, three visitors' chairs, a few potted plants and a large couch. On the wall opposite the desk, an antique clock ticked away. Always set ten minutes fast, it allowed Webley to end meetings a bit sooner than scheduled. A detailed map of Gundarland filled another wall.

As if expecting to pose for a portrait, Webley always dressed formally in a cutaway suit with identically colored cummerbund and ascot. Today's color was lilac.

Except for a small adjacent room occupied by secretaries, the office occupied the entire fifth floor of the presidential palace and the windows on all four sides gave splendid views of Gundarland's capital city. Unfortunately, most of the views showed the city in the embrace of a low-hanging cloud of smog generated by the peat-fired furnaces in the factories and the cooking fires in homes.

The door opened and Francesco Rodrigs entered. Webley smiled at his chief-of-staff, an elf. Webley loved smiling. He did it often because it was one of the two things he did well. His other talent was getting elected to public office. So far he had been elected by landslides to the offices of Deputy Mayor of Dun Hythe, Mayor, Senator and lastly

President. And that didn't count getting elected class president in every year of his school days. In his first campaign in kindergarten, he ran on a platform demanding longer nap periods. After that, naps became his lifelong interest.

Webley gestured to a chair in front of the desk and Rodrigs sat down. He wore his usual outfit: a black linen suit, a white shirt with a stiff collar. Today, he added a pea-green bow tie. He carried a notebook and a sheaf of loose papers.

"Good morning, Mr. President." Rodrigs was tall, lean and green-haired.

Webley, a human, prided himself on the diversity of his staff and cabinet. "Hello, Frankie. I hope you don't have unpleasant news for me."

"Just the usual stuff. The *Gundarland Times* published an editorial today demanding you do something about the city's pollution."

"As if I can. To do what the paper wants, I'll have to shut down factories and that'll throw vast numbers of workers onto the unemployment lines. And those workers vote, you know."

"The *Dun Hythe News* demanded that you abdicate."

"Hah!"

"Perhaps, you should call a cabinet meeting to address the pollution problem," Rodrigs said. "Surely, the cabinet members can produce some ideas."

"I don't like cabinet meetings." Webley grimaced, something he hated to do. "They all expect me to make decisions. Why can't those people understand? I put them into office so they would make the decisions, not me."

Webley frowned at the sound of a knock on the office door. "Who's that? It's almost time for my nap."

"That'd be Boudreau. I asked him to stop by for a few minutes. We have an issue to discuss with you." Rodrigs walked to the door and opened it.

"Oh, dear. It's a problem, isn't it?"

Benoit Boudreau, the half-pint Treasury Secretary waved a hand at the President and took a chair facing his desk. He wore the traditional half-pint garb consisting of tan linen breeches and a white pullover tunic. Like all half-pints, his bare feet didn't reach the floor when he sat on a normal-sized chair. Boudreau swung them back and forth. His long toe hair had been recently curled.

"Well, Boudreau." Webley gave him a campaign-type smile. "Making any money?" Webley chuckled at his own joke.

"We need to talk about Crumlish and Sfiore," Rodrigs said, referring to the Defense Minister and the Interior Secretary. "Their infighting is getting worse and it harms your administration and Gundarland."

"They're megalomaniacs," Boudreau said. "Rodrigs and I agree that you should sack them."

"If I sack Crumlish and Sfiore, then I'll just have to find replacements, won't I?"

Rodrigs sighed. So far, after three years in office, Webley had yet to make his first official decision. Even cabinet appointments weren't the result of a presidential decision. Rather than face up to a number of selections, he procrastinated on the cabinet positions and eventually filled them with the lame ducks from the previous administration. The Treasury position, empty when his presidency began, remained so until Rodrigs chose Boudreau after Webley ordered him to stop nagging about the appointment and take care of it himself. Rodrigs never expected to become the chief decision maker in Gundarland when he graduated from Wizardry and Liberal Arts College and went to work on one of Webley's early election campaigns.

"Nevertheless," Rodrigs pressed the point one more time. "I think it's time to call a cabinet meeting. You haven't held one in two months."

Boudreau nodded his head.

"Why so soon?" Webley turned pensive and tapped a manicured finger on the desk top. He looked at his appointment calendar and then at the wall clock. "I see it's almost time for my afternoon nap. I'll think about the cabinet meeting while I rest."

Rodrigs sighed again. He and Boudreau stood up to leave.

# # #

Higginbottom leaned against the wall outside the town hall. The first floor of the two-story wood building contained her office, a pair of jail cells, a telegraph office, the mayor's office and desks for the town clerks. The mayor had living quarters on the second floor.

As a youngster, she mused, she had often joined her father when he patrolled the town. On those outings, she wore a miniature constable's cap and carried a small wooden sword.

Higginbottom's mother was a dwarf and her father a human. As a result of her mixed parentage, she was, at almost four feet, taller than the average dwarf. Yet, she was also much leaner and her beard was skimpier than the beards of full-blooded female dwarfs.

Skensfirth was a lower-middle-class town with a mixed population of three thousand souls counting the farmers in the fields surrounding the town. The shop-owners were all elves, the farmers and politicians were half-pints and the town dwarfs were mostly day laborers, working in the fields and on the odd construction job. Skensfirth had few human inhabitants.

She saw MacDrakin leave the general store and pulled a face. She could picture herself as an old-maid. All the intelligent young male dwarfs left Skensfirth as early as they could rather then stay and spend their lives in drudgery. The ones who didn't leave were the ones without any ambition or spunk. They worked for a pittance at hard labor and died at a young age, either worn out by the work or killed in a drunken accident. She couldn't picture herself in that sort of marriage because her children would be doomed to the same fate.

She decided to walk down and talk to MacDrakin again about the yuks. Maybe she could get him to change his mind about helping out. Before she could do that, the mayor, Luc Jehan, came out of the building. He wore a green sash, his badge of office, over his white tunic. Like all half-pints, he didn't wear boots so he could display his hairy feet, a come-on to female half-pints for some strange reason. Half-pints were as tall as dwarfs but only half as wide. Unlike dwarfs, half-pints didn't grow beards. Their slender builds and mild-mannered features belied their strength, both mental and physical.

She acknowledge him with a nod.

"Hrmph." Luc cleared his throat. "Did I show you the latest addition to my collection?" He held out a hand with a small reddish pebble in it. "I found it on the banks of the river."

Higginbottom stared at the stone. "It's very pretty. A fine specimen." She never understood why half-pints were such compulsive collectors. Every one of them collected something, often trivial items.

"Constable?" Luc jerked a thumb over his shoulder. "What are you doing about the two dwarfs in the jail cells? They're snoring so loud my clerks can't work."

"They're just sleeping off a binge. They'll wake up in a little while and I'll release them. I only locked them up so they wouldn't hurt themselves."

"Hrrmph. I think I'll pass a law making public drunkenness a crime."

"You can pass a law, but it won't do any good. You can't legislate folk's behavior. If you want to cut down on drunkenness get some better jobs for the dwarfs in this town."

"If we had less public drunkenness in town, I'd be able to bring in better jobs."

Higginbottom shook her head. It was a debate the two of them often had in the last month.

Luc scowled as he stared at the general store. "That damned elf had another midnight delivery last night. Woke me up. You should do something about those deliveries instead of chasing drunks."

"Why? It's not against any law to have night deliveries."

"You know elves always have a finger in illegal things. Those wagons that come here after dark must be filled with stolen goods otherwise the wagon would show up during the day. And dealing in stolen goods is a crime."

"You don't know they're stolen and not all elves are crooks."

The mayor stomped back inside, slamming the door. "Constable?"

She turned around to see MacDrakin leading his pony. "Yes?"

"I've been thinking about what you said before."

"And?" She raised an eyebrow.

"Since you're concerned about yuks, why don't you and me ride close to the border tomorrow? Just to check that everything is quiet. Besides, I know the tribal chieftain over there. We served in the military together and we see each other a few times a year. If we run across him, I can ask about any yuk raiders."

"That's a splendid idea." Higginbottom smiled at MacDrakin. "Don't you have to work in your mines?"

"I need a break from digging in the tunnels," he replied. "I'll meet you here early in the morning? Maybe we can get in some hunting."

"Sure. I'll see you in the morning." She ran inside. It wouldn't do to let MacDrakin see how excited and pleased she was with his offer.

# # #

While the *Black Carrion Flower* slid into orbit to analyze the surface of the planet, Yunta retired to her cabin. She fell onto her cot and lay there. Her small compartment contained the cot, a table, a closet, a computer console and a large wall-mounted monitor.

The medicine she had taken lessened the headaches, but her periods still played havoc with her body. She regretted feeling so lousy just when her management and entrepreneurial skills would be required now that a potentially profitable site had been found. Her mission was to find and mine deposits of minerals such as monazite, bastnasite and gadolinite. From these minerals, rare elements such as Cerium, Thulium and Ytterbium could be extracted. The *Furshtanker Corporation* was the biggest zaftan provider of these rare elements. After returning to Zaftan 31B, the minerals would be processed to remove the rare elements which were then auctioned off to manufacturers. If the voyage's profitability target was met, the crew earned a bonus. As the leader of the voyage, she would get credit for a successful mission and that could lead to a promotion. Over the course of her career, her corporate tree had grown from a seedling to a sturdy, medium-sized tree. With one more profitable voyage, she would be in line to become a fleet admiral, a necessary step in her path to CEO. No CEO of the *Furshtanker Corporation* had ever been appointed who wasn't a former fleet admiral.

A profitless voyage would damage her chances for promotion, and that would derail her fast track to the top of *Furshtanker*. Like all ambitious zaftans, she had no compunction to show mercy to her crew when profits were concerned. If this planet gave any indication that it held the valuable minerals she sought, she would drive the crew ruthlessly to finding the deposits and transfer them back to the ship in as short a time as possible.

The wall monitor beeped. "Yes?"

The engineer's image appeared. "This planet looks much more promising than we hoped. Besides the terrain types we have found useful on past missions, we can breathe the atmosphere."

Yunta opened her mouth and clicked her teeth. "Good."

The engineer replied by also clicking his teeth before continuing, "But there is liquid water on the land surfaces."

"Is this good or bad news?"

"I do not know. We never ran a mining operation on a surface with liquid water. Also, the planet is inhabited. The natives appear to have reached the early stages of a technological civilization."

Yunta bunched two tentacles at the news. Zaftans believed they had a moral right to crush inferior races and enslave them. Over the eons, zaftans had never found a race they didn't consider inferior. They had developed two methods of overwhelming these inferior beings. One was the military approach and the second used a corporate strategy. In the second, the central government assigned a native race to a corporation for exploitation. The corporation sold the natives sophisticated devices at outrageous prices, prices so inflated that the natives could never pay without taking out loans -- from the corporation -- at exorbitant interest rates. While that process went on, other programs plundered their mineral, cultural and artistic wealth. Within fifteen years, the corporations owned everything of value, and the natives swam in debt owed to the corporation. Anyone who didn't obey corporate orders would have that debt called in. Everyone knew zaftan debtor prisons had few survivors.

With the military option, they simply invaded the planet and destroyed the native's ability to resist. In combat, zaftans had a huge advantage; they were extremely hard to kill because of their multiple brains. Besides the usual one in the top of their torso, every major muscle group had its own processor. All of these brains were linked, but could operate independently. To kill a zaftan, all eight brains had to be destroyed. If one was left intact, it could activate a chemical and hormonal reaction that would grow replacement processors and new body parts.

Usually *Furshtanker's* mining operations took place on uninhabited planets and barren asteroids or moons. An unknown native population complicated matters. To her knowledge, no *Furshtanker* ship had ever attempted to mine a planet inhabited by natives who weren't primitives. A native population that had achieved technological advances made the situation trickier; they would have a level of sophistication that would make them harder to dupe. She would need all her entrepreneurial skills to turn this mission into a success. The planet and the natives might be worthy of a corporate takeover later on and if so, their discovery would be credited to her. "Tell Mivex about the water. Perhaps it will mean something to him. How long do we have before we must start the return voyage?"

The engineer played with a console. After a few seconds, he replied, "We have fifteen rotations of this planet before our fuel and food supplies will be half consumed." He put a map of the planet's surface on the screen. "The planet consists of one large land mass and a number of small ones. The large one is the best place to start because it has many of the types of terrain we always look for."

"All right. Do a quick survey to identify the best location to start explorations."

Five minutes later, the monitor beeped again. Shtap, her second-in-command filled the screen. He also served as the ship's negotiator and emissary to other races.

"What is it, Shtap?"

"I just learned the planet has native populations. Do you intend to negotiate with them before we begin exploring?"

"What do you recommend?" Shtap was the only officer she had confidence in.

"I think we should attempt to negotiate a mining treaty with the natives. That will also allow us to make a threat assessment. We can find out the technological capabilities of their weapons."

"That is good advice, Shtap."

"We will need to train the language computer to speak the native tongue before I can open negotiations."

"All right, but you must learn the language quickly. Will two natives be enough?"

"Two will be fine. One will come from what appears to be the capital and the other from a likely mining site."

"Tell Drek to pick up the natives. Anything else?"

"We need a strategy to get the natives to agree to our explorations and mining activities. I suggest we pretend to be experts on pollution control because all the urban areas show signs of heavy pollution. In return for mining concessions, we will offer to teach them how to control pollution. Long before we finish studying the pollution sources, the ship will be loaded with minerals. We can give the natives whatever it is we found out by then."

"An excellent plan." Yunta laughed and clicked her teeth. "Do it." She thought of her corporate tree. A regiment of bugs dropped dead and fell off it. "But never mind doing any pollution studies."

The screen shut off.

She sat on her cot deep in thought. Things definitely looked brighter, but much had to be done quickly. The *Black Carrion Flower* didn't have much time to orbit the planet.

CHAPTER THREE

Higginbottom hummed a ditty while she packed a basket with a green salad and fried chicken she had cooked last night. The only sounds besides her humming came from an occasional bird song and from the Skensfirth River gurgling a hundred feet away. Wide and sluggish, the river had a number of islands, both large and small, in the middle. Many could be reached by wading and offered great places to hold a picnic or to go fishing.

While she put in the cutlery, she looked out the window of the small house she had grown up in. The early morning promised a glorious summer day. She put on her constabulary cap, adjusted it to a jaunty angle, strapped on a belt with her sword and her baton, picked up the basket and left the house. High Street was a five minute walk up a slight rise.

She had looked forward to the scouting expedition with MacDrakin ever since he proposed it yesterday. He was so different from the other dwarfs in town. The locals were only interested in her because she had a job and earned fifty silver pennies a year. Most of them earned a few copper pennies a day working as farm laborers or odd construction jobs. Most of what they earned they immediately spent on ale.

MacDarkin, on the other hand, had property, an education, military experience and was descended from the most famous dwarf hero in history. And if that wasn't enough, he was pleasant, good-looking and well-mannered. She pegged his age as a few years older than her thirty-five years, the prime of life for a dwarf. So far, she'd never had a serious male friend. A few casual acquaintances was all. It was hard to get serious with a male in Skensfirth when you knew he wouldn't be in town very long or would end up with a menial job and a drinking problem.

She had known MacDrakin's father, MacFergus, a crusty old dwarf who became friendly with her own father. MacFergus had come to dinner several times and always acted properly towards her. The dwarf had died the month after she took up her position in Ashton. From what she had heard, by the time MacDrakin resigned from the military and reached his land, a dozen squatters worked the gem mines. MacDrakin drove them off and settled in.

Halfway up the rise, she paused because a strange sensation coursed over her body. A tingling started at her head and traveled down to her feet. A bright, golden light enveloped her. She gasped for air. Her feet stopped tingling. She glanced down. They were dissolving! She clutched the basket to her chest as panic fought the tingling for control of her mind. Her calves dissolved next. Whatever had gotten hold of her was working its way up her body. She tried to scream for help but couldn't get enough air to let out more than a modest squeal. Her peripheral vision narrowed, as if she looked through a tube. Dizziness overwhelmed her and everything went black.

# # #

Benoit Boudreau ignored the budget problem sitting on his desk. Instead, the half-pint treasurer examined a new scroll. He had bought it yesterday from a dealer, but hadn't looked closely at it until now. It contained a history of the reign of King Alsam the Ghastly, a petty ruler in southern Gundarland three centuries ago. Boudreau collected history scrolls and books and studied them zealously. The objective of these studies was to gain a better perspective on what made governments tick.

The scroll was in poor condition and he hesitated to open it until he had the time to give to the delicate work of un-rolling it.

His office, in the vaults of a former bank, held his history collection. The rarest and most delicate scrolls and books were stored in glass cases while others lay on every horizontal surface available. He put the new one on a shelf temporarily, sat at his desk and sighed. Another day of dealing with never-ending demands for money. Cash in Gundarland was like water in a desert; there was never enough of it to satisfy everyone's thirst.

Boudreau chewed on a nib of a pen while analyzing a column of figures. A metallic clunk interrupted him, a knock on the vault door. "Come in."

With a sound like fingernails on a chalkboard, the heavy vault door slowly creaked open. A clerk, puffing from the exertion of pushing open the door, stood outside the office waving two envelopes. "Marked most urgent," the clerk gasped, "and addressed to you."

"Bring them here." Boudreau waved a hand inviting the clerk to step over the lip of the vault door.

The clerk delivered the letters and Boudreau grinned as he saw they were from the Minister of Defense and the Secretary of Interior. Boudreau never got messages from either one that didn't make his day more interesting. He opened the one from Crumlish and read it. The silly dwarf demanded that Interior transfer to his ministry all the border police along with their funding. According to Crumlish, this move simplified the country's overall command structure.

Sfiore's message insisted that Defense fork over a half-million silver pennies so that she could increase the defensive capabilities of the local constabularies through more training and by equipping them with heavier batons.

Boudreau looked at the clerk who stood awaiting replies. "Were these messages logged in?"

"Well, since they were marked urgent, no one wanted to be accused of slowing down their delivery, so no, they weren't logged in. I'll do that after I leave your office."

Boudreau held one letter by a corner and mumbled a spell. The document burst into flames and turned into a small pile of ashes on the desktop. He did the same with the second message. "No need to log anything in since we never received either message. No doubt they were lost somehow."

The clerk, clearly troubled by the disappearance of two official messages, knuckled his head and left.

Boudreau chuckled to himself. Nothing was as much fun as screwing up the plans of his idiotic and self-serving colleagues.

# # #

When she recovered, Higginbottom found herself in a windowless room with metal walls. One wall bulged outward and another one had the largest door she had ever seen. The room smelled like dead fish had been stored in it and the air was cold. She put down the basket and rubbed her arms to warm them up. A bright column of light appeared in a corner. To her amazement, the dazzling air coalesced into a figure. A female half-pint stood in the room, blinking and gasping. While the two of them recovered their wits, a sound from the door startled them. A small window opened near the top and Higginbottom knew someone, or something, inspected them.

She got a grip on her emotions, took a few deep breaths and said, "Hi. My name is Leslie Higginbottom. I'm the constable in Skensfirth. Do you know what happened to us?"

The half-pint continued to examine the room while identifying herself. "Alix Cyr." She sounded angry. "I'm from Dun Hythe." Alix had a dumpy figure with brown hair and eyes. She wore long pants and a sweater. Her bare feet had elegantly curled toe hairs. "I was food shopping," Alix continued. "Where are we? If you're a constable," she pointed to Higginbottom's sword and baton, "you should know."

"I wish I did, but I know as much or as little as you do."

"Whoever did this won't get away with it." Alix stood with her fists on her ample hips. "When I get back to Dun Hythe, I'll tell everyone what happened to me. Including the police. What's in the basket?"

"Lunch." Higginbottom sniffed and fought to hold back tears. "I was going on picnic with a male. I wonder if he'll get mad when I don't show up."

"If he gets mad, tell him to take a hike," Alix said. "He ain't worth it in that case. Let's eat. I didn't finish shopping." Alix scratched her head. "Whoever did this don't know who they're dealing with. I'm the Treasurer of the Furniture Workers of Dun Hythe Labor Movement. I have a lot of clout in Dun Hythe."

Higginbottom gave Alix a chicken leg. Between bites, the half-pint said, "I guess you ain't married since you were going courting. I'm married. I have two kids. A male who's seven and a female who's nine." She paused to swallow. "I don't know who'll take care of them while I'm here. My husband is pretty useless. All he ever does is sit in cafes and guzzle ale while telling everyone how unfair life is because he wasn't born rich." Alix sighed. "He is a handsome rogue though."

"Do you collect stuff?" Higginbottom's curiosity about this half-pint activity overcame her fears.

"Sure. I collect empty flower pots. I must have close to a hundred of them.

"Why do half-pints collect things like that?" Higginbottom smiled at Alix. "Our mayor collects pebbles."

"I don't know." Alix shrugged. "Maybe it's in our blood. My husband collects ale mugs. Mostly he steals them. My kids collect--"

The door crashed open and a huge, slimy, creature entered. The horrifying figure towered over them and resembled a squid Higginbottom had once seen in the fish market in Ashton. The creature's eye stalks moved to inspect each one in turn. The only article the creature wore was a silver medallion hanging on a silver chain. Higginbottom pinched her nose because of the creature's stench and struggled not to gag.

Alix threw up.

"Whoa!" Higginbottom talked without taking her fingers away from her nose. "You are an ugly sucker."

The creature looked at her and she got the impression it was pleased.

Higginbottom pumped up her nerve some more and said, "If you ever show up in Skensfirth, I'm arresting you for kidnapping." Her father had always stressed the need to pay back anyone who did her an evil turn. She hoped someday to be able to get even with the revolting creature.

"Hey, slimeball!" Alix wiped her lips with the back of one hand then shook a fist at the creature. "You'll regret snatching me. I can promise you that."

The hideous creature left. A minute later, a machine came into the room and cleaned up Alix's mess. The machine astonished Higginbottom. No one operated it. It moved by itself. Was it magic? Who were these creatures? What kind of powers did they have? What did they plan to do with her?

# # #

MacDrakin rode to the town hall, dismounted and tied his pony to a hitching rail. He leaned against the rail and looked around for Higginbottom. The early morning sun cast long shadows of trees and buildings along the dirt streets. He whistled an old dwarfish tune and smiled at the Skensfirth folks who passed by.

An hour later, MacDrakin stomped back and forth in front of the building. He had checked the constabulary office a while back, but it was empty. He didn't like to be kept waiting; it made him feel foolish. He was about to go back to the mines but decided to delay a while longer in case the guy had overslept. MacDrakin had suggested today's ride to help out Higginbottom. The least he could do was to show up on time.

An occasional caterwaul came from inside the town hall and MacDrakin wondered what that was about. He paced some more and almost collided with the mayor, Luc Jehan,

as he exited the building. "Hrrmmph!" Jehan looked furious. "MacDrakin! Have you seen the constable?"

"No. I haven't."

"Hrmmph! She locked up five drunks last night and now
they're awake and want out. They're making so much noise
my clerks can't get any work done." He looked up and down
High Street. "Don't just stand there." Jehan made shooing
motions with his hands. "Go find the blasted female."

MacDrakin gawked at the mayor in consternation. "The
constable's . . . a female?"

"Of course she is. What are you an idiot? Or are you
one of those . . . deviants?"

MacDrakin gave the mayor a hard stare and raised an
eyebrow. He was slightly taller than the half-pint, but twice
as wide. The battle ax on his back made him look even more
formidable.

Jehan turned red-faced and stammered, "I . . . I didn't
mean anything insulting."

MacDrakin ignored the mayor and walked away, his
mind in turmoil. Dwarf romance was fraught with peril because both males and females grew beards. Unless the females wore a dress or had a female first name it was difficult
to tell males from females. In Higginbottom's case, the
name Leslie could indicate male or female. The constabulary uniform included pants, so another vital indicator, a
dress, was missing. Whenever a male dwarf mistook another
male for a female, it always resulted in a ferocious fist fight.
He had seen enough of those. He had also been in two of
them. He triggered one of them after having too many ales.
In the other case, some dwarf had put the moves on him
thinking he was female.

Knowing Higginbottom was female raised interesting possibilities. She was attractive and she wouldn't be a constable if she wasn't also smart and educated. Who would have thought he would find an eligible and desirable female in Skensfirth?

MacDrakin walked up High Street to the general store. He entered and called to Geno Aterrano. "Have you seen Constable Higginbottom?"

Geno shook his head. "And that's strange. By now, she's usually patrolling up and down High Street."

MacDrakin had an ominous feeling. "Where does she live?"

"Her house is the one closest to the water." Geno pointed towards the river.

"I'll see if she's home. Maybe she doesn't feel good." MacDrakin left the store and walked towards the river, trying not to look like he was hurrying. He found the house and knocked on the door. When no one answered, he tried it second time. After a third knock, he tried the latch. The door opened. He loosened his ax and went inside. The house was empty and showed no sighs that anything was amiss.

He went back outside and bit his lip while looking around at her herb garden. Something bad had happened. He could sense it.

# # #

Luc Jehan walked back into the town hall which his family had controlled for generations. He considered the office of mayor as his personal fiefdom. His father, grandfather and great-grandfather had all been mayor in their time. In

Skensfirth, politics meant the Jehans. When a Jehan ran for mayor, he ran unopposed most of the time.

Over many years, the family had bought up property in town and were now the largest land owners in Skensfirth. They owned most of the property and buildings on High Street including Kate's Inn and the general store.

He was disgusted with Higginbottom. She was forever acting against his wishes, as if she didn't have to listen to the mayor. How many times had he explained he didn't like to see drunks in the cells when he came to work in the morning. He ordered her to wake them up and kick them out of the jail cell before he got there. Did she do that? No. And now she was nowhere to be found so he had to listen to a mob of dwarfs moaning about their headaches.

He walked to his office in the rear of the building. Along the way, he chatted with the clerks and minor officials. Everyone who worked in the town hall was a close relative of his except Higginbottom. The big problem was that the constable didn't report to him. She reported to the regional constable in Ashton and ultimately to an official in Dun Hythe. Consequently, Higginbottom looked on his commands as suggestions. He had tried to pull strings in Dun Hythe when the last constable died. He wanted his brother-in-law to get the position. His brother-in-law was not very well endowed in the brain department and would do whatever Luc told him to do. That made him an ideal constabulary candidate to Luc's way of thinking. Unfortunately, his efforts were in vain and he was stuck with Higginbottom and her independent ways.

Maybe he could bribe some folks in Dun Hythe to have her replaced.

CHAPTER FOUR

Higginbottom turned up in the exact spot where her horrible experience had begun. She guessed she had been gone for a day and a half. Her first priority was to find MacDrakin. Besides explaining why she didn't show up, he was the only one in Skensfirth she could talk to about what had happened to her. She couldn't talk to the locals. Few of them had ever been outside the immediate area. They were stubbornly close-minded and reluctant to accept new ideas or conditions. She knew many of them wouldn't even listen to her story.

Perhaps MacDrakin would understand what all this was about. Maybe he could explain what was going on.

She hoped she could express her fear for Skensfirth. The smelly creatures were certainly up to no good and only she and Alix were aware of their presence. With a start, she realized that, except for the kidnapping, nothing really had happened. The two women sat around talking. Eventually, they were taken out of the room one at a time. The squid with the silver medallion spoke to her and told her to come with him. Then he escorted her down a long curved corridor, and Higginbottom realized that she was in a ship of some sort. In another room, a second creature -- this one with a bronze medallion -- pushed her onto a corner and the disappearing act started again.

She was dismayed at how advanced the squids were. Every where on the ship she saw machines and flashing numbers and desks filled with buttons and small lights. She couldn't tell if her trip to the ship and back was the result of technology or magic.

She walked around the outskirts of Skensfirth to avoid meeting anyone. She didn't want to explain her disappearance to them. At least, not right now. She forced herself not to cry from her frustration. It wouldn't do if someone saw the constable with tears running down her face. Outside of town, she climbed the road leading up the mountain.

# # #

MacDrakin, covered in muck, sluiced a pile of dirt when he saw Higginbottom walking up the road. He suffered a bout of nervousness because he now knew she was a female. He was also confused by conflicting emotions. One part of him was mad because she hadn't shown up to go scouting with him. Another part was happy that she had come to see him.

He dropped the sluice gate. While he waited for her he tried to wipe some of the dirt from his arms and face.

She reached him, threw herself into his arms and sobbed. Shocked, he patted her back hoping he didn't get her too dirty.

"MacDrakin! You'll never guess what happened to me." She pulled back and wiped her nose on her sleeve. Her eyes were rimmed with red. "I was kidnapped by some gruesome creatures. They look like giant squids. I think they're going to do something bad. Maybe attack Gundarland."

"Kidnapped?" MacDrakin wondered how he was supposed to handle an upset female. All his limited experiences with females seemed useless in this situation. "Really?"

She stepped into his arms again. "They're so powerful. We could never prevent them from doing whatever they wanted to do. They're going to do something terrible. I just know it." Tears rolled down her cheeks. "They're hideous. And they stink. They smell like rotten fish. They kidnapped two of us. I think they were listening to us talk so they could learn our language. That's why I think they plan to do something nasty."

She told him about her companion, Alix. "What a feisty half-pint. So different from the folks in Skensfirth. It must be because she's from a big city. She never stopped carping about the violation of her privileges as a citizen of Dun Hythe. It was like living in Dun Hythe entitled her to rights that didn't apply to folks living in Skensfirth."

MacDrakin only half-listened to Higginbottom talk about Alix. He didn't know what to think. Higginbottom was serious, that much was apparent from her agitation, but he had never heard of squid-like creatures. He didn't think she had imagined it. What if she was correct and the creatures threatened Gundarland or even Skensfirth? If the creatures invaded the town, Higginbottom could be caught in the middle of a dangerous situation.

Several thoughts burst into his mind and fought for attention. Could this be the beginning of an adventure like his ancestor had? Was he about to become the second hero in the family? Did Higginbottom hug him because she was glad to see him or because she was frightened? The answer to the last question seemed more important than the first two.

# # #

Shtap, ready to begin negotiating, slithered his way through the narrow passageways of the *Black Carrion Flower* toward the gymnasium.

He had learned the art of deceptive negotiating at the tentacles of his parents, both high-ranking members of the diplomatic corps. Many of their double-crosses were considered classics and students studied them in negotiating classes. To zaftans, pulling off a well-designed betrayal was a sign of superior intelligence and worthy of a mention on one's resume. Successful treachery was celebrated with media attention along with praise from superiors. Promotions often followed. Someday, Shtap hoped to demonstrate to his parents that he was a worthy son by triggering an unspeakably loathsome betrayal of a native population.

Shtap wondered what kind of reception he would receive from the captain. When in a mellow mood, zaftans were merely hostile. Of late, Yunta had been the queen of bitches, even by the truculent standards of the zaftans.

He pushed open the door and saw Yunta working out on a treadmill with four tentacles while lifting weights with two others and using a communicator with the remaining two. These simultaneous activities were possible because of the multiple processors the zaftans possessed. "Greetings, Captain. I hope you are well."

"Shtap." Yenta acknowledged his presence by shutting down the communicator.

"The two language assistants were very helpful. Besides teaching the language computer enough words to allow me to negotiate, they also disclosed much valuable information about the politics and the culture, such as it is." The language computer had downloaded a data base into Shtap's medallion which would operate as a simultaneous translator.

"Excellent. When will you begin?"

"As soon as you give me leave to transport to the surface. I've identified the building where the political leader lives, thanks to the natives. I assume his office will be on the top floor. That is where I'll land."

"Very well. Have Drek send you on your way." She flapped a tentacle at him. "You can't be sure the natives will be friendly so have Drek cloak you in a ward for protection in case you are attacked. Remember, we must be quick. We don't have much time."

Shtap slapped the sides of his head with two tentacles splattering slime in all directions. The gesture was the traditional sign of obedience and respect. He slipped out of the gym and headed for his cabin to prepare for his journey. He had high hopes for the coming negotiations. Perhaps this planet was where he would gain fame as a consummate deceiver.

# # #

Drek sat erect on the couch in the transportation chamber and stared at the displays on the console in front of him. One monitor showed a view of the biggest city. He pointed a tentacle at a large building. "Is that where you want to go?"

"Yes," Shtap replied.

"That should not be too hard." Drek concentrated on the monitor, looking for possible obstacles. "I hope the natives gave you the right information. It will be embarrassing, and perhaps dangerous, if you show up in the wrong place."

"Yunta wants you to cloak me with a ward."

"A wise precaution." Drek operated switches and pushed buttons. "I will do the ward and then send you on your way."

All zaftans had eight processing units. Seven of them were subordinate to the main processor in their head. Before a zaftan could perform complicated maneuvers such as quick slithering or rising from a couch, the main processor established links with one or two other processors. Once the maneuver was accomplished, the links were broken. A few zaftans had the capability of linking two or three processors on a continuous basis. These were the scientists, philosophers and the insane. A very small number could establish simultaneous linkages between all eight and keep them established as long as necessary. These rare individuals became shamans. With the eight processors linked, the zaftan became a living and powerful parallel computer. The configuration was so robust, it could warp reality around the shaman who then manipulated the unreal space surrounding him to obtain unreal capabilities or to generate fantastic effects. Different linkage combinations yielded different results. Being surrounded by unreal space became an ordeal after a while and extended exposure could lead to bizarre mental states.

Drek had used one linkage configuration to send the natives back to the planet's surface. He now focused his main processor and established a different linkage. He waited a few seconds for the unreal space to establish itself, then he forced a portion of unreal space to wrap around Shtap, thus providing a protective ward that would last for two hours. Next, he set up the linkage he had used with the natives, closed his eyes and concentrated on seeing Shtap in the large building on the planet's surface. He felt a reduction in pressure as unreal space escaped from his immediate surroundings. He opened his eyes, and, as expected, confirmed he was alone. He checked the display and noted that all went well with the transfer.

Now he could relax and await until Shtap signaled he wanted to return.

# # #

Alix Cyr had returned to the street corner where she had disappeared. Looking around, she didn't see anyone she knew. Of course, in mid-afternoon most people in this section of Dun Hythe would be at work in one of the many factories. She waited a while, hoping for someone to talk to, but no one showed up.

She left the corner and walked down a muddy, garbage-strewn street. The old, dilapidated buildings were packed so close even the rats had trouble squeezing between them. The five- and six-story buildings blocked the sun from reaching parts of the street. Constantly in shade, strange things grew in these areas, especially in the slimy pools of stagnant rain water.

She was weary and hungry from her ordeal. The only food she had during her time with the kidnappers was the picnic food the nice constable had. She sat down at an outdoor table at a cafe and ordered coffee and cheese. She worked up a mental list of things to do. First, she would check on her apartment. No one should be home in her one-room flat on the fifth floor of a tenement. Her husband should be at work and her two children in school. Perhaps, one of them left a note for her. After that, she would go to the factory and apologize for missing work. With luck she wouldn't be sacked. Third, she would look in at the office of the Furniture Workers of Dun Hythe Labor Movement. She was the Treasurer of the union and her chores must have piled up in her absence. Finally, she would go to a police station and file a report on her kidnapping. No smelly, squid-like beings were going to kidnap her and not pay the price.

A female neighbor spotted her. "Alix? We missed you. Where were you? And what's his name? Who would have thought that you would run off for a few days with a male? You've always been so respectable." The neighbor giggled and look expectantly at Alix. "Come on. I want to hear every delicious detail."

"I wasn't having an affair. I was kidnapped."

"Oh, that's even better. Tell me. Everyone has affairs and, after a while, hearing about them gets boring."

Alix told her about the abduction.

"That's ridiculous, Alix. If you had an affair, just say so. Never mind telling folks this cock-and-bull story."

Alix chewed her lip. What if the police thought the same way?

CHAPTER FIVE

Webley sat in his office getting his afternoon briefing on Gundarland and the rest of the world. Across the desk, his Chief-of-Staff, Rodrigs, presented a review of events that he gleaned from newspapers, telegrams and reports from other bureaucrats. Rodrigs, wearing a mustard-colored bow tie, stopped in mid-sentence to listen to screams of terror coming from the secretaries' area outside the presidential office. The clomping of several pairs of running feet followed the screams.

"I'll find out what's going on." Rodrigs stood and placed his folder of reports on his chair.

"Not yet. It's almost time for my nap and I don't want anything to disturb it. You can tell me after I wake up." Webley yawned, stretched and loosened his orange cummerbund.

Rodrigs sat down and started to read from another report when the office door crashed open and a nightmare creature overflowed the door frame.

Both men gaped at the intruder with its grayish-black skin covered with green, oozing slime. It stood on eight tentacles. Eyestalks bounced around as they inventoried the room. A silver medallion hung from the creature's neck and a gold metallic belt covered with strange squiggles encircled the middle of its torso. It held a small, black, metallic device in one of its tentacles. The creature's eyestalks focused on Webley. After a few seconds, it slithered forward and approached the desk. Webley pushed his chair backward until stopped by the wall behind his desk. He had trouble breathing and his gut felt as if it was trying to digest a large rock. A violent urge to vomit seized him. The stench from the squid-like figure reminded him of dead fish baked in the hot sun for a few days.

Rodrigs stared pop-eyed at the apparition. He recovered and pushed his chair away from the desk. He gagged and retched.

"Whoa!" the creature said to Webley. "You are an ugly sucker."

Webley's fear morphed into anger. "This monster calls me ugly?" He glared at the stranger while struggling to control his bile.

A sudden aroma of coffee filled his nostrils and delighted his olfactory sense. He glanced at Rodrigs and saw that he too looked more at ease. Obviously, the elf had cast wards to protect them against the stench.

"My name is Shtap. This belt identifies me as the negotiator for the brilliant and beautiful Captain Yunta. Instead of destroying the planet or enslaving you pathetic creatures, she offers to trade with you. You may grovel at my tentacles to show your respect and gratitude." Squeaks came from the creature's beak but the words came from the medallion.

"Rodrigs! What is the point of having an appointment calendar if no one follows it. My calendar clearly states that it is now nap time. Why is this . . . this thing in my office?"

"Maybe he doesn't think he needs an appointment."

"You're a wizard. Cast a spell and get it out of here."

Rodrigs thought that was a very bad idea. It would require a lot of magical power to move a creature that big. The kilo-necromans required to cast such a spell would be more

than he had ever used at one time. The recoil from launching such an amount of power would be dangerous.

"Come on. Do your stuff."

While the creature stared at Webley, Rodrigs gathered
ten kilo-necromans of his magical resources, aimed them at
the creature and wove his hands in a removal spell. The recoil almost knocked him backwards out of his chair. An
opaque cloud of magical particles flew towards the intruder.
It rebounded off Shtap, engulfed a potted plant and changed
it into a pink dragon puppy. "Uh-oh," Rodrigs mumbled
aloud. The appearance of the dragon pup puzzled him. How
had that happened? Shtap didn't notice the spell. He must
have a protective ward, but the ward wouldn't account for the
transformation of the plant into a dragon. Producing a
dragon required much more power than the ten kilo-necromans he had used. Somehow the intruder's ward must have
amplified the power of the spell. Was that even possible?
He had never heard of such an occurrence.

The pup snorted a puff of steam through one nostril and
charged Shtap. It skidded to a halt a few feet away, sniffed
and yelped in consternation. It ran two circuits of the office,
yapping the entire time. At the end of the second lap, it
made a flying leap at Rodrigs' ankle and clamped down with
its needle-sharp puppy teeth.

Shtap's eye stalks rotated to follow the action.

Rodrigs, howling in pain, hopped on one foot with the
puppy clinging to his ankle and flapping its tiny wings to
maintain its toothy grip. He pried the puppy's teeth off his
ankle and dropped it outside the office until he could think of
something to do with it. He walked back to his seat, noticing
that Shtap towered over his own six foot height. "Where are
you from?"

"Zaftan 31B."

"We don't know where that is," Rodrigs said. "We never heard of it."

"Never? Your civilization is more ignorant than we thought. You are fortunate we are here. We come from far away. The other side of the galaxy."

"Galaxy?" Rodrigs frowned at the implications of that statement. "You mean like one of the stars?"

"Well, that's preposterous," Webley said. "How could they travel from a star?"

"We came on a ship."

"You have a ship out in the harbor?" Webley raised an eyebrow. "I think I would have heard about that."

"You mentioned trade?" Rodrigs changed subjects to get Webley off the ship idea. Letting the creature get a glimpse of Webley's thought processes wasn't a good idea.

"We want to explore the land and mine minerals if we find them."

"You mean like gold and silver?" Rodrigs asked.

"No. We seek minerals your backward civilization will not need for a long time and may never need. Like monazite and gadolinite."

"I never heard of them," Webley said. "Have you, Rodrigs?"

"No, I haven't. Why here? Why not in a different part of our world?"

"This land has the most diverse terrain types giving us the best chance of success."

"What do we get in return?" Rodrigs asked.

Shtap slithered to the closest window.

Rodrigs noticed the rug smoldered where he had been standing.

Shtap pointed a tentacle at the dirt-colored smog billow-
ing from a nearby factory. "We will teach you how to clean
up your pollution. Also how to keep your water clean."

"How long will you stay?" Webley asked.

"Until our ship is filled. Meanwhile, we will study your
pollution problem and teach you what to do before we
leave."

"How many of you will do the exploring?" Rodrigs
asked.

"We use robotic explorers."

"What are robotics?" Rodrigs asked.

"Machines, to your backward civilization."

"How many?" Rodrigs wondered how folks would react
to seeing machines roaming the land.

"Ten should be enough."

"Then there will be ten machines and ten others like you
to operate them?"

"Just the machines. There is no need to send down operators."

Rodrigs frowned. How could machines work without
someone controlling it? Was this magic or technology? He
wished he knew. He didn't like getting in situations where
he didn't understand what was going on. He needed more information. "What about private property?" Rodrigs asked.
"Will these machines respect property rights?"

"What are . . . property rights?"

"Homes, farms, gardens, orchards. Land that individual
folks own."

Shtap paused momentarily, then replied, "Ah, land. We
will respect property rights."

"Where will you start?" Rodrigs sensed that Shtap
replied to questions in a way that concealed much informa-

tion. The entire situation made him most uneasy. There were far too many unanswered questions, not to mention the unknown questions.

"We will analyze your land mass to identify the most promising area to find minerals. We will start there. If we find what we need, we will not have to explore further."

Webley cleared his throat. "We will think about your offer."

Rodrigs knew the prospect of cleaning up pollution appealed to Webley. It was a major issue with the voters. If Webley received credit for solving the problem, it would help his reelection campaign.

Shtap nodded. At least Rodrigs thought he nodded. It was hard to tell since he didn't really have a head, just eye stalks on the top part of the torso. "I will return tomorrow for your answer. I will require a large-scale map of your country." He pointed a tentacle to the wall map. "Like that one." He tapped the device held by a tentacle.

"Make sure you don't show up at nap time when you come back." Webley drummed his fingers on his desk top.

To their amazement, Shtap dissolved in a column of golden air.

Rodrigs shook his head in wonderment at the awesome display of power. "We need to have a cabinet meeting, sir," he said.

Webley stroked his chin. "I suppose we'll have to. Set it up for after my nap. And don't include everyone. Just Treasury, Defense and Interior. We don't need the rest of the buffoons."

# # #

When Webley and Rodrigs entered the presidential conference room they found the others already there. Bright afternoon sunlight flooded the window-filled room. A large polished table dominated the room and was surrounded by a dozen heavy, padded chairs. The dragon puppy, now named Pinky, trotted at Rodrigs's heels. Just to be sure it didn't get into mischief, he had the puppy on a leash with a collar. Rodrigs's greatest fear involved Pinky getting loose in the city since dragon pups were notorious troublemakers. Pinky would terrify old folks, stampede horses, start garbage fires and generally raise hell. He was responsible for its sudden appearance and he felt an obligation to protect the pup -- and the city -- from each other.

Owning a dragon pup, especially a rare pink one, was an exotic status symbol. Nobody else had one, but he had another reason for keeping the pup. After pondering the events, he concluded his spell, once it ricocheted from Shtap's ward, should have removed the potted plant to the waiting room. The spell was, after all, a powerful removal spell so something should have been removed. The alien's ward somehow altered the spell and that implied that Shtap's ward used a different type of magic than Gundarland's wizards used. Rodrigs had trouble accepting that premise. The existence of another type of magic was foreign to every textbook he had ever studied. Perhaps Pinky could help to unlock this mystery.

He tied the leash to a nearby chair leg, sat down and looked around.

Crumlish and Sfiore ignored Webley, Rodrigs and Pinky. They stared at each other like they waited for someone to ring a bell to start the fight. Nothing new there, thought Rodrigs. The two hated each other.

Medals festooned Crumlish's tunic; all were honorary, none had been earned in battle. The swagger stick under his left arm doubled as his wizard's wand. As a dwarf, he had to bend his neck backward to scowl up at Sfiore, an elf.

Sfiore wore a gold robe that reflected the sunlight making her appear like an independent light source. She resembled a walking treasure trove with her shoulder-length silver hair and amber eyes.

Boudreau sat with his feet up on the table and groomed his toe hairs with a small comb. He smiled at Webley and pulled his feet down. Boudreau raised an eyebrow to Rodrigs and flicked his head toward Pinky. Rodrigs smiled and shrugged. He'd explain later. Perhaps he'd understand more about the strange situation by then.

Crumlish and Sfiore broke eye contact and nodded at the newcomers.

"Let's get started," Webley said without making his usual preamble about how happy he was to see everybody in good health. "As you may have heard, I had a strange visitor earlier today. A really foul-smelling one. He claimed to be from a far-off world and flew here on a ship. Obviously, the creature takes me for a fool. Ships don't fly, they float."

"Excuse me, sir," Rodrigs said. "I understood him to mean a ship that is very different from the ones we are familiar with."

Webley frowned. "Are you sure?"

Rodrigs nodded and went on to describe what the visitor looked like.

"What did he want?" Boudreau asked. "Not money, I hope."

"Minerals," Webley replied. "Although I can't imagine why they want a pile of our rocks."

"In return," Rodrigs said, "they promised to teach us how to clean up the pollution messes. They also promised to respect property rights when they explore and mine the land."

"We are here to make a decision." Webley tried to look stern, but his expression came across as a half-smile. "When this rather smelly visitor returns tomorrow, what do I tell him?"

"They expect to land in Gundarland to get rocks?" Crumlish pointed a finger at Webley. "I suspect treachery. They will land under the guise of friendliness and then launch a surprise attack."

Webley's mouth fell open.

Sfiore coughed to get everyone's attention. "If they land here to explore for these rocks, I will need at least two of Crumlish's infantry regiments and one cavalry regiment just to keep track of their activities." She paused and watched Crumlish turn red. "I will also require his funding for these units." She grinned as Crumlish had a fit of coughing.

Out of the corner of his eye, Rodrigs watched Boudreau struggle to keep from laughing out loud.

"This . . . elf . . . is out of her mind," Crumlish finally replied. "Not only is she not getting my troops, but I will need to recruit and arm more units to defend the country from these treacherous invaders. I will require additional funding of at least one and a half million silver pennies each quarter from now on just to be prepared to defend Gundarland."

"Your charge is to defend the country from an external attack." Sfiore glared at Crumlish. "I am in charge of internal security. If these visitors are perfidious, I will command your troops."

Crumlish tugged his beard braids in anger.

Boudreau grinned at Crumlish. "To increase your funding that much we will have to raise taxes."

"What!" Webley almost came out of his seat. "We can't raise taxes. I'm up for reelection next year. A tax increase is out of the question." He looked hurt, as if someone had insulted him.

"If I can make an observation?" Rodrigs said.

Everyone turned to look at him.

"We have no reason to suspect that these visitors are treacherous. If they have technology to fly here from other worlds and if they can fix our pollution problems, then we must assume they also have powerful weapons that are beyond our comprehension. We must be very careful to keep from irritating these visitors."

"Really?" Webley blinked rapidly as he looked at his chief-of-staff.

"So where does that leave us?" Boudreau asked.

Rodrigs heard chewing sounds and looked down at Pinky. A chair tottered on three-and-a-half legs. A pile of wood shavings lay on the floor where Pinky worked on converting the chair leg from solid oak to scrap and sawdust.

"Where it leaves us is right back here." Webley assumed his stern, half-smile face again. "We need a decision. Do we let them land or do we refuse them? What is your answer?"

"A decision like this is beyond my authority," Crumlish replied. "You're the President, you must make this decision. I have no more time to waste on this meeting. I must put my forces on emergency alert." He jumped up and ran out the door.

"I must send telegrams to all my constables informing them to prepare for unexpected contingencies." Sfiore stood and walked towards the door. The motion made her gold robe shimmer.

"But what is your decision?" Webley said in a pleading voice.

"Whatever you decide, be assured my constables will be ready for whatever is required of them." Sfiore swished out the door.

Webley, with panic on his face, asked Boudreau," And you? Tell me what you think I should do."

"Do what you always do," Boudreau replied. "Follow Rodrigs' advice."

# # #

After the others left the conference room, Boudreau walked to a window and looked out at Dun Hythe. He loved the city. Besides being the political capital of Gundarland, it was also the cultural and financial capital. He loved going to operas, symphonies and stage plays. He loved sitting in cafes and watching the citizens stroll by. He sighed and broke his gaze from the window. Dun Hythe and Gundarland were in trouble. Deep trouble. While he feared the aliens, they were a secondary worry. Crumlish and Sfiore were his primary concern. They would use the aliens as a cover for increasing their own personal authority. Since both controlled armed forces, an all-out war between them was possible. Nothing was as important to them as protecting their own power and increasing it.

To him, one of the most fascinating historical aspects of governments was their complete disregard for governing. Governments were single-minded and interested only in increasing their control and any governance that come out of the government's actions was purely coincidental. This aspect of bureaucracy applied to governments as a whole, to the smaller branches within the government and went down to the individuals working in those branches. The lowest flunky as well as the most powerful bureaucrat was more interested in protecting his sinecure than in helping the citizens who coughed up tax money to pay the government workers' salaries.

While he was not shocked to learn from his studies that this environment applied to kingships and dictatorships, he was surprised to discover that democracies also suffered from the same symptoms. He would have thought that elected officials would give attention to the needs of the voters, but democracy worked exactly the way other types of governments worked. Bureaucrats in all forms of governments were too engrossed in either defending their turfs or attacking other departments to give anything but lip-service to the voters.

He dreamed of serving in a government that placed the needs of the citizens above petty office politics, but he was realist enough to see that his dreams were the stuff of fairy tales.

Boudreau was slender and wore a tan tunic that fell below his waist and black breeches without boots to display a luxurious growth of silky toe hair arranged in curls studded with jeweled pins.

Born to farming parents in northern Gundarland, he had won a scholarship to an exclusive university and graduated with a degree in accounting wizardry. In his first government job, he learned the hard way that introducing new ideas was a sure fire way to become unpopular with both his coworkers and his bosses. He had yet to discover that bureaucracies defended the status quo the way nobles defended their castles. He soon learned to plant the ideas on his boss and let that unworthy take the credit for it. This practice endeared him to his supervisors and he rose through the ranks. Shocked at the culture in which the organizations expended vast resources attacking other organizations instead of tending to their own affairs, he started delving into history to get a better understanding of how governments worked and how bureaucracies survived.

His appointment as the Treasurer came as a bit of a surprise. His old school chum, Frankie Rodrigs, Webley's Chief-of-Staff, selected Boudreau and provided Webley with the appropriate rationale. Rodrigs did this one afternoon when Webley was eager to take his nap. Boudreau still had problems grappling with the fact that, constitutionally, he was next in line for the Presidency if something happened to Webley. As interim President, he would have three months to run the country while organizing and holding a new election.

He jerked his mind back to the problem at hand. He identified several important issues in the current crisis. Perhaps most importantly, Webley's presence in the Presidential Palace represented a power vacuum. Even though Crumlish and Sfiore engaged full time in a power scrum, Webley would never assert his authority to rein in those two egomaniacs. Webley never listened directly to Boudreau. The President considered it a sign of weakness to listen to advice he didn't ask for. Boudreau also knew it was impossible to get Webley to make a decision. Boudreau saw himself as the principal advisor to Rodrigs who was, in truth, the chief decision-maker in Gundarland.

Boudreau used an extensive network of informants to keep abreast of events throughout Gundarland and within the government branches. He shared this information with Rodrigs. Between the two of them, they kept the country in reasonably good condition, despite the efforts of other bureaucrats.

He paced the office for almost an hour before he came up with a plan. Not a very good plan, but the best one he could develop under the circumstances. First, he would have to thwart the power grabs of Crumlish and Sfiore. That aspect sounded like fun, because he loved to screw with those two. Second, he would have to continue to feed Rodrigs plenty of advice and urge him to get Webley to listen to it. If Webley didn't act, then Rodrigs would have to make decisions for the President. Rodrigs had done it in the past, and now Gundarland's future depend upon the elf continuing to be the shadow president.

CHAPTER SIX

Yunta nodded to Shtap when he entered the flight deck on the *Black Carrion Flower.* She ignored the two crew members monitoring the condition of the ship and its orbit.

"I had a second meeting with the natives," Shtap said, "and all goes well, Captain."

"If everything is going well as you claim, why is the ship still empty of minerals?"

"We make progress, as I will show you." He pointed to a wall-mounted monitor. "The ship's computer scanned the map I got from the natives today. It analyzed the geographical features and made a recommendation on where to start exploring. The location is marked on the screen."

"Good," Yunta replied. She felt a bit better, but she didn't know if that was a result of her periods receding or if the heavy dose of recreational drugs had kicked in.

"We will start in this valley. It is surrounded by mountains and the area has forests, rivers and plains. We should find something. This small town will be the center of the exploration. We think the name is pronounced Skensfirth. The computer recommends an initial load of fifty explorers. That many robots will allow us to identify mineral deposits in a very short timeframe. However, we may have a problem with the natives. The robots cannot identify private property and that is a major issue with the natives. They brought it up again at today's meeting."

"The natives will simply have to adjust." With the tip of one tentacle, Yunta punched a button on her communication unit.

"Mivex. Yes, Captain?" The officer's image appeared on the screen. Mivex had responsibility for the engineering and propulsion sections.

"Have cargo pod number one prepared for a mission. Program fifty robots for mineral exploration and load them into the pod. You will launch them from the air, not on the ground."

"Very good, captain. I will see to it immediately."

"What about the propulsion system?" Like all the equipment on the *Black Carrion Flower*, the engines were old and worn. "You failed to provide me with a scheduled report."

"There is nothing to report. Nothing has changed since my last report." He sneered at her. "I know you are busy and I did not want to burden you with trivial reports. If anything worth noting had occurred, you would have been informed."

Yunta struggled to keep from ordering the fool thrown overboard. Mivex was another expense reduction. Zaftan ships required a propulsion shaman because the sub-fusion propulsion reactor pile needed a periodic and healthy blast of external energy to keep it burning properly. Mivex claimed to be intimate with every aspect of the reactor pile. No one in the crew believed him.

She pushed a button and the screen turned black. Yunta inhaled deeply. She shouldn't let Mivex irritate her so much, but she couldn't help herself. She made a mental note to read the personnel folders of the sub-shamans. Perhaps, one of them could be promoted to propulsion shaman. If so, she could strand Mivex on the planet. That thought raised her spirits.

She turned to Shtap. "We must do this quickly. We have only twelve rotations of the planet left before we reach the midpoint of the voyage. Find minerals and fill the ship, otherwise, we will not earn a bonus. I will not mention what our superiors will put in our performance reports in that case." In her mind, she could picture a blackened, dead corporate tree. "We are entrepreneurs and entrepreneurs take risks. We cannot waste time negotiating with property owners for permission to search their land. The robots are to chase down any trace of minerals they find and they are to ignore the natives. You can stall the natives with negotiations until we finish loading the minerals."

PART TWO:

CONFUSION

INTERLUDE ONE

In the beginning, the great god Gundar created recreational drugs and pronounced them good. He also created an in-space spherical swimming pool, a lounge chair and a sunlamp. While resting on the chair after a swim and while working on His tan, He snorted a double dose. This made Him sneeze a godly sneeze. The nodules of spittle flew through the nothingness of space and eventually solidified into suns, planets, comets and other celestial bodies. Gundar looked over His newest creation, shrugged, took another hit and turned His mind to His newest project; creating a female companion. Later the two became known as The Holy Duo.

Scientific authorities called the creation of the universe the Big Achoo. Medical authorities argued that infectious diseases resulted from this unsanitary beginning. Religious authorities countered that such talk was blasphemous and that the medical authorities should accept infectious diseases as Gundar's holy will. Ordinary folk thought the authorities had too much free time on their hands and ought to get jobs.

Religion always played a big part in people's lives. The biggest festival occurred in the spring when Snotists celebrated the birth of the universe. Know as the Sacred Snot-Fest, the ritual culminated in temples with all the believers simultaneously inhaling crushed pepper to generate a giant sneeze. Doctors loved the festival; many of them made more money in the month following the Snot-Fest than they did in the rest of the year. Oddly enough, the priests all wore masks during the ceremony.

Gundarland was the largest land mass on the planet. Other smaller land masses served to keep the oceans separated.

Diverse races such as dwarfs, humans, elves, half-pints, yuks and a few lesser races populated the land and lived cheek-by-jowl. Over time, the races achieved numerical equality, more or less. This ended the favorite past-time of bigots, persecuting a race because of their smaller population, an obvious sign of racial inferiority to the bigots.

Yuk society consisted of a single social class, the poor. They struggled to get food and basic needs. Some, more aggressive or smarter than the average, went out into the world to make a better life. Those that didn't get hung for stealing occasionally made a success of themselves.

All social classes need another social class to look down upon, a group that makes them feel socially superior. As long as someone is lower than they are, folks are content and put up with the situation. Yuks served this need in Gundarland; all other races looked down on the yuks and felt themselves to be socially superior. The yuks didn't mind and felt sorry for the others; they knew they were superior to all the other races.

The various races had different strengths when it came to the organized scrums known as wars. Elves were adept at using longbows while dwarfs usually fought as ax-wielding foot soldiers. Humans fought as swordsmen or in cavalry units. Half-pints made admirable scouts, spies and thieves. Yuks, on the other hand, didn't take to organized combat. They preferred to fight as individuals. The best a yuk general could hope for was that the majority of the yuk troopers under his command attacked in the direction he pointed to.

Magic always intrigued folks in Gundarland. As a consequence, wizards were held in high regard, even the incompetent ones. Wizard schools, early on, offered double majors in imitation of the combat schools. At first, the secondary course of study was perfunctory, but that changed when the dukes and counts began installing wizards in positions of power. The theory was that if a wizard couldn't figure out a solution to a problem, he could magic the problem out of existence. This theory proved to be catastrophically wrong.

Meanwhile, a group of wizards too lazy to work, called themselves philosopher-wizards and spent their time drinking wine and pondering the laws governing magic. Eventually, their findings were published to the dismay of many wizards who wanted everything about magic to be kept secret from the masses.

Penelope Hogsfoot formulated the Three Laws of Thermo-Necromancy: Magic can be altered, but it can't be created or destroyed; The universe never gets tidier; When it's really, really cold out, magic is hard to do.

Sheldonthorpe the Killjoy, in his Laws of Natural Magicks, postulated that there are only two types of magic in the universe, black and white. Another of his laws stated: If unspelled white and unspelled black magic come together, they will neutralize each other and release a large amount of chaotic energy.

CHAPTER SEVEN

Higginbottom patrolled High Street. It was the second morning after her return and the bright sunshine and warm temperature did little to lessen the memory of her ordeal. She still shuddered whenever she thought of what she had been put through. She had been cold and terrified the entire time. She had also been hungry after she and Alix finished the picnic basket. Why she had been chosen out of all the folks in Gundarland and for what purpose was a mystery to her.

Did the government in Dun Hythe know about the strange beings? Did the unusual telegram she received this morning have anything to do with the visitors? What if it didn't? What if it referred to something else? What if Dun Hythe didn't know about the squids? Should she send a telegram to the Secretary of the Interior, her ultimate boss? Would Dun Hythe believe her? They might even sack her for being delusional. For the first time in her life, she felt indecisive, and she didn't like the feeling. She wanted to make decisions and to act on them, but she didn't know enough about the squids and their motives. Were the smelly creatures evil? She thought they were, but she couldn't be sure. She also wished she could decide whether to send a telegram to Dun Hythe.

She passed farmers and their wives pushing hand carts or steering ox-driven wagons towards the market square at the north end of town. She knew all of them and she nodded and smiled at each half-pint couple as they went past. Very few folks had moved into Skensfirth during the three years she had trained in Ashton. She thought about that for a moment. MacDrakin was the only new resident that she could recall.

The cheerful attitude of the folks made her feel better. Perhaps she overreacted to those slimy creatures who had kidnapped her. All they did was listen to her and Alix talk. And answer some questions about the leaders. Maybe they wanted to learn the common language to talk to the big shots in Dun Hythe. Maybe there was nothing sinister about the event. She convinced herself she overreacted. After all, Dun Hythe must know what was going on. The capital was filled with smart people and they must have events under control. Her mood improved and she forced her mind off the ordeal.

After her patrol she planned to go to MacDrakin's mountain and get their picnic back on track. She wanted to get to know him better.

"Good morning, Constable," Geno Aterrano said from the door of his general store. "It's a glorious morning."

"It is indeed," Higginbottom replied.

"Did you enjoy your vacation?"

Higginbottom started. She hadn't told anyone but MacDrakin about her kidnapping. Geno must have assumed she took a few days off. "Yes, I visited with some . . . acquaintances."

"I got in a shipment of muffin tins last night."

"Thanks, Geno, but I don't do a lot of baking."

"That's odd." Geno stared at the distant sky with a frown on his thin, long face. He pointed to the north. "What are they?"

Higginbottom followed the elf's finger and saw three small cloud-like objects floating north of town. They were too high to discern any details. While she looked, two more appeared. All five formed a straight line with the first one a bit lower than the others. She glanced up High Street. Other folks looked at the sky and gestured. Voices started to get loud. She recognized incipient panic in several voices. The folks in Skensfirth didn't like changes or unexplainable events.

The number of falling objects increased to ten. With the appearance of each additional object, Higginbottom's anxiety increased. She gulped air in an attempt to slow her rapid heartbeat.

"Hrrmph. Nice of you to show up for work, Constable." Luc Jehan, the mayor, stood with hands on hips and glared at her. "We had to hire a lock-pick to open the jail cells and let the drunks out." He looked around the street. "Why is everyone making a fuss?"

"Because of those things." Higginbottom pointed to the sky. The first line had stopped at ten, but a second line began forming closer to Skensfirth.

"Hrrmph. What are they? Are they dangerous?"

"I don't know." Higginbottom suspected the strange, and very vague, telegram was a warning about the objects.

One or several areas, the telegram read, *may experience periods of unusual activity by robots, a harmless type of machine. They are exploring for minerals. They have been instructed not to harm anyone or their property. Constables are not to interfere with the robots as they go about their explorations and are to prevent citizens from likewise interfering with the robots.*

Higginbottom thought the first part sounded like a weather forecast, not an invasion alert.

The robots, the cloud-like objects and the squids must be connected, she decided. The telegram meant Dun Hythe knew about them. Did that mean the creatures and their machines weren't dangerous? She didn't believe it. She harbored deep fears about the squids, but she couldn't explain why she did; her sense of danger was instinctive. How could she protect Skensfirth? Were these robots an invasion force? What in the world did a robot look like?

# # #

Gorya sat with his back to the judgement tree, awaiting members of his yuk tribe to bring a complaint against another tribal member. The tree, an ancient oak, had seen a large number of criminals and trespassers of all races dangle from its stout branches. It sat on top of a slight rise and overlooked the village. Gorya was the chieftain of the tribe and his holding consisted of fifty homes made of wood and thatch. His territory extended eastward to the Gundarland border twelve miles away.

Gorya's immense, over-muscled shoulders gave his five-foot frame a top-heavy appearance. Like all yuks, he was bald except for clumps of wiry black hair scattered randomly over his green-skinned torso. Every other race considered the yuks the ugliest creatures in the world. Yuks, in turn, felt sorry for the frightful appearances of the others. Many people considered yuks to be stupid because of the way they fractured the common language. Those with experience knew the yuks were quite smart, Machiavellian and crafty negotiators. Few ever got the better of an exchange with a yuk.

Gorya's black, beady eyes surveyed the immediate area looking for plaintiffs, not that he wanted to listen to complaints, but it was part of his job.

His wife Kiska sat at his side. If a complaint came from a female, Kiska would help him decide the case. She wore a burlap sack that exposed acres of muscles and skin while he wore the traditional garb of yuk males: canvas breeches held up by a rope.

"Uh-oh," Kiska said. "Dere comes complaint for sure." She pointed to their six-year-old daughter, Zoya, running towards them. The yukling had a murderous look on her face.

Gorya sighed. Zoya, unlike any other creature in the world, could wrap him around her finger.

Zoya skidded to a stop in front of her father, placed fists on her skinny hips and glared at him.

"Why ya give me dirty look?" Gorya asked.

"Stas, him pinched me butt. Me demand death penalty for me brother." She stamped one bare foot on the ground.

"Private fights not da bidsness of dis judgement tree, and fightin' not against de law."

"So ya gonna let him get away wid it?" Zoya looked like she was about to cry.

"Him pinch yer butt, you gotta punch him inna mouth. It's da yuk way."

"Me punch him inna mouth, him gonna pound me inna dirt."

"Life's tough bein' a yuk."

"Ya pa's right," Kiska said. "Ya can't expect us to fight yer battles. Gotta stand up for yer rights."

Zoya crossed her arms, tapped a foot a few times then turned and ran back the way she came. "Stas! Ya gonna die."

"Dat one could be tribal chieftain after me," Gorya said with a heart filled with paternal pride. "She gonna be tough enough."

Kiska agreed.

A minute later, Zoya came running back in a state of excitement. She grabbed Gorya's hand and pulled. "Pa. Get up. Ya gotta see dis." She pointed to the sky with her other hand.

Gorya stood up and ran a calloused hand over the girl's bare head. "Wot ya talkin' about?"

"Pa, dere's stuff fallin' from da sky. Ya can't see dem from here 'cause of all de trees. Some of dem not too far from da village."

Gorya scowled while he thought through the ramifications of the news. While he didn't understand what the child referred to, he couldn't, as chieftain, ignore a possible threat to the tribe or its land. "Us go see. C'mon." He followed Zoya downhill until he could see the sky to the north. His mouth dropped open. Two lines of white objects floated in the sky. The line farthest away was closer to the ground and looked like it would land on the other side of the Gundarland border. The closest line would come down on tribal land.

"Me count ten of dem in each line." Zoya grinned, proud of her accomplishment.

"Dat good countin'," Gorya said, pleased that he didn't have to count them now.

The village males came to stand by Gorya while the females congregated in the village square. Every one kept their eyes focused on the unknown objects.

"Pa! Wot are dey?" Zoya asked.

"Don't know. Passin' strange, me thinkin'."

"Dere's somethin' hangin, underneath de white mush-rooms," she said. "Looks like a barrel." His daughter had sharper eyesight than he did.

"Barrels not supposta fall from de sky." Gorya scratched his chin. "Dis not a good thing." He didn't like strange events. Especially strange events that involved him or his tribal responsibilities because the villagers would expect him to come up with explanations and solutions. If he didn't, they would think he was getting senile and needed replacing.

"Watcha gonna do? Can me go wid ya to catch a barrel thing?"

"Nope. Too dangerous. Gotta scout dese things out first." He pointed to his three best hunters. "Go get weapons. Us gonna check dis out."

"Maybe dose barrel things have food in dem," Zoya said.

Zoya's comment puzzled Gorya. Why would food float down from the sky? Who would send it? Whatever they were, he knew in his gut they were not going to help him or the villagers.

# # #

MacDrakin climbed out of the mine tunnel holding two sacks of dirt. He blinked in the bright sunlight, dropped the sacks and paused to take a few breaths of fresh air. While he worked in the tunnel, his mind constantly thought about holding Higginbottom in his arms. She certainly was the best looking female dwarf in Skensfirth. Perhaps in the whole area. He had always assumed that his extended family would arrange his marriage to some distant cousin. That frequently happened in his clan. It would happen soon if he didn't tell the elders that he had someone in mind because the family expected him to breed a warrior son who would carry on the MacDrakin lineage.

When his eyes acclimated to the sunlight he gave a startled gasp. To the south, two lines of small white clouds filled the sky. The unusual thing about the clouds was their uniform shape and movement. They stayed aligned in their formations as they fell and they moved at a constant rate, like military units on a parade ground. If they were real clouds, the winds would affect the formations and make them ragged. He turned around. To the north, he saw more clouds. Some had fallen close to the ground and he noticed they had a barrel-like package tethered to the bottom.

The clouds to the south were much higher than the ones to the north, and the furthest line would surely fall in Yuk-land. That would really annoy the border yuks. Another thought hit him like a punch to the head. Were these clouds what Higginbottom worried about? Did these clouds come from those squids?

He carried the sacks of dirt to the sluice and dumped them into the trough. Suddenly he whirled around and studied the clouds more intently. At least one, and perhaps two of them, would land close to his mine shafts. Did each cloud have one of those squid creatures Higginbottom described? Or something else?

He wasn't sure what was dropping near his land, but he wanted to be prepared for whatever happened next. He hurried to his shack and took down his ancestor's battle ax. As he gripped the handle, he had a premonition that his big adventure had started.

# # #

Yunta, not quite recovered from her multiple periods, squeezed her bulk into the crowded engineering section to observe the landings. Two crew members, with headsets covering their audio receptor holes, sat in front of consoles filled with signal lights, switches and monitors. Each console had communication links to the robots. The electronics, the console operators, a section supervisor and Yunta overloaded the cooling systems. The temperature in the small room grew uncomfortably hot. Mivex, the engineering officer, had to stand outside because of the crowded conditions. He tried to peek over heads.

Yunta patted each operator on the back and breathed deeply to sooth her nerves; landings were fraught with danger for the robots and could result in lost machines. Landing on rough terrain often damaged the robots and made them inoperative. This planet presented additional hazards. It had flowing water and extremely large plants. It was possible for a robot to become lodged in the plants and the water presented an unknown danger. Native populations presented further unknown perils. No one could predict how these natives would react to the robots exploring the land. In case of problems with the locals, she had ordered Shtap to be ready to meet with the native leader to solve the problems. No one in her crew had ever mined a planet with an intelligent native population. Shtap believed he had everything under control, but she didn't trust the natives.

A row of lights on the nearest console changed from red to yellow. "Captain," an operator said, "the units in the first group are almost on the ground." A few lights changed from yellow to green. A moment later, "All ten units are on the ground and undamaged." He paused then added, "And the units have activated the search programs."

"Excellent." Yunta relaxed slightly.

"Unit 15 has not landed," the second operator said. "I think it is stuck in something, possibly a large plant. It will have to use its tools to try to extricate itself. Unit 27 lost contact right after it landed in liquid water. Possibly, it was destroyed in the landing."

Soon, all the robots landed and contacted the ship. Only two units were unaccounted for. The remaining units began to scour their assigned sectors except for the one still stuck in a plant.

"Well done," Yunta said as she heaved her bulk out the section door.

She now had a good feeling about the mission. She was confident the robots would soon discover the minerals that would turn the voyage from a financial disaster to a profitable mission.

# # #

Unit 15 found itself dangling from a tree ten feet above the ground. On a command from the mother ship, it activated a problem-solving program and analyzed the predicament. The program found no danger and ordered the parachute latches to release. Unit 15 dropped to the ground, bounced, fell over and rolled downhill until it slammed into a tree trunk. It righted itself and ran an integrity check on all systems. With everything in working order and with only a few dents noted, it sent a status report to the mother ship. After receiving a confirmation message, it moved forward to the closest boundary in its assigned grid and turned on the search-and-analyze program. Its mission involved working back and forth between a pair of boundaries while slowly making forward progress. The search was complicated because it had landed in a rocky forest that prevented straight-line movement. Undeterred, its onboard transmitter sent powerful radar waves into the ground. It compared reflected signals to a database to determine if it matched a reflection from one of the dozen minerals it sought.

Three feet tall, painted a dull gray and generally round, its midsection contained a tool chest. The communication and function control processor, much smaller than the tool chest, sat above it. The robot's pair of optical detectors, one for visual and one for infrared, and its sound detectors were contained in this small upper unit. The legs consisted of an open steel framework that ended in motorized tractor treads. Two flexible arms completed the assembly. A metallic belt circled the torso below the tool chest and held a variety of grips for the unit to use at the ends of its arms.

Unit 15 rolled over small rocks, detoured around large trees and boulders and crushed saplings in its path. After seventy-five passes, it emerged from the forest and searched a meadow. On the far side of the meadow, it entered a wheat field, its progress marked by parallel lines of flattened wheat. Near the end of the field, it picked up a reflection that partially matched a database pattern. It continued its search pattern and found more indications of a possible mineral deposit near the center of the search grid

Unit 15 continued to move from boundary to boundary, but each time it crossed the center area, reflection patterns found a match. It emerged from the wheat field and, close by, identified a native habitat. The closer Unit 15 came to the habitat, the stronger the reflection match.

A female native stood in the habitat's doorway watching as it worked its way towards her. The female stood as tall as

Unit 15 and had hairy, bare feet. The unit took pictures of the native and sent it to the mother ship for analysis and possible further instructions. It noted the habitat was a dome-like structure made of bricks.

The next leg of the sweep included the habitat. Unit 15 stopped at the doorway, still filled by the native. It gave her a move-aside warning beep. The creature obstinately stayed in the doorway. Programmed not to harm native life-forms unless necessary to continue the mission, Unit 15 beeped in a threatening manner, to no avail. Finally, it backed up a few feet, switched to high speed mode and charged the doorway. The female made sounds and jumped back into the habitat. Unit 15 followed and stopped in the center of a large, round room with a wood floor. A radar probe confirmed that it stood over a small mineral deposit. It opened a compartment in its tool chest and took out a woodworking tool. After it cut a hole in the floor, it replaced the wood tool with a digger from its tool belt. This tool was nothing but a fat drill point. Unit 15 inserted the tip of the drill into the dirt in the hole and turned it on. It spun into the ground, sending dirt flying out of the hole. A mound of dirt quickly grew and covered much of the floor. The female native made noises and ran around the hole while jumping up and down.

After the hole reached a depth of twenty-five feet, Unit 15 stopped and probed with its radar. The reflection indicated it had reached the mineral deposit. It extracted a sample and dropped it into a small dish that slid into its built-in analysis laboratory in the tool chest. A quick chemical scan indicated the mineral existed, but in such diluted quantities that mining the deposit would not be cost-effective.

Unit 15 filed a report, beeped an apology to the native and left the habitat. It headed for a field filled with large green stalks. It zigzagged through the corn field as it contin-ued its search pattern.

#

Bitting her lip and clenching her fists, Higginbottom watched the last line of objects disappear behind hills and trees to the south of Skensfirth. It was a sure bet the objects would land in Yukland. The yuks were touchy about border integrity and she wondered how they would react to an inva-sion of their homeland. She sighed and decided it was time to earn her salary, even if it was only fifty silver pennies a year.

Two lines of objects had bracketed Skensfirth, one to the north and the other to the south. The northern one landed across the Skensfirth River and in a forested area, but the southern one landed in the town's farmlands. She walked to the stables by the river, checked out the municipal mule and saddled it. The animal was used occasionally to haul a cart filled with dirt or garbage and wasn't used to having a rider. Higginbottom had difficulty getting it to move.

Outside of town, she passed several farms before she found a trail of flattened corn. She rode the mule through the corn field, careful not to overtake whatever it was that she followed. The trail frequently and abruptly reversed direc-tions. She wondered why. The idea that she might face pos-sible danger sent adrenaline soaring through her veins. Her blood roared in her ears.

She came out of the corn field and recognized the farm of Guy Dupre. A gray object -- it could only be a robot men-tioned in the Dun Hythe telegram -- had finished sawing through the top rail of a split-log fence surrounding a pony pen. Even though alerted by the telegram, the sight of a machine operating without anyone controlling it upset her. Was it magic? Or an advanced technology. She didn't like it when she didn't understand the situation.

Six ponies retreated from the robot and stood huddled near the domed stable that formed one side of the pen. The hair on her neck rose. What if every floating mushroom had landed one of these things? About the size of an average dwarf, it didn't have feet. Instead it had some sort of moving platform. And one of its hands was a saw blade.

Higginbottom frowned. Dun Hythe said the robots wouldn't damage property, but this one had trampled a field of corn and was sawing through a fence. She had to protect Dupre's property. It was her job.

"Hey," she yelled. "Leave that fence alone." She rode closer to the robot until she towered over it on the mule. She wondered if it had weapons. Even more important, was it hostile or friendly? Riding this close may have been a mistake.

The robot turned. It resembled a small barrel, that was the only way she could describe it. A pair of dark circles focused on her. It made a string of whistling sounds and went back to sawing. The middle split-log fell in two and the thing attacked the lower one. Once it sawed through the lower log, it brushed the logs aside and entered the pen. It rolled towards the stable. The animals whinnied and bucked to get around the thing. They charged for the broken fence and ran into the corn field.

"Now look what you've done," Higginbottom called out. "Stop what you're doing and help me round up the ponies. I thought you robots were supposed to respect property rights?"

The robot ignored her and sawed through the side of the stable. Brick dust clogged the air as it cut out a section of wall and entered. A few seconds later, she heard more sawing. The robot obviously needed a lesson on what doors were used for. She rode around the stable and watched it move away. She dismounted, went inside the stable and found six sets of harnesses. She remounted and started off rounding up the ponies. Once she got back to Skensfirth, she would send a telegram to Dun Hythe. She needed instructions on what they wanted her to do.

If the high and mighty in the capital responded to the telegram, she had an ominous feeling she wouldn't like the instructions.

# # #

MacDrakin finished sluicing the dirt and pawed through the rock remains searching for gems. His battle ax nestled in a harness on his back.

He kept glancing at the path leading down the mountain, expecting a trespasser. He looked at a few rocks and realized he had looked at the same rocks several times. He still hadn't decided if the rock required a closer inspection or should be thrown over the side of the mountain. He took a deep breath and gave up looking at the rocks. He couldn't concentrate. His mind was filled with the idea of someone or something trespassing on his land. His father had always told him that a landowning dwarf had only one primary job and that was to defend that land. He intended to follow his daddy's philosophy. No matter what came up the mountain, he would fight it to defend his land. As a descendent of the legendary Drakin, he had an added incentive; he couldn't disgrace his heritage. To allow Higginbottom's squids to trespass would be a double violation of his responsibilities: to his father's memory and to his heroic ancestor.

Along with those responsibilities, he had a gut-wrenching sensation that whatever happened today was only the opening event in an important and dangerous adventure that would make his name as famous as the original Drakin's name. Or, possibly, he would become infamous. Or even dead and forgotten.

He wondered if Higginbottom had met any problems because of these unknown creatures. After he cleaned up, he'd ride down to Skensfirth and check if she needed any help. He hoped she could cope with the situation until he got there.

Something crashed through the woods that paralleled the road. He realized he had heard the noise for a while, but it hadn't registered in his mind because of his concentration on the other issues. The noise wasn't constant. It alternated with periods of silence and it had grown louder over time. He leaned against the side of the sluice and drew his ax. Placing it on the ground between his legs, he flapped his wrists to loosen them up.

A metallic figure appeared on the path. It looked like one of the barrels he had seen hanging below the small clouds. Instead of feet, it maneuvered on a pair of continuous belts. How could the thing operate without someone to guild it? How could it move without an animal or a driver? It stopped and examined the area, then moved to the right as far as it could go without falling off the edge of the foothill, turned, and worked its way back to the left, close to where he stood. Its actions puzzled him. It looked like it searched for something. But what could a machine do by itself? It reached the other edge, turned again, paused to examine MacDrakin momentarily then started another trip to the right. How did the thing know when it reached the edge? MacDrakin picked up the ax.

MacDrakin flushed with anger at the apparent dismissal by the mechanical thing. With a shock he noticed his hut stood in the new path of the machine. He sprinted to the hut, beat the barrel by a few seconds and took up a defensive position in the doorway. The machine meandered to within ten feet of the hut and paused as if sizing up MacDrakin's intentions. It gave three shrill blasts. MacDrakin sensed the thing sounded a warning. He frowned as he thought through the implications of that observation. The machine had intelligence? How could that be?

The machine stopped making noise and moved towards MacDrakin.

MacDrakin hefted the ax into a strike position. No one or no thing came into his hut without his invitation.

The machine continued forward and appeared intent on pushing past MacDrakin.

He timed the machine's approach and swung an overhand blow. He aimed at the round part on top that had two eye-like circles. The ax smashed through its metallic skin between the circles. The machine stuttered to a halt and squealed. The noise made MacDrakin's skin crawl. It sounded like a cry for help, like a wounded bird or animal might make. It turned in a circle while grinding noises came from the left belt that no longer worked. It shuddered and fell on its right side. A small square of shiny material fell out of the gaping wound. So did a few other strange items. After one more squeal and another shudder, it stopped making noises. MacDrakin watched it warily for a few minutes. When it remained inert, he grabbed the frame near one of the bottom belts and pulled it to the closest cliff edge and rolled it over the side. He watched it bounce and burst apart until it reached the bottom, nothing more than a pile of parts.

MacDrakin realized he had just rolled Fortune's dice, but he couldn't see if the dice showed a winning or a losing number. It would be a while before he knew the result of the dice roll. Whatever it turned out to be, he couldn't disgrace his ancestor.

He saddled his pony and headed down the mountain. He chewed on a beard braid while he worried about Higginbottom.

# # #

Gorya led his hunting party back to their village. One of the hunters, using a rope slung over his shoulder, dragged their captured prey behind him.

The village children screeched in joy and ran to meet the hunters. Gorya greeted each of his four yuklings with hugs and head rubs. Other children got a pat on the head or on the shoulder.

"Whatcha catch, Pa?" Dima asked. He was the first-born and at nine was almost ready to start his hunting apprenticeship.

"Don't know. But it trespassed onna tribal lands so it don't matter wot it is."

"Can us keep it. Like a pet?" Dima asked.

"Me don't know if it can be trained. Might not be housebroken. Dat'll get Ma pretty angry. Us better off killin' it."

"Can us eat it?" Zoya, his daughter asked.

"Don't think so. Dey gotta tough skin. Don't think it gotta lotta meat."

Zoya walked up the beeping robot and knocked on the skin with a knuckle. "Dis one sound mad." She nudged it with a toe. It beeped again. "Hey Pa! Maybe dis thing like a crab. It gotta a hard shell but after ya cook it and crack de shell dere's good stuff in it."

"Maybe so." Last year, Gorya attended a meeting of tribal chieftains. It was held on the west coast and he took his whole family there. "How ya cook crabs? Anyone remember?"

"Ya drop 'em inna big pot of boilin' water," eight-year-old Ziv replied.

"Okay. Zoya, run back and tell ma to get a pot goin'. Us'll cook dis one to see if it's got any good eatin' inside. Dere's a lot more of dese things runnin' around in de woods. If dey ain't good eatin', us'll leave dem where us kill dem."

"Pa, can me go onna next huntin' party?" Dima asked.

Gorya rubbed his chin and looked at his eldest son. "Dat a good idea. Dese things ain't too dangerous and ya can get some experience."

# # #

MacDrakin found Higginbottom in the town hall building. In her office he could barely fit in the tiny room already filled with her desk, two chairs and stacks of wood boxes filled with loose papers. She looked distraught. She didn't see him at first, so intently did she stare out a small window that opened into an alley.

"Constable? Are you all right?"

Higginbottom jumped at the sound of his voice. She turned in her chair and gave him a wan smile. She stood and said, "This is the worst day of my life. I need a hug." She came around the desk and embraced him. MacDrakin, taken by surprise, froze momentarily then wrapped his arms around her and gently squeezed. He was surprised again at how good it felt. He couldn't recall ever getting hugged before Higginbottom started doing it. It wasn't something his family did.

"Is this a bad day because of those mechanical beasts running around?"

Higginbottom drew back far enough to look at him. She grimaced and nodded. "I can't do the job I've dreamed of all my life. When I was a little girl, I used to go with my father on his rounds and he'd always say, 'The most important thing I do is protect folks and their property.' Well, I'm not allowed to interfere with the robots and they're destroying property. Folks are afraid of them. I spent most of the morning chasing ponies one of them let loose on the Dupre farm."

"Robots? Is that what the things are called? And why can't you interfere?"

She reached over to her desk and snatched a sheet of paper. "This telegram to all constables came from Dun Hythe. It said that robots would show up somewhere and that we were not to interfere with them. It also said the robots wouldn't hurt folks or property. But they are. I saw one of them do it. And I'm not allowed to stop them." She crushed the telegram into a ball and hurled it across the room. "Let's go outside. It's too cramped and stuffy in here."

On High Street, folks gathered in small groups and whispered amongst themselves. To MacDrakin, they looked

as dispirited as Higginbottom, and many of them looked
fearful. As another sign of the town's mood, the market
square at the end of the street had only three vendors instead
of the usual dozens.

"Up on my land, one of these robot things tried to enter
my home," MacDrakin told her.

"What happened?" Higginbottom held a hand in front of
open mouth.

"I bashed it with my ax." He reached over his shoulder
to touch the handle. "Then I rolled it over the side of the
hill. Maybe you can't interfere, but no machine is going to
trespass on my land."

Higginbottom looked aghast. She wondered what the
consequences of that action would be. Certainly, MacDrakin
hadn't broken any laws in destroying the robot. She had a
faint hope that more folks would do that, but she knew that
most of them didn't have the MacDrakin's spunk. Another
concern popped into her mind. Would the squid-like
creatures retaliate for losing one of their machines? "You
destroyed it?"

"Aye. I killed it." MacDrakin pointed south. "Some of
the robots looked like they were landing across the border.
The yuks'll kill them all."

"I don't know what to do." She sighed. "I wouldn't
mind taking my sword to a few of them. I sent a telegram to
my supervisor in Ashton and asked him to forward it to Dun
Hythe. I told them what the robots were doing and asked
how I'm supposed to do my job. He wrote back that he sent
it along and added one of his own saying much the same
things I did. Maybe that will get some answers from the
capital."

"Do you think it'll do any good?" MacDrakin raised an eyebrow.

"Oh, I hope so. I'm so frustrated." She gave him a smile. "Let's walk down High Street. Maybe, if the people see me on the job, it'll calm their fears."

# # #

That evening, Busby Abercombie, an elderly, gangling, bald human, banged his pewter mug on a work bench. "This meeting of the First Skensfirth Militia will come to order."

Eleven other old males sat around on empty ale kegs in a dilapidated stable near the river. Outside, a thunderstorm dropped water in drenching sheets, the first rain in two weeks. The roar of thunder shook the frame of the building. The militia held meetings irregularly, whenever they had collected enough dues money to buy a keg of ale and a pound of pipeweed. That happened several times a week.

"Wait," a half-pint corporal said. "We didn't tap the keg of ale."

"We will hold off on the ale until we discuss an important business issue." Abercombie's eyes blazed with determination, awaiting a protest over his keg-tapping edict.

"The roof's leakin'," a dwarf private said.

"That's 'cause it's raining out," Paddy Stuart replied. The white-hair burly dwarf was the Militia's first sergeant. "It always leaks under those conditions."

"The maintenance committee was supposed to fix that. I remember votin' on it."

"The maintenance committee died a while back," Stuart said.

"He did? I don't remember that," the dwarf said.

"Fell off the roof while trying to patch it up," Stuart replied.

"You was at his funeral," a half-pint corporal said. "We all was."

"I was? Oh well. All dead guys look alike."

"Can we get back to business?" Abercombie banged his mug a few more times.

"Iffen we can't drink the ale yet," Josh Biddle said, "let's bust open the pipeweed so we can have a smoke while you run off at the mouth." He was a human and, as head of the refreshment committee, wielded much influence within the militia.

"I second that motion," an elf private called out. "It's the only intelligent thing I've heard all day."

Biddle grabbed a small cloth sack, took out his pipe and filled it from the sack. He passed the sack to the closest member and lit his pipe with a candle. Soon the fragrant odor of pipeweed filled the area and the militia became slightly less hostile.

Abercombie tried again to get everyone's attention.

"Ahh, let's listen to the old windbag," said a half-pint private, "so we can get to the main business of the night. Drinkin' ale."

Abercombie glared at the half-pint for a second before saying, "It is time to start planning for the Militia Day Parade. This year will be the fifteenth annual parade."

"The other fourteen was cancelled," Stuart pointed out.

"Due it unforeseen circumstances," Abercombie replied.

"Yeah, we was all too hungover to walk, let alone march," Stuart said with a laugh.

"That is why this year I propose we not have a meeting the night before." Abercombie expected a angry reply to that suggestion and he got one. The First Skensfirth Militia stood up as one, booed and shook their fists at their leader.

"I demand that we table this agenda item and tap the keg," Stuart called out.

"I second the proposal. All in favor raise your hand," the dwarf private called out.

The proposal passed unanimously.

Abercombie gaveled the work bench. "Wait a minute --"

"Abercombie, shut up, sit down and drink your ale," the half-pint corporal said.

CHAPTER EIGHT

"See, Dima." Gorya pointed to a path of crushed and broken bracken in front of them. "Dese things don't care about coverin' dere tracks. Dat makes it easy to hunt dem. And dey always go back and forth, like dey lookin' for somethin'." He squatted down behind some brush and indicated to Dima to do the same. "Us wait here for da thing. It'll come back soon."

"Can me shoot it?" the yukling asked.

"Naw. Ya gotta watch and learn first. 'Sides, dis thing too heavy for a yuklin' like you." Gorya hefted his custom-made triple crossbow. The bows were stacked on top of each other and could be fired individually or in a volley of three.

Gorya looked around to ensure the others in the hunting party had taken proper positions.

Soon, he heard sounds of snapping twigs and parting shrubs.

Dima, squatting behind a bush, bounced on his heels and giggled.

Gorya placed a hand on Dima's arm to steady the lad and quiet him down.

In another minute, the prey emerged from behind a wall of shrubs. Gorya stuck the front end of the crossbow through the brush and waited for his prey to walk into the weapon's line of sight. Gorya pulled the volley trigger and, with loud twangs, three bolts shot forward and slammed into the target, one in the head and two in the torso. It jerked backward, spun around and tumbled on its side.

The other hunters howled a victory paean. Dima jumped up and down and imitated the hunters' howl.

Gorya walked over to the target and prodded it with his foot. It made strange noises, like metal scraped across metal. "Dima come here." He loaded one bolt into the crossbow and handed it to his son. He helped the yukling hold the heavy weapon. "Aim at de head, if dat's what it is. When me tell ya, pull da trigger."

Dima stuck out his tongue in concentration and pointed the crossbow at the target.

"Now," Gorya said.

Dima pulled the trigger and the bolt crashed into the prey's left eye. It shuddered. Blue sparks shot out of its eyes along with green smoke. A small explosion came from somewhere inside.

Gorya kicked it again and got no response. He smacked Dima on the back. "Ya got ya first kill, son."

# # #

"Captain?" Shtap said. "We have discovered why two of the units stopped communicating with us. Some of the information is very puzzling." They were back in the engineering section.

"How did you get this information?" Yunta wondered why Shtap hadn't included Mivex in the meeting since he was in charge of the section. It must mean she was about to get bad news. She didn't need more of that. While she was just about recovered from her menstruations, her metabolism was still a bit out of whack. What she needed was rest, quiet and some peaceful time alone.

An engineer cleared his throat. "All the units continuously upload audio and video streams of whatever they come across." The engineer spoke while he manipulated switches on a console. "We do not normally look at the video streams and they are stored in the auxiliary memory banks until we need to look at one of them. After units 18 and 44 went dark, I retrieved the streams and looked for clues."

"Very good." Yunta clacked her teeth and patted the engineer on her shoulder. "I like initiative. Give Shtap your name and ID number. I will put them in my communicator for future reference. Now show me."

"This is the last few minutes of video from unit 18." The engineer operated switches and the screen lit up to show a short, hairy native standing in a doorway.

"What is in the native's hand?" Yunta asked.

"A weapon," Shtap replied.

The unit examined the native briefly then beeped a warning. The native ignored the warning, and the unit moved forward. The native swung his weapon and the last sound from unit 18 made was the noise of quantum electronic chips shorting out and sizzling.

Yunta's eye stalks snapped back and forth seeking something or someone to destroy.

"It appears the native did not understand the unit's warning," Shtap said.

"That idiot Mivex did not program the robots to give warnings in the native language?" Yunta bunched two tentacles and squeezed until she felt pain. It helped her control her anger. "Can we download language programs into the robots?"

"No, Captain." The engineer's eyestalks bobbed left and right. "That can only be done on board the ship or a cargo pod."

"Sending down a cargo pod to program the robots would involve recalling all of them and delay the mineral exploration," Shtap said.

Yunta made a mental note to think of a way to make Mivex suffer a slow and painful death.

"The last reports from that unit," Shtap said, "disclosed a mineral deposit in the area, possibly a large one. We will have to send another robot there to finish mapping the area."

"Next, we have the end of unit 44," the engineer said. "This is disturbing." He threw a switch and the screen filled with a view of trees seen from below.

"What is this?" Yunta was puzzled by the action on the screen. "Can anyone explain what is going on?"

"We think the unit is laying on its back and being dragged along the ground. It has been captured by a group of natives." Shtap wrung a few tentacles.

"Now what are they doing?" Yunta watched the unit get strung up on a tree limb. Upside down, it dangled above a large cauldron of water over a fire.

"Apparently, the natives are preparing to cook unit 44."

"What is wrong with these natives?" Yunta snarled. "Do they not have any notion of civilized behavior?" Seeking a measure of composure, Yunta shook herself, spattering slime over nearby the cabinets and walls. "Do you have any more bad news?"

Shtap nodded. He looked crestfallen.

"Well, what is it?"

"We have lost contact with all the other units in 44's group of ten."

Never in her life had Yunta felt as depressed as she did at that moment. Her corporate tree was again infested with bugs. "Shtap!" She pounded a tentacle on the top of a cabinet. "Fix the problem."

# # #

In mid-afternoon, Rodrigs, wearing a copper-colored bow tie, sat in the presidential office reviewing national issues with Webley. The president's only interest in these matters was how they could affect his reelection campaign. Pinky chased its tail in tight circles. The puppy growled in frustration when it didn't catch it and howled in pain when it did. Rodrigs had an appointment with a dragon expert to get advice on how to train the dragon pup and to find out if Pinky was male or female.

A column of bright light formed in the middle of the office. Colors swirled around the outside of it. Inside the column, a shadow formed and then solidified. A horrible stench filled the office. Rodrigs snapped off a pair of wards before Webley or he could get sick from the smell.

"Oh, no! Rodrigs, tell me this isn't what I think it is." Webley shook his head. "At least it's not nap time."

"Whoa," Shtap said. "You are an ugly sucker."

"Has your race discovered appointment calendars yet?" Webley folded his arms across his chest and glared at the alien.

Pinky stopped running in circles when it noticed the visitor. It crouched down and moved closer, like a cat stalking a bird. It pounced and bit the end of one tentacle. The tentacle flicked and Pinky flew across the room, bounced off a wall, stood up and vomited.

Interesting, Rodrigs thought. Shtap's ward didn't extend to the tips of his tentacles. Could that mean something of importance? Something he could use?

"I have come to inform you that you are in violation of our treaty." One of Shtap's eye stalks rotated to keep watch on the dragon pup. "You court disaster. Captain Yunta has a violent nature when angered."

"What are you talking about?" Rodrigs asked.

"The natives are destroying our explorer robots. I assure you they are very expensive and Captain Yunta is not pleased."

"I find it offensive that you make accusations without providing any proof," Webley said.

"Wait a minute, sir." Rodrigs cringed at Webley's semi-hostile attitude. "Your robots landed in the Ashton-Skensfirth area?" He walked over to the wall map and tapped the area. "Here?"

Shtap confirmed the exploration site.

"We have reports from there that the robots are damaging private property." Rodrigs mentally thanked Boudreau for sharing the reports his spies had picked up.

"The cost of any property damage will pale compared to the cost of one explorer." Shtap slithered over to the wall map. "In this area," a tentacle slapped near the Yulkand border, "many robots are missing." Yukland smoldered from Shtap's slime.

"Ah," Rodrigs said. "That area is not part of the deal. It's a different country and the yuks are very hostile to trespassers. They'll root out every one of your machines and destroy them."

"Why were we not informed of this vital information?" Shtap slithered back to the front of Webley's desk. "You have not acted in good faith."

"You promised us the robots would respect private property, so how can you accuse us of not acting in good faith?" Webley replied.

"I think it's time to review the situation," Rodrigs said. "I'm sure we can clear up these misunderstandings."

"What do you propose?" Shtap asked.

"We will order the constables in the exploration area to protect the robots, but you must instruct these robots not to damage buildings and farms. In addition, they must not harm our folks."

"That is acceptable. See to it." Shtap tapped a tentacle on a small device. The column of light reappeared and Shtap dissolved.

"How does he do that?" Webley asked.

"I wish I knew. I can't tell if its magic or an unknown technology." He sighed. "I'll tell Sfiore to inform the constables they are to protect the robots." Rodrigs sensed the situation careened toward disaster, but he couldn't explain why he had the feeling.

# # #

A tall and lithe elf, Meria Sfiore stood over six feet tall. The Secretary of the Interior had amber-hued eyes and silver hair that draped over the tops of her shoulders. She wore an ankle-length hyacinth-colored gown and matching slippers. The gown had flowers embroidered into it, and they changed over the course of a day. Early in the morning, they were buds. By mid-afternoon, they were in full bloom. Late in the afternoon, they folded up.

The scent of newly mown hay permeated the office where she sat reading through reports.

Born into a family that dwelt in a forest area, she loved the outdoors and regretted the time she spent in her stuffy office. She much preferred to travel around the country and meet with people. At an early age, she had shown signs of magical talent and had been bundled off to a wizard's prep school. Later on, she graduated from the University of Magic and Husbandry. Entering government administration, she rose through the ranks by talent combined with treachery.

Her responsibilities at Interior included supervising all constabulary functions inside Gundarland as well as overseeing immigration and food production. Kincaid Crumlish, her nemesis, felt that his position as Defense Minister should include control over the constabulary. They fought over the issue at every cabinet meeting and engaged in guerilla warfare elsewhere.

Thinking of Crumlish made her hug herself in glee. Certainly by tomorrow morning at the latest, he would have learned about her plan to acquire six of his ships. That information would drive him berserk.

Crumlish would be even angrier if he ever discovered it was a hoax. One of her assistants had uncovered a spy in the department. Knowing that any agent had to be Crumlish's minion, she spread disinformation by letting the spy overhear her whispered discussion in the hallway.

Her personal assistant entered the office and dropped a pile of scrolls on the desk. The assistant smiled, turned and left. Meria frowned at the assistant's back. The assistant

posed a problem and she didn't know what to do about it.
When her Godmother learned of her appointment as Secretary, she gave her the highly trained assistant as a gift. She
wasn't her real Godmother, rather she was 'The Godmother'
to the entire tribe and her wishes were taken as mandates.
One didn't simply refuse a 'gift' from her. While giving the
impression of being a gentle female, the Godmother had ac-
quired a ruthless reputation. Meria knew the assistant reported everything to the old hag and Meria was helpless to stop
it. So far, she hadn't been approached by the Godmother for
a 'favor,' one that couldn't be refused, but Meria knew it was
only a matter of time before the old female requested repay-
ment for the gift of the assistant.

For a moment, she looked at the many prints on the
walls. All depicted scenes from nature: a meadow bursting
with flowers, a snow-covered pine tree, ivy climbing an oak
tree. One landscape had mountain peaks bathing in sunlight
and another showed the sun sparking off placid lake waters.
During the day, the sun traveled across the pictures' sky
changing the light and shadows. At night, a full moon did
the same. As always, the pictures soothed her nerves. She
pulled her eyes from the pictures and set to work. Crumlish
was sure to launch a counterattack and she had to figure out
what he would probably do so she could devise a strategy to
block it.

Before she addressed the Crumlish situation, she had to
consider the two telegrams on her desk. Webley had assured
the cabinet that the robots would respect property rights, yet
constables in Ashton and Skensfirth sent telegrams describ-
ing violations and damage. Apparently, these visitors used
technologies that bordered on magic to the constables. She
looked at the wall map covering most of one wall. Obvi-

ously, the visitors concentrated on the area in the southwest near the Yukland border. Sfiore tapped a long, exquisitely painted fingernail on her desk. The nail showed a yellow begonia. What to do? Her constables were charged with protecting citizens and their property, but at Rodrigs' insistence, she had sent a second telegram ordering the constables to protect the robots. The new telegram must have crossed paths with the ones she had on desk. Once the constables received the new one, they would be utterly confused. Of course, since she sent the telegram at Rodrigs's urging, her backside was protected in that matter.

Nonetheless, the telegrams presented her with a major problem, but, of more importance, the situation offered an opportunity to counterbalance that problem. Apparently, she was only one in Dun Hythe who knew about the awesome technology deployed by the aliens or that the robots destroyed property.

Knowledge is power. So, how could she use this information to force Defense Minister Crumlish to surrender some of his authority to her? Until she figured that out, she would refrain from answering the telegrams.

# # #

Alix Cyr, weary from working a shift in the furniture factory, trudged her way to the closest police station. It was the first chance she had to file a report since her return to Dun Hythe three days ago. As she walked along, she had to jump over the many filthy puddles of stagnant water. She kept her eyes looking straight ahead to ignore the folks, both male and female, who snickered at her. Her story of a kidnapping had made the rounds of the district and everyone knew about her claim. She held her head high and continued walking.

"Alix!" a friend called from a cafe. "Tell us yer story again and I'll buy ya a mug of ale."

What a bitch, Alix thought and made a note to scratch her from her list of friends. A number of similar comments had her seething by the time she reached her destination.

Inside the police station -- the only stone building on the street -- a cop directed her to the sergeant's desk. She felt uncomfortable. Folks in her district didn't have any reason to like the police.

"Wot can I do for you, missy?" the sergeant asked. He was a tall human with a sizable paunch and a face covered with stubble. His uniform blouse still showed signs of his lunch.

"I want to report a kidnapping." Alix smiled at the man even though she hated the idea of being nice to a cop, but she didn't want to annoy him before she filed the report.

"And just who was kidnapped?"

"I was."

"But yer here. So it looks like things worked out all right. How much was the ransom, iffen ya don't mind me asking?"

"I didn't have to pay a ransom."

"Well, iffen ya here and ya didn't have to pay anything, why bother with a report?"

"Because I want the kidnappers caught and punished."

"All right." The sergeant sighed as if exasperated by Alix. He rummaged through a desk drawer and took out a piece of paper. "Write down yer story here. Give us as much detail as ya can remember."

Alix sat a badly scarred table and wrote about her ordeal.

An hour later, she left the police station. Before the door closed, she heard the sergeant laugh out loud and call out to the other officers to read her report.

Alix's face reddened. Why wouldn't anyone believe her?

#

Kincaid Crumlish, the Minister of Defense, paced his office while contemplating alien opportunities. In addition, he schemed about how to steal assets from his arch-nemesis Meria Sfiore. If either project enjoyed success, it would add to his power and authority while weakening hers. It also gave him great satisfaction, as a dwarf, to defeat an elf, and Sfiore certainly was an elf. Why President Webley ever let an elf remain in a cabinet position was beyond his comprehension. It demonstrated the shoddy thinking that humans were capable of.

The aliens intrigued him. If they could come from a distant world, they possessed technology that could revolutionize weaponry and warfare. Armed with this technology, he could conquer the planet for Gundarland. Sfiore would be swept away like crumbs on the floor.

Crumlish wore a military tunic with gold lacing to depict his rank. His cavalry-style pants were stuffed into the tops of calf-high boots. His sky-blue beret with a large gold star hung from a hook on the wall. While he paced, he stroked his belly length beard with its three braids dyed red, green and white to match Gundarland's flag colors. No one would ever accuse him of being unpatriotic.

His office was shaped like a pentagram as was the entire building -- the better to repeal enemy spells in case of an invasion. The walls held portraits of his predecessors, all apparently painted while they suffered from indigestion. Scattered around the floor and on shelves were models of prototype weapons under development. One was a model of a compact, fast-loading catapult. Another was a blunderbuss that magically reloaded itself. So far, neither of these had proven effective. Crumlish suspected that the inventors were charlatans trying to dupe the ministry into giving them lucrative development contracts. To prevent getting cheated, he provided minimal funds to keep the projects going just in case the weapons worked as predicted. He had better uses for the scarce funds in the military budget. He needed money to attack Sfiore's Interior Department. His attacks kept the blasted female on the defensive and prevented her from attacking him.

Even if the new weapons worked, he would be reluctant to equip his forces with them. He preferred the traditional ways and worked to strengthen them. He had increased the number of wizard-advisors in every combat brigade. In the fleet, the number of wizards in each warship jumped from eight to twelve. Finally, he started elite assault units consisting entirely of wizard-warriors. These increases reflected his personal military philosophy: one can never have too much magic between oneself and the enemy.

He walked to a window overlooking Dun Hythe's harbor now in late afternoon shadows. Two new warships sat a-building on their ways. The iron-sided, steam-driven ships would be the most modern and most powerful ships in the world. The ships represented one of his few concessions to modernity. It would also bring to eight the number of iron-clad ships in the fleet. He decided to visit the harbor soon and check on the progress of the ships. An unannounced vis-

it would keep the builders on their toes and cut down on pilferage.

"Sir!" A clerk stood in the doorway.

"Yes. What is it?"

"There is someone downstairs who claims to work for
you. He has an important message he says."

"Did he give a name?"

"Only that he is Agent 13."

Crumlish closed his eyes and frowned in concentration.
He snapped his fingers and held out his hand. A paper on his
desk flew into the hand. He opened his eyes and scanned
down the list. Agent 13 was assigned to the Interior Department. "Send him in." Crumlish wondered if the agent
would provide him ammunition to attack Sfiore. He tamped
down his excitement so the agent wouldn't notice it.

A minute later, a tall, slender human dressed in a dark
suit and foulard slunk into the office. His furtive glance took
in Crumlish and every object in the office.

"What is it?" Crumlish asked.

"I overheard the Secretary talking to one of her deputies.
As soon as I could get away from the job I came straight
here."

"Tell me."

"She wants to snatch six ships from your ministry to use
in controlling immigration and smuggling."

Crumlish's mouth dropped open. He blinked several
times before waving a hand for Agent 13 to depart. Once he
was alone, he kicked a trash bucket and sent it flying across
the room. All thoughts of alien technology flew from his
mind. How dare that bitch covet his ships! How dare she
think she could pillage his empire! If Meria Sfiore wanted

war, he would give her a war. She would regret this brazen
attack.

CHAPTER NINE

Yunta lunged with her rapier and Mivex knocked it aside with a shield. Both zaftans carried a pair of shields, a rapier and a cutlass. The two dueled in a cargo hold still empty of minerals. Idle mining machines lined the walls of the hold. Yunta used the exercise to burn off some of her stress. The voyage would reach the midpoint in eight rotations and they still didn't have any minerals. A second reason for the workout was to punish Mivex for his gross stupidity. He had failed to program the robots with the native language and he hadn't turned on the stun gun features in the robotic control programs. If he had, she wouldn't be facing the loss of so many expensive robots putting even more pressure on profits. Her corporate tree needed fertilizer as profits instead of infestations of bugs known as loses.

Mivex slashed at her with his cutlass. Yunta blocked it, slithered forward and smashed her second shield into his torso, splattering his slime. She withdrew, and clicked her teeth at her opponent. He looked winded and the blow with the shield hurt him. He rubbed the area with the back of the tentacle holding the cutlass. Excess slime glistened on his body, a sure sign of exertion.

The door to the cargo hold opened and Yunta jumped back to glance at the door. She didn't trust Mivex. He was capable of assassination if he sensed an opportunity or if he thought he was in danger. Shtap entered. "Greetings, Captain." He bobbed his eyestalks to Mivex.

"I hope you bring good news for a change, Shtap." Yunta pointed the rapier in his direction.

Shtap shrugged, a gesture that made his tentacles quiver. "Some good, some bad."

"Let's hear it." Yunta attacked Mivex who had relaxed his guard while listening to the conversation. He yelped in pain when Yenta drove her rapier through one of his tentacles.

Yunta's mood improved and she clacked her teeth a second time. This was more fun than she had anticipated it would be.

"The good news is that a robot has found a source of minerals. The bad news is it's a small deposit."

"How small?" Yunta circled Mivex searching for more places to stick him.

"Estimates say it will only fill two percent of our capacity, but the find is gadolinite which has a high profit margin."

"Mivex!" Yunta faked an attack and a panicked Mivex threw his two shields together to from a defensive wall. Too bad she hadn't thought of workouts before today. It was so enjoyable. Maybe she would bring in Drek for a therapy session tomorrow. "Have your engineers uncovered the reason we couldn't contact any robots for a time the other day?"

"Not yet," Mivex replied. "It's a mystery to my staff."

"Everything seems to be a mystery to your department." A wicked idea formed in Yunta's mind. "Mivex! Attention for orders!"

Mivex lowered his shields and weapons and stood at attention.

"Prepare cargo pod two with mining equipment and robot drivers. Then load ten more explorer robots. We will intensify the exploration. Make sure these explorers have the native language programmed into them and their stun weapons activated. Send one robot to the mountain where we lost unit 23. Order it to finish mapping the area. You can program that one to harm natives." Yunta tightened the hold on the tentacle grips of her shields. "Then send the machines to mine the deposit."

"I hear and obey, Captain," Mivex said.

"You may show your respect by bowing in the old-fashioned way."

Yunta waited until his bow bought his eyestalks parallel to the floor. "This is for screwing up so badly in the past." She slid forward and slammed her shields against both sides of his inclined head. Mivex emitted a gurgling sound. His eyestalks bounced around wildly while his eyeballs rotated crazily. He slumped to the floor.

"Damn! That felt good."

She dropped her weapons and walked out of the cargo hold.

She thought about all the destroyed robots and now regretted another of her expense reductions: not taking any heavy weapons on board for the voyage. A few blasts from a ship-mounted laser cannon would subdue the natives and protect the remaining robots. Unfortunately, all she had was hand-held stun guns and a few laser rifles.

# # #

Meria Sfiore walked up the main street in Dun Hythe toward the old city walls to meet Boudreau. An out-of-doors meeting offered a location safe from office spies listening in. Long ago the city had outgrown its walls and now they formed a dividing line between the old city and the newer sprawling suburbs. The land directly inside the walls had been converted into a narrow park that circled the inner city.

Her silver earrings, three heavy concentric rings, jingled as she moved. A matching set of torcs encircled her neck and her forest green gown left a trail of pine scent.

A melancholy mood had taken hold of her since she had heard about the robots damaging property. It could give her nemesis Crumlish an opportunity to denounce her administration as incompetent. She needed a way to defend her organization from his imminent attacks and to launch an offensive. Her meeting this morning could go a long way to further the campaign against the maniacal dwarf. Meanwhile, she hoped her constables uncovered an alien secret. Possession of the secret would allow her to demonstrate her superiority over the idiotic Crumlish.

Besides the usual inter-department warfare issues and the possible opportunities, the aliens caused still more problems for her and she silently cursed their arrival. Her affairs had been under control and moved ahead smoothly until the aliens showed up. All her training and experience had focused on controlling known problems. The aliens and robots presented novel situations that eluded her control.

The arrival of the aliens also complicated her plans to run for the presidency. Instead of recruiting influential supporters, she now wasted time and resources on the aliens and the problems they caused. She suspected that Crumlish would also be a candidate, so her attention to building her supporter base became ever more important. She had to fix the alien problem so she could spend more time on her main priority. Unless of course, an alien secret came into her hands. That would change a number of areas for the better.

On top of everything else, her personal assistant delivered a note from the Godmother this morning. The hag
had heard rumors of strange events in the south and she
wanted Meria to apprise her of potential moneymaking opportunities.

She spotted Boudreau sitting on a bench eating nuts. His
support could help solve her problems. She noted his toe
hairs looked recently groomed.

Sfiore pasted a smile on her face and greeted him. For
his part, Boudreau seemed genuinely glad to see her and that
aroused her suspicion. Why would he be glad to see her?
What was the runt up to? She sat on the bench and looked
down on the much shorter Boudreau. "Thank you for meeting with me," she said. "I want to share an idea with you."

"'Ill be glad to listen and offer advice." Boudreau threw
a nut to a squirrel. Two pigeons demanded equal treatment.

"This concerns the alien situation. Webley has promised
to protect their robots, even though they are damaging and
destroying property. I've received a note from Rodrigs
telling me to order my constables to protect the robots from
attacks by our folks. I sent a telegram to that effect to all my
constables, even though I think it is a mistake."

"Yes, I've heard about Rodrigs's order."

Sfiore paused to absorb that information. How did
Boudreau know everything that went on the government?
Who was his source? She suspected Rodrigs. The two frequently acted like old friends. Did they actively plot against
her? How could she get them to plot against Crumlish instead?

"My problem is that by protecting the robots the constables will have to ignore their oath to protect property. I'm
not sure they'll be willing to do that. In any case, Ashton has

two constables and Skensfirth only one. That's not enough to protect all the robots that were reported landing in that area."

"So what do you propose to do about the situation? Webley is serious about keeping the aliens happy so they'll tell us how to fix our pollution problems. He's even made a decision on the issue, if you can believe that. He'll insist your constables protect the robots."

"He wants the pollution problem fixed so he can run for reelection. Is that it?" Webley's campaign would present another obstacle to her plan to become president.

"Indeed. That seems to be the case." Boudreau flipped a few nuts to the pigeons. The squirrel gave him a bunch of noisy static for wasting tasty tidbits on birds.

"To the problem at hand," she said. "The only way I can protect the robots is for Crumlish to lend me a regiment of foot soldiers . . . but that gives him an opportunity to demand that his troops remain under his control and that he take over responsibility for protecting the robots, a clear violation of both our mandates."

"Hmm. Ordering soldiers to protect the robots isn't a bad idea, although it could set a dangerous precedent."

"If Crumlish comes with the soldiers, I don't want them."

"The issue isn't what you and Crumlish want. The issue is what's best for Gundarland. I wish you and Crumlish would consider that aspect of your jobs occasionally."

She ignored the comment and said, "Can I count on your support to transfer the troops to my command?"

"I'll promise to consider it, but nothing more right now."

Sfiore jumped up, setting off a symphony of silvery noises from her earrings. "I knew it was a waste of time talking to you." She strode off towards her office.

Along the way, she decided to assuage her anger by jerking Crumlish around. She would use Crumlish's spy to pass on more disinformation. She smiled as she came up with an idea that morphed into a plan before she had walked a block. The plan would garner her many style points.

Plotting skullduggery improved her mood and allowed her to admire the flowers planted in pots on street corners.

# # #

Karl Crumlish, wearing his sky-blue beret, watched a formation of Swine Riders perform intricate maneuvers. Except for his beret, he was uniformed like the dwarf riders in a tan military tunic and gray cavalry pants. He stood near his field office in the Dun Hythe Military Base a few miles outside the city walls. Back in his official office, he felt like an overworked clerk wasting his time shuffling papers. Here, he felt like he truly belonged to the military.

Much to his amazement, he had grown to like the idea of war in the years since he took over the Ministry of Defense. Of course, the best part was that he got to give the orders without facing any battlefield danger.

He always thought it curious that he held the top position in the military when he had never wanted to study warfare. Instead, he wanted to be a poet. That ambition led to beatings from his father, a hoary army veteran of many battles. His family had provided officers to the military for many generations, and his father wanted that tradition to continue. Studying the family history convinced Crumlish that the military was a fool's career since most of these officers died early from combat wounds. As a compromise, he and his father agreed he would go to the School of Sorcery and Military Arts. A degree from that institution meant a career in military administration rather than combat duty.

A Swine Rider captain galloped his mount straight at Crumlish and skidded to a halt with his lance tip only feet from the minister. "Sir!" The captain snapped his M13A lance up to a vertical position before jumping from the mount and standing at attention. "The next exercise will involve simulated combat between two units using blunted lances and dull swords."

"Very good, Captain. I'll look for you personally to perform courageously." Crumlish returned the salute and watched the captain mount up and trot away. He loved to watch maneuvers, especially when they involved the Swine Riders, his favorite unit. It consisted entirely of dwarf warriors mounted on trained swine, it was the elite unit in Crumlish's arsenal. Too bad he had nothing for them to attack.

Another innovation of his involved warrior-wizard units. They consisted of foot soldiers armed with swords and wands. He staffed the new unit after a research wizard came up with a standardized formula for launching combat spells, one that greatly simplified the spell-casting process. A caster needed to determine the target's elevation, azimuth and range and include that information in the spell. The spell also needed a power level. The standardized process allowed the casting wizard to mutter the values in sequence without adding the names and the measurements of the value. Using the new process greatly increased the number of spells launched in a given time along with their accuracy.

A few minutes ago, he had watched a sham battle between two squads of warrior-wizards and was pleased at their skill with both weapons. He had also formed a unit armed with blunderbusses, but the weapons took too long to reload to be useful in combat. They did however put on impressive displays for the civilians

While waiting for the troops to begin he brought up a picture of the hated Sfiore. What would he give to unleash the Swine Riders on her organization. Let the dwarf riders and their swine hack and chew their way through her army of useless clerks. Since such an attack had a very low probability of getting approved by Boudreau or even Webley, he had to do the next best thing, psychological warfare and undercover attacks against Sfiore.

With a great splintering of lances, screams of angry swine and shouts of traditional dwarf curses, the two units of Swine Riders crashed together. The units broke apart and regrouped on opposite ends of the field. Four dwarfs lay unconscious on the grass and hospital orderlies rushed forward to get them off the field before the next charge occurred. Traditional training doctrine called for the charges to continue until a predetermined number of riders had been brained. Today's number was nineteen.

Crumlish watched three more charges. With the exercise needing only two more casualties to call it a day, he turned toward his tent. Later, he would present a trophy to the unit with the fewest number of injured riders. He entered his field office, a large canvas tent. He had had it erected to show solidarity with the troops who lived in tents whenever they were in the field. Of course, their tents were much smaller and didn't have carpeted floors, a full service bar or a four-poster feather bed equipped with a mosquito netting. He sat down at his desk in a deeply cushioned chair and contemplated how best to attack Sfiore. As far as he could calculate, she was a few tricks ahead of him. If nothing else, he had to admit she was creative. He had to get even with her and then pull a few more stunts to gain a lead. It was un-seemly for the Defense Minister to be bested by the Interior Secretary.

# # #

When Mivex's eyeballs stopped rotating, he watched Yunta and Shtap leave the cargo hold. His hatred of the cap-tain had almost forced him to react violently to her unwar-ranted attack. With a great deal of restraint, he managed not to retaliate.

He had signed onto this mission in hopes of displaying a talent that would gain him a successful reputation. That hope had been crushed by Yunta who was disrespectful of his skills. No one told him the robots needed a language download. No one told him the robots should have been armed. How was he supposed follow orders when the orders didn't give him all the information he needed?

This mission didn't different from other events in his life: a failure. All his life, others had either blocked his way or caused him to fail. When he was growing up, his friends all had wealthy parents while his were middle-class and de-cidedly un-rich. How could he succeed with that handicap? It was a testament to his perseverance and talent that he got this far despite his parental handicap.

In the military academy where he studied engineering and science, he was caught cheating on an exam and unfairly expelled. It wasn't his fault he didn't have time to properly prepare for the exams. His female friend needed his atten-tion and the only way to pass the exam was to cheat. What else could he do? The bigots on the academy board of dir-ectors refused to listen to reason.

It always came down to others forcing him to fail. Like his many incompetent teachers who couldn't properly explain the subjects. Or the superiors -- like Yunta -- who gave vague, imprecise orders and then blamed him for failing to understand what the orders really entailed. It was unfair. All his life, he did exactly what folks told him to do, nothing more, nothing less. And he didn't have a thing to show for all his hard, dedicated work.

His most recent mistake was listening to Yunta's pitch about the importance of the voyage. He signed on believing he was on a historic mission to the far reaches of the galaxy. It went to the far reaches, but it wasn't historic. Apparently, it wouldn't be profitable either. He had hoped the voyage would provide enough riches to get him started on a new life. Another failed hope.

He sighed. Someday his talents would be recognized. Someday, he would be rich and powerful. All he needed was a single break. Then perhaps he could repay Yunta for the drubbing she had just administered.

#

For lunch, Boudreau joined Rodrigs in the park across the street from the Presidential Palace. Pinky frolicked in a fenced-in dog run with a dozen canines. To get Pinky admitted to the dog run, Rodrigs had to make a healthy donation to the current mayor's reelection fund. Rodrigs wore a mint green bow tie that matched the color of his hair and eyes.

A statue in the center of the park dominated the area. It showed the four heroes who saved Dun Hythe from getting sacked hundreds of years ago. One of the heroes was a wizard named Brodwin and the other three were Vatsik, a knight-accountant, Burga, a warrior-chef and the legendary dwarf hero, Drakin.

Boudreau sat down on the bench and slapped Rodrigs on the knee. "What are you going to do with Pinky if she grows up to be the size of a mountain?" A wizard learned in the ways of dragons had recently examined Pinky and proclaimed the pup a female, but couldn't predict how big she'd get.

"I'm hoping she'll turn out to be a miniature. If she isn't, I'll need a raise in salary just to feed her."

"If she gets big and snorts flames, maybe you can hire her out to construction companies looking for a fast way to clear away old buildings."

Rodrigs laughed at his old friend. "So, what's going on with the aliens?"

"Sfiore wants to snatch some troops from Crumlish to protect the robots. Crumlish won't let them go unless the troops remain under his control. I wish somebody besides the two of us would worry about Gundarland." Boudreau shook his head and sighed. "I don't like the idea of the military getting involved in internal affairs. That kind of stuff can led to the government getting overthrown by an ambitious officer or bureaucrat."

"Can you see Crumlish or Sfiore as dictator? Or even president?" Rodrigs opened a hamper at his feet and picked up two sandwiches. He handed one to Boudreau.

"I think Crumlish would love to be a dictator or the president. I'm not sure Sfiore would have time, what with how long it takes to paint her fingernails plus all her other primping."

"So do we send troops or not?"

"There is another issue to consider before you give Webley some advice."

"What's that?"

"How will the aliens react to seeing a squad of troops trailing each of their robots? They may get suspicious and decide we're planning a double-cross." Boudreau unwrapped the sandwich and took a big bite. "Don't you ever get sick of egg salad?"

Rodrigs didn't reply until he swallowed a bite of his sandwich. "You're right about the aliens getting suspicious. Let's leave things the way they are. No troops for Skensfirth. I'll get Webley to issue a memo to that effect just so those two are clear."

Boudreau laughed. "You mean you'll write the memo and sign Webley's name to it while he takes a nap."

Rodrigs shrugged. "Whatever works."

Boudreau stood up and placed the remains of the sandwich on the bench. "I'll tell Crumlish and Sfiore about 'Webley's' decision. You can give my sandwich to Pinky. I'm going to buy a salami on rye."

# # #

Crumlish sat in the comfort of his tent. The maneuvers went well and he had presented the trophy and retired to the tent to spend the afternoon planning his next moves.

He regarded the pilferage report on the desk and cursed to himself. The damned elf gangs stole everything that wasn't locked up and lately even locks didn't deter them. When he had more time, he had to address the issue, but the stealing was an irritation compared to his other problems, especially the aliens. That situation frustrated him. As hard as he tried, he couldn't find the lever he needed to use the visitors to his advantage. Every ploy he tried was blocked by Sfiore or Boudreau. He wondered if this implied an alliance between the two.

His greatest desire was to get his hands on a piece of alien technology. Unfortunately, only Sfiore's minions had access to the aliens and their machines. That fact was an abomination that could shift the balance of power in favor of the despicable elf.

"Minister!" A tall human stood at the tent flap entrance. The man's eyes never stopped darting back and forth.

Crumlish had seen the man before, but couldn't place why or where they had meet. "And you are?"

The man pulled back from the entrance and looked around the outside of the tent. When he stopped his inspection, he said in a stage whisper, "Agent 13."

Crumlish frowned, trying to recall why he recognized Agent 13 as important.

The man coughed. "I work Interior. Remember, sir?"

"Of course!" Crumlish snapped his fingers. "It's just that I have so many folks working for me. Have you learned anything?

"Aye. This morning I overheard Sfiore's supervisors talking about an alien secret that the constable in Skensfirth had uncovered."

Crumlish spasmed into a coughing fit. When he recovered, he croaked, "An alien secret? Are you sure?"

The man nodded. "I heard them say the secret will give Interior a lot of power."

Crumlish stared at a tent wall with his mouth open. After a few seconds, he said, "What's the constable's name? Do you know it?"

"No. I didn't hear a name."

"Find out the constable's name. Immediately. There's a big reward in it for you."

The man knuckled his forehead and disappeared behind the tent flap.

Crumlish paced the carpeted floor trying to control his rage. The selfish bitch! How dare she hold back alien secrets. How dare she accumulate more power. He was sure she would use the secret to screw up his bid for the presidency. Well, she wasn't going to get away with it. When he had the name of the constable, he'd send an agent to Skensfirth to pry loose the secrets. Then Sfiore wouldn't hold an unfair advantage.

# # #

MacDrakin rode his pony up High Street looking for Higginbottom. He hadn't seen her in two days and was concerned about her. She must have a plenty of pent-up anger and frustration because of the robots. He spotted her outside the town hall arguing with Luc Jehan, the mayor. He rode up, dismounted and tied his mount to a hitching rail, acting like he wasn't listening to the argument.

"Hrmmph. Here's MacDrakin," Jehan said. "He'll tell you the same things I'm saying."

"What's that?" MacDrakin asked.

"The constable says she now has to protect the robots instead of folks' property. Isn't that the dumbest thing?"

MacDrakin raised an eyebrow and glanced at Higginbottom. She looked mad and clenched and unclenched her fists.

"It's all Dun Hythe's fault." Higginbottom snatched a telegram from the breast pocket of her shirt and handed it to MacDrakin.

MacDrakin read it in amazement. *We in the Interior Department are dismayed by the reports that some citizens have taken matters into their own hands damaging and/or destroying robots. Such actions are strongly condemned and are to cease forthwith. Constables are ordered to protect all robots from attacks by citizens. In the event that a constable observes someone damaging and /or destroying a robot, the constable will make an immediate arrest. After placing the perpetrator in jail, said constable will inform Dun Hythe of the matter. Subsequent telegrams will instruct the constable how to proceed with the case.*"

MacDrakin handed the telegram back and said, "These people in Dun Hythe don't know their butt from a hole in the ground."

"See," Jehan said," MacDrakin agrees with me."

"I agree the order is dumb," MacDrakin replied.

"Oh, MacDrakin. I don't know what to do. I've never been so frustrated in my life. My daddy taught me this job and Dun Hythe won't let me do what he taught me."

MacDrakin's heart ached for Higginbottom. She looked so unhappy. She pulled a face and placed her hands on her hips.

He said, "Dun Hythe doesn't tell me what to do. If a robot trespasses on my land, I'll kill it."

"Good lad, MacDrakin," Jehan said.

"I don't know if I should be glad or sad about that." Higginbottom gave him a weak smile. "I guess if I saw you do it, I'd have a real big problem."

"Hrmmph. We need a plan to make the folks feel safe while these blasted robots are running around."

"I don't know what to tell you to do." McDrakin brushed his beard braids and frowned. After a few seconds, he said, "Maybe you can arrest a robot that damages stuff or hurts folks."

"My instructions didn't say I'm permitted to arrest robots." Higginbottom momentarily made a face, then gave MacDrakin a big smile. "But they don't say I can't. So I guess the only way to do my job and to still protect the robots is to arrest the machines that don't respect property."

MacDrakin felt a lump in his throat. He had never met a female so independent of mind, or so adaptable. What a mate she'd make for some lucky male. He wondered if any males in town were after her hand in marriage. He'd have to do some sniffing around on that score.

"But I can't cover the whole district by myself. I'll be lucky if I can protect the town itself."

"What about calling out the militia?" Jehan asked.

"Are you crazy?" Higginbottom gave him shocked look. "They can't help me. They're all old and feeble. And that's when they're sober."

# # #

Gorya sat on an empty ale barrel and leaned against a tree trunk while watching the youngsters kick around a ball made from hog skin filled with straw. He had nothing to do since he and his hunters had exterminated all the trespassers that wandered into his tribal territory.

He heard a shout from the other side of the village and stood up. A mule-drawn wagon approached the village driven by an old elf trader named Vinny. He showed up every two weeks with a wagon-full of supplies to trade for furs and crops. Vinny also brought the latest news from Gundarland and was the only trader allowed to enter the village.

Gorya walked over the wagon and shook hands with Vinny. "What's new, old friend," Gorya asked.

"I suppose you heard about all the mechanical things runnin' around Skensfirth. They're doin' a lot of damage, I tell you."

"Us had some over here, but dey're all dead now." Gorya pointed in the direction of Skensfirth. "Dey gotta problem?"

"Yeah. Those things are runnin' amuck, bustin' up homes, ruinin' crops and no one knows why"

"Me gotta idea. Me and me hunters go over dere and help dem out. Dose things lotta fun to kill."

"Don't think the folks in Skensfirth will like the idea of you yuks roamin' around."

"Me know a fellow over dere. Me in army wid him. Name's MacDrakin. Maybe him go huntin' wid us."

CHAPTER TEN

Just after sunrise, cargo pod number two landed in a field of barley south of Skensfirth. The dull gray color of the hull blended into the morning fog. Despite the early hour, many folks in town saw the huge ship floating to the surface and they dreaded the new invasion.

After the cargo doors opened, five enormous mining machines lumbered out of the pod followed by a squad of robots. Powerful but cheaply made, the backhoe, auger, chain bucket and two dump trucks, had no intelligence and were designed to be abandoned by the mother ship if the mineral deposits were rich enough to justify loading more minerals in place of the machines. Each machine had a reprogrammed explorer robot sitting at a control panel to drive and operate the machine.

Another explorer robot spent thirty minutes crisscrossing the property on its tractor treads looking for the point of maximum mineral density. It found the point next to the farmhouse and sent a signal to the driver robots who drove the machines close to the house. Ignoring the pleas of the small natives, they flattened the house and tossed the debris to one side. A back-hoe opened the ground then a giant auger took over and drilled straight down. The dirt was dropped into the dump trucks and disposed of in a nearby field. Within an hour, the machines had dug a deep hole an acre in extent. Excavated dirt buried fields of barley.

After the mineral deposit had been reached, the machine with buckets on an endless chain extracted the mineral ore

and loaded the dump trucks. Once loaded, the trucks drove
back to the cargo pod, unloaded and returned to the hole.

By noon, the mineral deposit had been depleted and the
robots drove the machines back into the cargo pod. The
doors clanked shut and the ship slowly lifted off the surface,
leaving a formerly productive farm devastated.

While the mining operations continued, ten explorer robots left the cargo pod and deployed toward their assigned
sectors and missions.

# # #

Crumlish approached the dingy waterfront tavern called
the *Groveling Shoat*. Reputed to be hundreds of years old,
there was no evidence to contradict the claim. Smoke had
turned the rafters and the plank board walls black. The dirt
floor held so many obnoxious stains that it appeared to be
uniform in color. The table surfaces were thin from knife
carvings and the annual cleaning.

Crumlish wore old work clothes so no one would recognize him. A turtle neck sweater covered his multicolored
beard braids. Upon entering the tavern, he forced himself to
ignore the foul smell of old ale, vomit and stale pipe smoke.
On his left stood a dilapidated and heavily scarred bar with a
fearsome creature behind it. Dock workers, drinking their
lunch, stood three deep at the bar. Despite the summer's
heat, a roaring fire spewed light, heat and smoke in the rear
of the room. He saw his contact sitting at a table near the
fireplace. He sat down at the table and nodded to the dwarf
who dressed entirely in black. The dwarf had a full, dense
uncurled beard whereas, a month ago, he was clean-shaven.
Crumlish surmised the beard was false.

The dwarf took a pull from a leather mug. He was know only as Dagger. No one, including Crumlish, knew his real name. "Ya said it was important." Dagger's eyes displayed cruelty. So much cruelty that even Crumlish couldn't look him in the eyes. "Well, what is it?"

Crumlish bit his tongue to prevent a tart remark about respecting one's betters. Dagger was the best assassin in Gundarland and Crumlish had need of his services, even if it required putting up with the ill-mannered lout for a time. "It is of middling importance and only one of many projects I have underway." Crumlish had no intention of telling Dagger just how important this mission was. "There is a constable in Skensfirth named Leslie Higginbottom. She has learned a secret from the aliens that are exploring the region. I want the secret. Go to Skensfirth and get the information."

"What kinda secret? Technology? Weaponry? Treasure? It'd help iffen I had some idea what I was searchin' for."

"The question is irrelevant."

"How much pressure do I use? You want the constable dead? Or should I leave her alive?"

"I want the information. The constable's life is inconsequential. Just spare me any details of how you get it."

"Sounds like I should get paid more than usual."

"Don't be daft. It is just another assignment and I'll pay you the usual fee." Crumlish made a face.

"I'm thinkin' this one's more important. Why else would ya be demandin' that I drop everythin' and meet wid ya right away? I'm also thinkin' my bill should be twice the usual."

"Twice?" Crumlish growled and shook his head. "For twice your usual fee, I can hire an entire gang of assassins."

"Then hire 'em. Dagger smiled. "I ain't goin' to Skensburg for less than a double payment."

"Skensfirth. I'll give you a twenty percent bonus. Not a copper penny more."

"Fifty percent and we got a deal."

Crumlish frowned and shook his head. "For a simple mission? Fifty percent is robbery."

Dagger stared into Crumlish's eyes.

"All right." Crumlish shuddered at the lack of emotion in Dagger's eyes. "Fifty percent more than your usual fee."

Dagger drained his mug and stood up. "I'll be onna first train inna mornin'."

# # #

MacDrakin, using a pick ax, whacked at the vein of black rock and was rewarded with a small cascade of loose lumps. He dug in mine shaft three, the shallowest of his three. So far, the shaft hadn't yielded any emeralds but it did have a thick vein of coal. MacDrakin preferred the coal to peat for cooking and heating his home and he had used the last of his coal pile last night heating water for a bath.

During his work, his thoughts kept drifting to Skensfirth and Higginbottom. He worried about her. She was caught in a dilemma caused by the idiots in Dun Hythe. How could she protect all the houses and farms in the area from damage by robots while protecting the robots at the same time? It was unfair, and she had no one to help her. The militia was supposed to be there for problems like this, but they wouldn't be much help. They could be a hinderance since she would have to watch over them to keep them from injuring themselves.

Folks expected her to perform her constabulary duties to protect their lives and property and they had begun to mutter against her. One loudmouth wished Higginbottom's father was still constable. Higginbottom couldn't remain a constable unless she had the folks behind her. Her job depended on trust; she had to trust the citizens and they had to trust her. These alien robots were destroying that trust. Luc Jehan openly complained about the lack of protection she provided. Other citizens were taking up the mayor's complaint.

MacDrakin wondered what his heroic ancestor would do in this situation. His initial expectations that a great adventure was about to start hadn't happened. It frustrated him. Instead of going on a quest or an adventure, he spent his time digging in mine shafts.

He dropped the pick and filled a sack by scooping up the loose coal. He lifted the sack and his battle ax. He never went anywhere without the weapon since his encounter with the robot. He dragged the sack to the surface and stretched his cramping muscles. In mid-stretch, he stopped to gawk at the robot standing on the lip of shaft number two.

"Get off my property!" he roared.

The robot spun on its tractor treads to face in his direction. "Whoa!" it said in a metallic voice. "You are an ugly sucker."

Stunned by the voice, MacDrakin stared at the machine. How could a machine talk? What other amazing devices did the aliens have?

The robot turned back to the shaft and rolled forward a foot or two. It stopped and engaged in some activity unknown to MacDrakin.

"Last chance." He smacked the handle of the ax into his open palm. "Leave now or else."

The robot spun back to face MacDrakin and opened a door in its chest. It took out a gray metal device and pointed it in his general direction. "When I have finished my survey of this sector, I will leave. Do not interfere. I am armed."

"Leave now." He advanced on the robot, keeping his eyes on the device.

"Native! Do not interfere."

MacDrakin advanced another step and the robot moved the device to follow him. He felt a surge of combat fury and he dove forward and rolled to his left. A sound like an angry bee zipped past his left ear. He rolled again, jumped to his feet and found himself on the right side of the robot. He swung his ax at what he thought of as the machine's neck. It sliced through the robot and the upper part flew down the mine shaft. The rest of it remained motionless.

MacDrakin removed the machine's weapon, fetched a rope from his hut and tied it to the bottom of the robot. He hauled it over to the edge of the mountain and rolled it down to rust with its mate. The destruction of the robot assuaged his combat rage slightly.

He examined the weapon. He had never seen anything like it. L-shaped, it fit comfortably in his hand. He held it the way the robot had, and more by accident than purpose, pushed the trigger. A beam of orange light squirted from the device and ricocheted off the side of the mountain. He spotted a squirrel near his hut. He aimed and fired again. The orange beam hit the ground in front of the animal, bounced and enveloped it. The squirrel collapsed on the ground. MacDrakin approached it and bent over to examine it. It still breathed and seemed uninjured. He waited a few minutes to see what would happen. The squirrel's eyes opened and it looked around. It saw MacDrakin standing close by, jumped to its feet, gave MacDrakin a mouthful of squirrel curses and fled into the woods alongside the road.

MacDrakin reviewed what had just happened. A robot trespassed on his land and then attacked him. No one or no thing attacked him and got away with it. The attack meant war! This must be the great quest he had sensed was about to happen. A sudden thought jolted him out of his adrenaline-induced anger. Since the robots had weapons, Higginbottom would be in danger if she tried to arrest one of them. He couldn't let the machines hurt her. He didn't care what Dun Hythe thought or said. He would do what his ancestor would do; eliminate the threat from these robots so Higginbottom would remain safe.

He took a deep breath; his adventure had started!

First, he needed reinforcements, like his old sergeant major, but before he attended to that, he had to warn Higginbottom.

# # #

Higginbottom didn't like what she saw. People assembled on street corners and argued in whispers. When she approached them, the arguments stopped and they pasted phony smiles on their face. After she passed, she heard the cutting remarks some of them made. What really alarmed her was that a number of males walked around carrying weapons, either real ones like short swords or makeshift ones such as pitchforks. Skensfirth was moving towards a violent reaction to the robots and their destruction of property. Her contradictory orders didn't help. Somehow, everyone knew Dun Hythe had ordered her to protect the robots instead of the town folks. She was viewed with suspicion by folks. If she followed the new orders, Skensfirth would de-test her; if she didn't follow the new orders, her superiors would take her to task and perhaps fire her. Her frustration made her as tense as a coiled spring. She wanted to fight with someone or something just to lessen the tension.

It broke her heart to see and feel the animosity of her friends and neighbors, folks she had known all her life. Fear drove them. They'd all heard tales about robots violating the sanctity of homes and destroying property. The news about the recent brutal destruction of a farm didn't help. So far, the robots had avoided Skensfirth, but she didn't think that would last. Not with the new report that more of them had landed.

On top of everything else, a new, vague message arrived last night from Dun Hythe. It urged her to uncover a secret from the robots or aliens.

She came to the general store and saw Geno Aterrano talking with Luc Jehan. If she joined them, she would get a raft of grief about her actions or non-actions. She pressed forward though; she needed to gauge the mood of leading citizens like these two.

"Constable." Aterrano's voice wasn't as friendly as it was in the past.

"Hrmph".

"Have you heard what the aliens did to the farm?" Ater-rano looked down his nose at her. "Just to get some minerals or some such nonsense."

"I did. I wish I knew when this would stop."

"What I want to know," Jehan said, "is whether you plan to protect Skensfirth or the aliens. You can't do both you know and, right now, you're not doing either."

"I wish I knew what to do." Higginbottom's eyes welled up from her anguish. "I don't want to protect the robots, but I have no choice. At least, the robots have stayed away from town."

"I fear that won't last much longer," Aterrano said. "After all, this is the only place they haven't been."

Higginbottom knew the shopkeeper was right. Her personal hell hadn't started yet. She decided to send another telegram to Dun Hythe. Those people must have no idea how bad things were in Skensfirth. Perhaps, they would send her new orders, ones she could enforce without breaking her heart.

# # #

MacDrakin rode his pony into Skensfirth. He greeted the folks standing in groups on the street corners and was surprised by their curt responses. He could feel hostility in the air. The attitude of folks reinforced his belief that going to war with the robots was the correct thing for him to do. It was what his ancestor would have done, but he didn't think the original Drakin would have waited so long before taking action. He would have begun when the first robot trespassed on his land.

He spotted Higginbottom near the town hall. He jumped off the animal and tied it to a hitching rail. Higginbottom saw him. MacDrakin noticed she looked even more upset today than she had been yesterday. He was afraid she might crack under the pressure if the situation didn't change. The corners of her mouth flicked upward into a brief smile then curved downward again. She met him in the middle of the street.

"Have you gotten any new orders from Dun Hythe?" he asked.

"I just sent them a telegram," she said. "I told them how bad the situation is here. Maybe, they'll reconsider and send me different orders." She sighed. "How are things with you?"

"Another robot trespassed on my land a little while ago. This one talked and had a weapon. It tried to attack me." He reached into his pocket and pulled it out. "I don't think it kills, it just knocks you out for a while. At least that's what it did to a squirrel."

"That's terrible. What did you do?"

"I killed it and threw it over the side of the cliff."

Higginbottom chewed her lip. "I guess I can call that one self-defense." She gave another flimsy smile. "What are we going to do? I can't stand much more of these robots. Or my orders."

"Your orders don't apply to me. I'm going to war with the robots. I'm sending a telegram to my old sergeant major asking him to round up the discharged soldiers living in the area and meet me here. I'm going to wipe out all the robots."

The town folks started yelling and pointing. MacDrakin looked up High Street and saw a robot traveling towards them. Every few feet it stopped as if briefly examining something before moving on.

"Oh! What am I going to do?" Higginbottom cried. "I've dreaded this moment. If someone attacks the robot, I've got to arrest him."

MacDrakin's initial reaction on seeing the robot was to go over and kill it, but Higginbottom's wail stopped him. He recognized the awful position that would put her in.

The folks gathered in a crowd close to the robot.

"Leave it alone," MacDrakin called out. "I ran into one this morning and it had a weapon. Stay away from it."

The robot crisscrossed High Street. The crowd fell back as it moved deeper into the town. On one pass across the street it came up to Higginbottom and MacDrakin. It stopped and examined them. "Whoa! You are an ugly sucker."

Higginbottom's mouth dropped open. "That's what I said to an alien when they had me on the ship."

"Move away," the robot said.

"Don't move," MacDrakin said. "Let the thing go around us."

The robot beeped twice then brushed against Higginbottom. She staggered backward a few steps and grabbed onto a hitching rail to keep from falling.

In one smooth movement, MacDrakin reached over his shoulder, grasped the handle of his battle ax and swung it overhand. The ax split the top of the robot down to its middle. It ceased moving and fell on its face.

"Damn!" Higginbottom covered her mouth with her hands. Her eyes were wide with alarm. "Now what am I going to do? You killed a robot."

MacDrakin saw her expression. He seethed at her intransigence. "You aren't going to arrest me, are you?" He had to yell because of the cheering from the folks. He looked around. Males pounded each other on the back while females hugged and squealed.

"You killed a robot. My orders are to arrest you and tell Dun Hythe."

"The thing attacked you. I wasn't going to let it get away with that."

"Three cheers for MacDrakin," Luc Jehan called out.

The crowd responded with lusty roars.

"I think this crowd will get out of hand if you try to arrest me," MacDrakin said in a quiet voice after the cheering died down. "Write it up as unprovoked attack by a robot. Even the idiots in Dun Hythe should be able to understand that."

"I'll ignore it this time, but don't you dare touch another robot. You hear me?" Higginbottom, hands on her hips, glared at him.

"I'm going to kill every one of the damned things I can find," MacDrakin snarled. "I'm going to war. So I guess you better stay away from me."

"Oh! Males are so stupid!" She spun on her heel and stomped off towards the town hall.

"Males are stupid?" he yelled at her back. "And what about how stubborn females are?" MacDrakin gnashed his teeth and yanked at his beard. Females were so flighty. How was anyone supposed to figure out what they wanted? He waited until Higginbottom disappeared inside the building then followed her so he could use the telegraph located across from her office. Even though her office door was shut, he heard her sobs. His anger melted and he paused wondering if he should knock on her door. No, he thought, she'd just yell some more. Instead, he went to the telegraph operator. "I want to send a telegram to a guy who lives outside Ashton."

CHAPTER ELEVEN

Webley sat his desk calculating how much of his life had been spent in his most enjoyable task, napping. Besides the eight hours of sleep each night, he estimated he napped two hours a day out of the remaining sixteen. That meant more than ten percent of his waking hours weren't spent awake. Overall, a splendid achievement. He set himself a new goal; by the end of the year, to increase his nap time by a half-hour yielding a fifteen percent napping rate.

Rodrigs entered to give Webley a report on the overnight happenings. Pinky trotted alongside chewing on a secretary's boot. The secretary, from the adjacent office, yelled threats at Rodrigs's back.

"Ah, Rodrigs. It's wonderful to see you again." Webley gave his Chief-of-Staff a dazzling smile. "I like the color of your bow tie. Huckleberry, isn't it?"

"It's good to see you also, sir. Yes, huckleberry is the color. Made especially for me."

"I trust Gundarland spent a quiet night." Webley's cummerbund and ascot were lemon colored.

"Not too many problems last night. A train derailed down south and--"

A column of bright light appeared in the middle of the room.

"Bloody hell," Webley muttered. "We'll never get the smell out of here if he keeps popping in."

Shtap appeared. "Whoa! You are--"

"I know." Webley held up one hand with the palm toward the alien and pinched his nostrils with the other hand. "I'm an ugly sucker. Where did you get such an idiotic greeting?" He nodded to Rodrigs in appreciation for the ward that now surrounded him.

"Idiotic? A native greeted me with that expression the first time I presented myself to the captives."

"Captives?" Rodrigs started. "What captives?" The idea of captives shocked and angered him. Or were the captives really hostages?

"We picked up two natives to learn your language. That is how we do things."

"Where are they now?" Webley asked.

"They were safely returned before I came here for the first time. They were unharmed."

Pinky dropped the boot, now in tatters, and stalked Shtap.

Shtap cleared his throat, a nerve-grinding noise. "I am here to demand payment for the robots that have been destroyed by the natives. So far, we count thirteen and they are very expensive machines. My captain is upset and is considering retaliation. Trust me, she is bloody-minded."

"Wait a minute," Rodrigs countered. "You dropped a group of them in Yukland. The yuks destroyed them, not us."

"We don't acknowledge your artificial boundaries and thus reject your argument. It is nothing more than an attempt to evade responsibility."

Rodrigs had to refute the alien's argument quickly, before he gained a negotiating advantage. "It's premature to discuss payment," he said. "First, we have to tally the cost of the extensive damage caused by the robots. Then we will swap bills and see who owes who and how much."

Shtap tapped a tentacle and stared out a window.

Pinky half-leaped, half-flew to attack Shtap and crashed into his midsection. With a loud zapping sound, the dragon pup flew backward, hit the floor and cart-wheeled three times before slamming into a wall.

"This creature of yours is not too smart," Shtap said.

Rodrigs noticed Shtap's' ward and had a strange idea. He pondered the implications, especially the danger if the alien detected Rodrigs' actions. Gently, so as not to attract Shtap's notice, he probed the ward to determine the nature of the spell used. To his shock, it was as foreign to him as Shtap was. An unknown type of magic! How was that possible? According to his instructors at Wizardry and Liberal Arts College, there were only two types of magic, black and white. According to the Laws of Natural Magicks formulated by Sheldonthorpe The Killjoy, these were the only two permitted in the universe.

"I will tell my captain of your concern about damages. I assure you that she will not tolerate losing more robots. If another one is destroyed, she will order retaliation. Be warned." Shtap disappeared. Rodrigs kept the wards intact until the alien's stench dissipated.

Rodrigs had a knot of anxiety in his stomach. The situation was careening out of control. Boudreau had slipped him a note last night that said the population in Skensfirth verged on rebellion and may soon take things into their own hands. Boudreau was sure that meant attacks on the robots.

"Sir, I think we need a cabinet meeting."

"For once, Rodrigs, I think you are right about a cabinet meeting." Deep lines creased Webley's forehead. "I have no idea how we can force these creatures to pay for their damages. Why, they could simply fly away after we give them the bill."

#

A dispirited Higginbottom sat in her office, her head resting on her arms. Never had she felt so low. All because of Dun Hythe. She liked MacDrakin and hoped to spend a lot more time with him in the future. He was the most unique dwarf in Skensfirth for number of reasons: he made a living, he didn't intend to move out of town, he was good-looking and he came from a good family.

Unfortunately, his sense of duty included killing the same robots she was ordered to protect. She couldn't ignore Dun Hythe's orders and still live with herself, but she didn't know how she would live with herself if she lost MacDrakin. If they remained on their differing courses, she could see herself as an old maid. That thought depressed her even more.

It all came down to Dun Hythe. If they regained their senses and allowed her to do the job she was trained to do, she and MacDrakin wouldn't be at odds. Then their paths and their lives could converge. What would she do if MacDrakin killed another robot in front of her? Could she arrest him and hold him for a trial? Would he resist if she tried to arrest him? Would the two of them end up in a street brawl? She knew instinctively if she tried to arrest him, it would end any possible relationship they might have.

She decided to patrol the town. She put on her cap, but was so distracted she neglected to set it at its usual jaunty angle.

#

A troubled MacDrakin sat alone.

He rested on a bench outside his hut drinking a cup of coffee. His decision to go to war against the aliens weighed on his mind. He was alone and had no idea how powerful the enemy was. The robots proved that they had an awesome advantage in technology and that implied their weapons would be unimaginable to him. The possible enemy strength was another worry, but his relationship with Higginbottom could be the first and most important casualty of his actions. He knew she wanted to fight against the robots, but her dedication to duty made her suppress that desire to follow orders no matter how stupid they were. Similarly, their relationship may be sacrificed on her altar to duty. He regretted that possibility. She was the first female he truly felt comfortable with. He could visualize the two of them spending many years together. He pictured a tribe of dwarflings running around the mountain having rock fights while Higginbottom tried to get them in the house for baths. Of course, he would have to build a new much larger house to replace the small hut he now lived in.

He sighed. He had to stop thinking about her and concentrate of the task at hand. He reviewed the two major imperatives demanding that he prosecute the war. The first was his father's belief that a dwarf was nothing if he didn't protect his land. If the stupid robots had asked permission, he would have allowed them to explore. Their acts of trespass showed disrespect for him and his rights as land owner. That couldn't be tolerated without disgracing his father's memory.

Then there was his revered ancestor. According to the legends, the original Drakin never backed down from a challenge, no matter what the odds and no matter how formidable the enemy. It was now his turn to uphold this family tradition. He had the hero's ax, now he had to prove to himself and to the world that he had the hero's courage and backbone. He had to demonstrate his spunk even he had to fight alone. He hoped his sergeant-major would bring in a few volunteers, but whether the old soldier came alone or with others, he had to face the aliens. It could come down to himself, back to a tree or wall, fighting off a horde of aliens. If that was his fate, so be it.

He stood up and cocked an ear downhill. Something moved on the road. Another robot? He hoisted the battle ax and stationed himself behind the hut, out of sight from the road. He listened intently and heard the noise of multiple robots. His adrenaline spiked upward. The robots were ganging up on him. So, the aliens had declared war on him! He grinned. Here was a chance to demonstrate his mettle.

"Hey!" a rough voice called out. "Anybody home onna hill."

The voice surprised MacDrakin. It couldn't be, but it was. Yuks were here on his mountain. "Gorya! I heard you a hundred yards away. You're lucky I didn't go downhill and attack you from the rear. You never were any good at sneaking up on anyone."

"Hah! Dat from de worst officer inna battalion." Gorya's head showed on the road, as ugly and brutal-looking as MacDrakin remembered from the army days when they worked together.

MacDrakin ran forward and embraced his old comrade. "What brings you here? Didn't the people in Skensfirth chase you away?"

"Naw. Me tell constable me here to meet wid old army buddy. She tell me where ya was. Us go around de town so us not scare folks." He pointed to the three yuks following him. "Dese guys me best hunters and fighters."

MacDrakin's hopes fluttered upward. He had a hunch why Gorya had shown up. "What brings you all this way?" He held his breath for the answer.

"Us kill all dem strange things in Yukland. Me wondered if ya had a problem wid dem. Us wanna kill more of dem. Dey fun to hunt."

"I declared war against the robots and the aliens who sent them here."

"A war!" Gorya whooped and pounded MacDrakin on the back. "Dis get bedda and bedda."

# # #

Rodrigs arranged the cabinet meeting for later in the day, inviting only Crumlish, Sfiore and Boudreau. He didn't look forward to the meeting. Gundarland was facing a critical situation and he anticipated that Crumlish and Sfiore would try to use it to increase their personal power and prestige.

"We have some unique problems," Webley said to open the meeting. "We need answers. Has to do with the aliens, of course. Rodrigs can explain it better than I can."

Rodrigs outlined Shtap's demand for compensation for the destroyed robots. He also mentioned Shtap's threat about retaliation.

Pinky snorted an occasional puff of steam while she prowled the room searching for prey.

It is clear," Crumlish said, "that Sfiore's minions have botched things up." His tunic was covered with enough gold lacing to drowned him if he ever fell into a lake. He banged the butt of his combination marshal's baton and wizard's staff on the table. "Her constables are incapable of controlling the situation. The only possible solution is turn things over to me." With a theatrical flair, he dropped his baton on the table.

"It is clear," Sfiore said, "that Crumlish has finally passed beyond the boundaries of saneness." Her silver robe showed scenes of a meadow in spring sunshine. Whenever she moved, the flowers and grasses bent as if caressed by a breeze. "This crisis has been precipitated by his refusal to augment my forces. That would have allowed my constabulary staff to control the situation and none of this would have happened."

"The female deserves to be whipped for those vicious lies. Under my command, the augmented constabulary force could have prevented this situation." Crumlish pounded the table with a fist. His baton jumped off the table onto the floor.

Pinky pounced, grabbed the baton in her mouth and crunched down with her teeth. She yelped.

The room filled with yellow and green smoke along with a hideous low humming sound.

When the smoke from the burst of magical energy dissipated and the noise stopped, the conference room had been transformed into a bordello. The table was now a huge feather mattress. Red curtains covered all the windows. One empty chair contained skimpy, black leather costumes. Another held a pile of whips and handcuffs.

"Just what do you use that wizard's staff for?" Boudreau asked. "I think we need a new conference room."

Crumlish turned beet red.

"That reminds me," Rodrigs said. "We have another potential problem and it could be very serious. While Shtap was here, I examined a ward that covers his body," Rodrigs said. "It is as alien as he is. It's a completely different form of magic than ours."

"What nonsense," Sfiore sneered. "There are only two types of magic, black and white."

"You must have done something wrong," Crumlish said. "For once, I agree with the honorable Secretary of Interior."

"I too was taught there is only black magic and white magic," Rodrigs replied. "But now I know there is at least one other kind no matter what Sheldonthorpe the Killjoy says. And we don't know anything about it."

"Even so," Webley said, undisturbed by the magical problem. "I am worried about the situation in Skensfirth. I want all of you to go there and see it for yourselves. Take control of the situation and fix the problem."

"Sir!" Rodrigs said in alarm. The others stared at Webley in disbelief.

"What?" A puzzled Webley looked at Rodrigs.

"You made a decision."

Webley blinked a few time. "So I did." He chuckled. "I suppose this crisis has served to sharpen my leadership talents." He paused. "Or maybe it was the magical whatever it was that just happened."

Everyone gawked at Webley.

The idea of him having leadership talents was even more mind-boggling than his making a decision, Rodrigs thought.

"Well, I can't leave Dun Hythe until the day after tomorrow," Crumlish said. His eyes swept the room looking for anyone who would dare challenge his statement.

"I have important meetings tomorrow," Sfiore said, "that can't be postponed. It'll have to be the day after tomorrow."

"I'm concerned about Rodrigs's claim of a strange magic," Crumlish said. "I'm taking a squad of warrior-wizards with me."

Sfiore almost leaped out of her chair. "If you do, they will report to me." She glared at Crumlish.

"More female nonsense," Crumlish snarled. "You wouldn't know what to do with them."

"Wait a minute." Rodrigs interrupted the argument before the two started launching spells at each other. "I have a suggestion."

Crumlish and Sfiore stared at Rodrigs.

"I think bringing warrior-wizards to Skensfirth is a good idea. In order to keep you two from fighting about who is in charge, the squad should report to Boudreau. He's neutral in this squabble."

"A half-pint in charge of my elite forces? You are as crazy as she is." Crumlish tugged his beard braids in frustration.

"That's a wonderful solution," Webley said. "Boudreau is in command of the warrior-wizards during your trip to Skensfirth." He looked at the others. "Oh dear. I did it again, didn't I?" He yawned. "Decision-making is tiring. I need a nap."

# # #

Dagger sat in the tap room drinking an ale and eating a sandwich for dinner. After his train had arrived in Ashton in late afternoon, he leased a mule and rode the ten miles to Skensfirth where he rented a room in Kate's Inn, the town's only public house. From his table, he observed High Street through a small, dirty glass window. He hoped to get a look at his target, Leslie Higginbottom, and size her up before he made any moves. Crumlish had emphasized the need for speed on this assignment, but he had no intention of moving until he thoroughly scoped out the operation. After all, Crumlish's life wasn't at stake, his was. As a disguise, he was clean-shaven and wore a fake, single red beard braid. The local folks would remember the colorful braid, but, after he completed his mission, he would change and wear the traditional triple-braided full beard.

In the fading light of early evening, he saw a tall female dwarf wearing a blue constabular cap. She walked up the middle of the street and greeted everyone who passed. Many of the townsfolk ignored her greeting. An unpopular constable? How interesting. That could simplify things for him. Perhaps no one would care if she went missing. On the other hand, she carried a sword. That presented an unanticipated danger.

He beckoned to the serving female. "Watch my food and drink. I have to talk to the constable."

He stood up, went outside and waved to get Higginbottom's attention. She stopped and waited for him to come close.

"Good evening, Constable. My name is Ernst Bauer. I'm a businessdwarf. I came to Skensfirth because of the aliens and robots. I am most interested in learning the secrets of these visitors."

"Secrets?" The constable looked puzzled. Another one looking for secrets? What was going on? "What secrets? What are you talking about?"

"Secrets that can earn someone a substantial amount of cash if they are revealed to me. Do I make myself clear?"

"No, you don't."

"Come now, Constable. You've dealt with the robots. You must have uncovered a secret or two from them. Haven't you?"

"I don't know what you're talking about, Mr. Bauer. Have a nice stay in Skensfirth." Higginbottom continued her stroll up High Street.

Dagger returned to his sandwich and ale. The constable was good-looking and that would make dealing with her more interesting. He reviewed her answers to his questions. She deflected the one about knowing any secrets. Instead of answering, she claimed she didn't know what he was talking about. And then she walked away when he pried more directly. Was she afraid she would disclose too much information? Was she leading him on? Perhaps, she was trying to increase the cash value of the secret by acting coy. He found it informative that she neither denied nor confirmed that she knew secrets, but that was to be expected. After all, if she admitted to it, the secrets wouldn't be secret very long. In retrospect, she had responded exactly the way someone protecting a secret would respond. He would have to find an appropriate private spot to interview the constable more intimately

Dagger felt a pair of eyes staring at him. He looked around the dim tavern and saw an old man observing him. The man stood up and approached his table. "How do? New in town, are you not? We Skensfirthers don't see many strangers. Why are you here?"

"My business is none of your business, old fellow."
Dagger gave him a hooded stare. "And I don't like nosey
people, so just go back to your ale and leave me alone."

"Hah! A rude and pushy stranger. I'll wager you're from
Dun Hythe. Everyone up there is rude and pushy." The man
walked back to his table, drained his mug and turned toward
the door. On his way past Dagger, he winked and said, "I'll
keep an eye on you, so don't do anything suspicious."

Dagger cursed to himself. Already the job had gotten
complicated. He may have to eliminate the old man before
he could take care of the constable.

# # #

Busby Abercombie, his bald head turning red, used his
mug as a gavel and banged it on an empty ale keg. "I hereby
call the meeting to order. The First Skensfirth Militia will
stand and salute."

"Where's the ale?" an elf private called out. "Me mug is
dry."

"And my pipe is empty," a dwarf corporal whined.
"Break out the pipeweed already."

"We have important business to conduct. The ale will be
held until we conclude this business."

"Abercombie, you're getting senile," a corporal said.
"Drinking ale is the militia's business."

"Stand at attention, you rabble." Paddy Stuart, the
white-haired, burly dwarf first sergeant, stood with hands on
hips and glared at the other ten members of Skensfirth's militia.

"We elected you sergeant, Stuart, and we can un-elect
you, so don't you forget it." The angry half-pint private

sneered at the sergeant while jabbing his pipe stem near Stu-art's paunch

"Come on, guys," Josh Biddle said. Josh was a human and the head of the refreshment committee which consisted of him. "Let's get this business over with so we can get to the ale drinking."

"Good advice from a human. How odd," an elf private said in a stage whisper.

Abercombie banged the mug twice more.

"You're gonna have a hard time drinking ale if you bust your mug," Stuart pointed out.

"If everyone will come to order, I won't have to bang my mug." Abercombie was so angry a vein in his head throbbed.

"So let's hear it already."

"It has come to my attention that Skensfirth is rapidly ap-proaching a crisis. What with aliens and robots and destruc-tion of property, the town is in severe danger."

"We ain't blind, you know. We knew that."

"Well, I propose that this situation is exactly why the First Skensfirth Militia was formed. We must come to the aid of our town."

"I wouldn't mind whacking a robot with my sword," an old dwarf called out.

"Hah. You swing a sword, you'll fall over and break something."

"I believe that physical action is beyond our talents," Abercombie said. "I plan on something less strenuous."

"I hope it involves drinking ale," a private yelled. Everyone laughed except Abercombie.

"I propose we keep Skensfirth free from spies and enemy agents."

"Why would a spy come to Skensfirth?" Josh Biddle asked. "That don't make any sense."

"Much that concerns spies makes no sense to ordinary folk like us. Nevertheless, spies exist and one is here right now in Skensfirth. I saw him in the tavern this evening. He's a clean-shaven dwarf with a single beard curl and wears a cape. He looks ridiculous. He's also rude and pushy so I guess he's from Dun Hythe and everyone knows that Dun Hythe is overrun with spies."

"So what are we supposed to do with this spy?" an elf private asked. "Can we lynch him? Skensfirth ain't had a good lynchin' since I was tyke."

"No, we can't lynch him. We have to respect the rule of law. I propose we organize watches and keep this stranger under constant surveillance. Any suspicious activity will be reported to me and I will pass it on to Constable Higginbottom. Of course, this project will have to take preference over the Militia Day Parade."

"I second the motion," Sergeant Stuart said. "And I propose we toast the project by tapping the ale keg."

"Hear! Hear!"

"We need a code name for the operation," Stuart said. "That's how the military does it."

"All right," Abercombie said. "How about . . . Operation Dagger?"

"I second the motion," a private called out. "Now tap the damned keg."

# # #

Late at night and alone in her cabin, Yunta modified her Profit and Loss report to see the effect of the minerals already loaded. The bottom line on the report put her in a foul mood. Because the loss of robots showed up on the expense side of the ledger, she now needed to fill the ship to eighty-five percent of capacity just to break even. Every day, more robots dropped out of contact with the ship. History showed that short voyages averaged fifty percent profit margins. Long voyages averaged a shade over thirty-five percent. Even if she filled the ship to capacity, the profit margin would be considerably lower than normal. Someone had to pay for lowering her profitability.

The monitor on the wall flashed twice indicating a call. "Answer," she snarled.

Shtap's head filled the screen. "Captain. I have a little bad news and much good news." He clicked his teeth tentatively and softly.

"Good news is a change. What is it?"

"We have discovered two more mineral deposits. Both of them are much larger than one we have already mined."

"Ahh! Where are they?" Yunta opened her mouth and noisily clacked her teeth.

"On that mountain north of Skensfirth, we knew there were minerals. We have now identified it as a large deposit of bastnasite, a very profitable find. And, you won't believe this, beneath the town itself is a huge deposit of monazite."

"Monazite! That will yield any number of rare elements. It looks like our luck has finally changed to the good." Yunta bounced on her cot in her excitement. She suddenly stopped and glared at Shtap. "What's the bad news?"

"We sent a robot up that mountain to check on data received from unit 23. The new unit confirmed the find, but was destroyed by the same native who destroyed 23. And this second robot could speak and its stun gun program was active."

Yunta cursed to herself. The new loss of the robot moved her break even point even higher and moved her maximum profit even lower.

"Finally, the robot that discovered the deposit under Skensfirth was also destroyed. By the same native. I suspect this native is a fierce warrior."

"What!" Yunta seethed. How dare a lowly native endanger her career. How dare this benighted creature interfere with her plans. She tapped a tentacle on the floor. Finally, she told Shtap, "Before we leave, I will teach these natives to respect their betters. Meanwhile, prepare a plan on how we proceed to mine these deposits. Bring it to me first thing in the morning."

PART THREE:

CONFLICT

INTERLUDE TWO: GUNDARLAND

When the provinces united to form the People's Federal Republican Government of Gundarland, the petty wars of the local leaders became a thing of the past. The outbreak of peace caught most folks by surprise and caused major disruptions to many portions of the economy. Weapons and armor manufacturers, many of them one-anvil blacksmith shops, went bankrupt from the lack of orders. The Camp Followers Guild, which furnished the armies with food, drink and entertainment while in the field, saw its primary markets vanish. Dens of iniquity lost many of their profitable, iniquitous customers. Ripple effects troubled other economic sectors. Ale brewers laid off workers in response to the hordes of still thirsty but now penniless ex-warriors. The garment industry suffered from a glut of skimpy, rip-away costumes favored by the Camp Followers Guild. The surviving blacksmiths offered reduced rates to sharpen kitchen knives and scissors leading to an alarming increase in marital homicides.

While elves, half-pints and humans all felt the effects of non-war, dwarfdom suffered the most. Dwarf warrior unemployment shot up to historic highs causing hardship, worries and a frightening rise in highway brigandage. Both freight wagons and train traffic suffered equally showing that the dwarf ex-warriors were up to technological adaptation since train robberies required new and different techniques than wagon robberies. The turmoil decreased traffic and brought on more unemployment along with an increase in economic hardships.

Besides the unemployment problem, many dwarf families felt a further economic pinch because their sons or husbands no longer sent home loot from pillaged castles, forts and towns.

The dwarf warrior caste was now left without many career options. Since only a small number of bandits could make a living by robbery, some of the warriors sought jobs in their home towns, but most of those jobs were already filled by others. The rest of the unemployed dwarfs flocked to the large cities, especially Dun Hythe. There they lived in squalor, worked in factories, when they could, and bitched about how unfair life was. For entertainment, mobs of angry dwarfs often set up barricades and warred against the authorities or gangs from other parts of the city.

One of the first acts of the new government concerned Yukland. Rather than fight a war to annex the worthless swamps in the territory, it recognized Yukland as an independent country. Who knew the area held the only sizable deposits of peat, the substance that fueled Gundarland's Industrial Revolution? Compared to the cost of peat, the country's known deposits of coal were too expensive and difficult to extract.

The formation of a new type of government hastened the development of the Industrial Revolution and it brought both the good and bad to Gundarland. Telegraph lines crisscrossed the country carrying news, rumors and lies. Railroads transported goods in a day instead of a week. Factories, using peat-fired steam engines spewed out cheap goods and dirty air. Other factories dumped waste material into rivers and lakes.

Folks now looked suspiciously at the strange stuff floating in their drinking water and wondered why the air had a
nasty taste to it.

Conforming to the nature of politics, two major parties
vied for supremacy: the Freedom Party and the Liberty Party.
The Party platforms were identical and consist mainly of
pointing out the idiocy of the opposite Party's actions and
positions. Given that there was little reason for voters to
choose between the two, the vote often went to the Party that
annoyed the folks the least in recent memory. With voters,
recent memory often recalled historical events as far back as
two weeks ago.

CHAPTER TWELVE

Dagger walked to the stables near the river to get his mule. Today he planned to scout the area to find an isolated spot where he could take Higginbottom and force her to reveal the alien secret she harbored. He stopped walking and bent over as if to dislodge a pebble from his boot. While he did that, he peeked behind and to the sides. He didn't see anyone following him, but he couldn't shake the feeling that a pair of eyes watched whatever he did, where ever he did it. He must be getting old. His nerves never acted up like this on previous assignments.

He saddled the mule and rode out of town heading west toward the farming areas. The day promised to get hot later on, but, in the midmorning, the air was pleasant with a slight breeze to keep him cool. He found a dirt road and followed it as it meandered through the farms.

While he rode, he reviewed his plans for the caper, searching for a flaw. After following Higginbottom yesterday, he knew enough about her to avoid surprises. She lived in a small house on the edge of town, making it easy for him to grab her without getting spotted. After tying her up and gagging her, he'd put her on the mule and bring her to where he could work on her in quiet. He still hadn't decided whether to let her live after he learned the secret. Maybe that would depend on how hard she made him work. If she lived, he had confidence his fake one-curl red beard would allow him to remain unidentified. The plan was perfect, he decided.

He rode past many farms, each with a round, domed house set back from the road. Adjacent buildings on the farms included a barn and a silo. While they were isolated enough, they were all occupied and not suitable for his project. Dagger had no intention of complicating the job by involving more witnesses.

The road ended in a pile of dirt, a few feet high. He rode the mule up on top and stared in astonishment at the extent of the dirt. This must be where the aliens destroyed a farm. He had heard folks talk about it in the tavern. In the center, a huge hole gaped. He rode to the edge and peered into it. He couldn't see the bottom. He shuddered at the thought of falling into it. On the other hand, it provided him with an ideal spot to get rid of the constable if that's what he decided to do with her. No one would ever find her down there. He looked around. At the far end of the dirt pile he spotted a round building, the only one in the area still standing. He prodded the mule and rode over to it. He dismounted and went inside. It smelled of grain. It must be the silo where the farmer kept his harvest. It was deserted and made a perfect spot. Now all he had to do now was to find an opportunity to snatch her.

#

Yunta lounged on a couch in the conference room. Her mood had improved remarkably since Shtap reported the mineral finds last night. She slept soundly for the first time since they had arrived over this planet. Soon, the ship would be filled with high-profit minerals, just in time before the midpoint of the voyage in five more rotations. Despite the heavy loss of robots, she could still turn a profit, but she had no margin for error. Another delay would be an entrepreneurial disaster. On the return trip she would create a situation report that emphasized the sheer difficulty of operating here. She would describe the hazardous terrain and chronicle the barbaric, treacherous natives. She would have the executives of *Furshtanker Inc.* marveling at her accomplishments. Yes, the situation was under control. She fingered the gold medallion hanging from her neck. Soon, it would be encrusted with diamonds.

She looked around the room. Shtap waited for her signal to begin his presentation. Mivex and Drek watched her from the corners of their eye stalks. They both sensed her dislike. Actually, she thought, she didn't dislike them. She abhorred them. They were the two worst officers she had ever commanded. Never again would she cut costs and hire mediocrities just to shave her expenses. She must think of an appropriate way to reward their lackluster performance.

She flexed an eye stalk at Shtap.

He stood up and bobbed his eye stalks to her before beginning. "You are all aware of the situation we are in. We have located two large mineral deposits, but both are in sensitive areas, native-wise. Underneath the town is a large monazite deposit and on a mountain north of there is a smaller find of bastnasite. Between the two deposits we will easily fill the ship."

"How long will it take to gather a full load?" Yunta asked.

"I estimate we can fill the ship to capacity in three rotations. Four, if we encounter difficulties."

"Excellent." Yunta felt her face sliding into a less hostile expression and she suppressed it. She mustn't let Drek and Mivex see her animosity relax. It might give them an idea that she liked them. "But we have little margin for error with the time situation. We must proceed quickly. How do you propose we do this?"

"I recommend that we concentrate initially on the mountain deposits and deplete that one before moving on to the other."

"Why?" The proposal puzzled Yunta. To her, it made sense to mine the largest deposit first.

"The native population is hostile and they have a warrior who has destroyed at least three robots. If we begin mining in the town, I suspect this hero will lead the natives in an uprising resulting in delays for us. Therefore, I propose we mine the mountain first. This is where the warrior has his home and he will defend the area. In all the confusion during the fight, I would not be surprised if one of the machines rolled over him."

"Brilliant!" Yunta clicked her teeth loudly. "With the hero out of the way, the natives will not have a leader. We can continue in peace."

"While we mine the mountain," Shtap continued, "we can recall the robots to an assembly point. They are no longer needed to explore."

Yunta clacked her teeth again while she stared at Drek and Mivex. "I may need your skills before this is over." The idea had come to her last night after she heard Shtap's report.

"How so, Captain?" Drek asked.

Mivex looked wary.

"Nothing must delay the mining operations, and, since the situation on the ground is tricky, I may need you two and some of your assistants to go down and protect the machines and their drivers from native sabotage. A show of shamanistic prowess will cow any hostile natives."

Drek coughed. His eyeballs rotated to look at Yunta and Shtap at the same time.

Mivex gasped, then replied, "I signed on as a propulsion shaman." He gave her a defiant look. "Not as a tentacle soldier."

"You signed on to follow my orders. Turn over the propulsion control to your second-in-command and brush up on your linkages. You do the same Drek, since you'll both be involved in mining the town. Mivex! You will load a cargo pod with the necessary machinery and dispatch it to the surface. We will begin mining the mountain immediately."

She stood and slithered towards the door. She hadn't felt this good in ages. Now all she had to do was find a reason to send those two idiots to the surface and leave them there when the ship left. Without their wages, due at the end of the voyage, her expenses would decline.

# # #

Higginbottom sat in her office drinking a cup of tea on her lunch break. She twirled a finger into one of her beard curls. She dreaded going back out on High Street. Luc Jehan openly sneered at her. Instead of smiles and cheerful greetings, she only saw frowns from the males. The females avoided looking at her. She had difficulty believing the job she wanted all her life had turned so bad so quickly. It was because of the robots and the smelly squids. Why couldn't they have landed someplace else? Someplace far to the north. Not only had they ruined her job and her reputation, MacDrakin and she were on different paths that would ultimately lead to the destruction of their friendship. And just when she had started to think they had something special growing between them.

Shouts interrupted her thoughts. She stood up and peeked out the office window. By standing in a corner and tilting her head, she could see a sliver of High Street. A couple stood looking into the sky. The male pointed at something. The female bit her lip.

She belted on her sword and stepped outside.

"Constable!" the male yelled. "What is that thing?"

Higginbottom looked up but couldn't see anything from her side of the street. She crossed over to the couple, looked to the northeast and gasped. Her stomach clenched into a knot.

Floating down near MacDrakin's mountain was a huge, elliptical, gray shape that filled part of the sky. It was so big, it blotted out the sun for a few moments. "Oh no," she croaked. "Not another one." The shape didn't make any noise and that was eerie. It moved silently. If it made a howling noise, Higginbottom didn't think it could be more terrifying.

"What is it?" The female's voice sounded on the edge of hysteria. "Do you know?"

"I heard a report that one landed near Dupre's land," Higginbottom replied, "and the next thing we knew, the farm was destroyed." She rubbed her hands up and down her suddenly cold arms. She had a feeling that the monstrous shape threatened MacDrakin. She thought of running up the mountain to warn him, but decided he didn't need a warning. He could see it as well as she could. Besides, she wasn't talking to him. Not until he changed his attitude. Not until he didn't make her job harder that it already was.

She pulled her eyes from the shape to examine the faces of the folks staring up in sky. They all looked like they were on the verge of panic. Then she spotted a pair of eyes that weren't looking skyward. They were staring at her. Ernst Bauer. Everywhere she went in the last day or so, she found him near by. The male always seemed to be studying her. She looked away.

As she walked back to the town hall, a movement caught her attention. A robot entered High Street from an alley and turned north headed towards the market square. Her shoulders sagged. The day was already a disaster and it was still early in the morning. When would these aliens go away? When would they leave her and Skensfirth alone?

# # #

MacDrakin stopped braiding his beard. His mouth turned dry as he watched the sky-filling gray object descend to the ground at the base of his mountain. Gorya, sitting alongside him, sucked in air.

He must have been crazy to think he could wage war against aliens with their awesome technology. Here he was, armed only with an ancient battle ax, pitted against robots and who-knew-what-else. It didn't seem likely that his dice toss would come up with a winning number.

He forced those negative thoughts from his mind. No matter what, these aliens weren't going to trespass on his land without a fight. Under-matched as he was, he would go down fighting to protect his land.

There was one factor in this situation that he didn't have information on, but it could influence the outcome. Did the aliens have combat experience? If they were here to dig minerals out of the ground, logically they must be miners or merchants not warriors. It was also logical to assume that the ship's officers had never led troops and had never been in battle. At least he hoped those assumptions were true because it meant he had a slight advantage in both his battle and command experience. He had observed that most soldiers were killed or maimed by the stupidity of their leaders. The enemy soldiers were merely the mechanism by which the stupid leaders got their troops killed.

"Dat thing mighty big," Gorya said. "Wot ya think is in it?"

"Nothing good, that's for sure."

The two friends leaned against MacDrakin's hut and listened to trees snap apart as the vehicle crushed them. Stout branches flew high up in the air.

"Whatever is in it," MacDrakin said, "is planning to come up here."

"Dat good. Me like it when da bad guys come to me. Don't like walkin' all over de place to take a whack at dem."

Gorya's presence made MacDrakin feel better, but now he regretted that he had invited the yuks to join him. He would be responsible for their injuries and possibly their deaths.

"Me gonna go down to da bottom and see wot's goin' on." Gorya hefted his triple crossbow and walked towards the road. "Be back soon."

"Be careful, friend." Drakin went inside the hut and fetched his ax. He rubbed a towel over the blade to wipe off a few motes of dust and took a half-dozen practice swings to loosen up. Gorya's three warriors lounged on the ground by their blankets. They grinned at MacDrakin. "Us gonna have fun later?" one asked.

"Something will happen, but I don't know how much fun it'll be."

The yuks started a fire and heated a pot with their version of tea. From experience, MacDrakin knew if he drank a cup he'd throw up and be sick for the rest of the day.

Several loud mechanical coughs and whines shattered the peacefulness of the woods below them. Minutes later, Gorya exploded into the camp. His green skin had turned so pale it looked white. He acted terrified.

MacDrakin's hair on the back of his neck crawled. He had never seen Gorya afraid of anything.

"Magic!" Gorya stammered. "Dos buggers usin' magic."

"Slow down," MacDrakin said. "Tell us what you saw."

One of his warriors handed Gorya a cup of tea. He drained in a single gulp.

"Dey got big, really big wagons and dey ain't got mules or horses. Dos wagons move widout de animals. Gotta be magic."

MacDrakin smiled to himself. Obviously, Gorya had never seen a train locomotive. "How many of these magic wagons do they have?"

"One more than dis many." Gorya held up a hand with five fingers extended. "And dem things dat are fun to kill."

"What are they doing?"

"Da magic things linin' up on de road. Me think dey comin' up here."

As if to emphasize Gorya's statement, groans came from trees before they shattered. Soon, the ground shook under their feet.

MacDrakin set his feet and gripped the ax's handle. The yuks checked their crossbows. Only Gorya had a triple bolt; the others had single bolt models.

"Are the robots walking in front or behind these wagons?" MacDrakin asked.

"Dey ridin' on da big things."

MacDrakin recalled a picture of the train station in Ashton: the huge locomotives, the plumes of smoke and the driver in the back of the locomotive. The robots must be driving the machines. "Listen to me." The others turned in his direction. "We have to kill the robots on top of the machines. Without the robots, the machines won't be able to move."

"Hah! Dis gonna be fun den. Us trap dem. Me kill first robot, den da others can't go up da hill." He pointed to two yuks. "Go down da hill and kill da last one so dey can't leave. Use dis side of da road so us ain't shootin' at each other." He pointed to the last yuk. "Ya stay with me. Us kill da middle ones after us do de first and last ones."

The two yuks nodded and ran into the woods on their left to work their way down the hill.

The first machine, producing a loud, low-pitched whine, poked its front around a bend in the road. It had a big sheet of metal mounted on the front. MacDrakin saw the robot high up on the machine. The robot spotted him and the machine accelerated as Gorya and his hunter slipped into the woods.

MacDrakin's mouth turned dry again. The machine was headed straight for him and at a speed that astonished him. How could something that big move so fast on a dirt road? It would reach him in a few more seconds. He sidestepped to his right two paces. He saw the robot's arms move and the machine swerved slightly, keeping him lined up with the middle of the metal sheet. MacDrakin realized the robot had orders to run him over. The aliens must be aware that he had destroyed some of their robots, and they put out an execution order! He gulped and hoped he been correct in assuming that the machines were controlled by the robots. His life now depended upon it.

He waited to let it get closer. The longer the robot concentrated on him, the less likely it would be to spot the yuks. When the machine crested the top of the road, just before he planned to break and run to his left, he heard the twang of weapons. The robot flew off the machine with four bolts sticking out of its body. It crashed into the woods and the machine skidded to a halt and the whining sound stopped. He heard the twang of more weapons and the sounds of machinery dissipated.

A few minutes later, the yuks reappeared, all grins and backslaps. MacDrakin hadn't participated in the fight, except to be a lure. Gorya and his warriors had done all the shooting. He felt guilty about them risking their lives to protect him. Nevertheless, they had defeated the aliens in the first battle. His exhilaration was in strong contrast to the depression he had felt earlier in the morning.

He inspected the inert alien machines. He had to walk in the woods because there was no room on the road. The sheer size of the machines amazed him.

"Ya gonna have a lotta trouble gettin' supplies up the road now," Gorya said.

MacDrakin frowned, his exhilaration deflated as fast it had appeared. The machines had to be immensely valuable; the aliens wouldn't abandon them. Someone would come back to recover them. The battle they had just fought was only the opening skirmish.

# # #

Unit 13, under orders to travel to an assembly spot north of Skensfirth, took the shortest route. It motored through the side streets and entered the wide, main street. It turned left. Along the way, it noted the many natives in different sizes and shapes. It also noted that the natives yelled and some shook their fists or waved farm implements. It assumed the natives urged it to do something, but it didn't know what they wanted. It took a few pictures and uploaded them to the mother ship.

Its master program had recently run a maintenance scan and reported ten major and minor areas that had to be serviced before long. All the problems were the result of liquid water falling from the sky. Twice, it lost communication links with the mother ship because its devices didn't work when soaked with the liquid.

Without instructions not to search for minerals, it continued to send radar scans into the ground and analyze the reflections. It noted it traveled over a massive mineral deposit and launched another message. Its treads churned up clouds of dust as it followed an especially rich vein. The vein branched off to the left. Unit 13 veered with it until it came to a stone wall where it stopped and looked around for an alternate path. Not finding one, it ran through a decision-tree program, opened its tool chest, took out a rock drill and attacked the wall.

A native came up and stood close by. The native seemed excited and made loud noises with its face. Unit 13 ignored the native and stepped back to get a better look at the gap it had created with the drill.

# # #

Dread and anger competed for primary position in Higginbottom's emotions as she watched the robot maneuver up the street. The folks in town yelled obscenities and cursed at it while some made stabbing motions with their pitchforks and shovels.

The movement of the robot puzzled her. It constantly changed directions, going back and forth across the wide street like a hunting dog following a scent. On one of those detours, the robot ran into the side of the town church, down the street from town hall. After a pause to examine the wall, it opened a door in its chest area and took out a tool. To Higginbottom's astonishment, the machine began drilling into the wall.

Her conflicting orders again presented her with a baffling situation. Should she protect the church or protect the robot from a lynch mob? She sighed and made a decision. The robot committed an act of vandalism. She wasn't going to allow the robot to damage a building in her town. Especially with so many of the folks watching. She had to do her job; her original job. She ran up to the robot. "Stop that!"

The robot ignored her and continued drilling. Behind her, she heard the muttering of the crowd growing louder. It was apparent that the citizens of Skensfirth wouldn't let a robot continue to damage the town church. She didn't know how one would manage to lynch a robot, but she was sure the folks were about to figure it out.

She wagged a finger and sputtered, "For the last time, stop drilling. Or else."

The robot stopped and lowered its arms, but only to examine its progress. It soon continued drilling.

"That's it." She stamped her foot. She had enough of these robots and their destruction of property. "You asked for it." She spun around and ran into the town hall. Within a minute, she returned with two stout lengths of rope. She dropped one of the ropes on the ground and made a noose in the one she held. Higginbottom dropped the noose over the robot's head and lowered it until it dangled around its upper arms. She pulled the noose tight and looped it around the robot's body three more times before tying it off.

The robot squealed and beeped and tried to raise its arms.

"I ordered you to stop. Did you listen? No." Behind her, she heard the folks clapping.

The machine turned to face Higginbottom who was busy making a noose in the second rope. When it was ready, she moved behind the robot, dropped the noose over its head and pulled it tight around its legs just above the tractor treads. She jerked the rope and the robot fell on its face. She pulled the squawking machine along the ground and into the town hall accompanied by cheers from the crowd.

Inside the building, she hauled it into a jail cell and tied the loose end of the rope to a ceiling beam, leaving the robot's treads several inches off the ground. To make sure the machine didn't dig its way out of the cell, she pried open the lid of the chest with the point of a dagger. She took out all the tools and threw them on the floor outside the cell. She slammed the cell door and lowered the locking bar into place.

She leaned against the door and thought about the consequences of her actions. Dun Hythe certainly wouldn't approve of her arresting a robot. She probably had ruined her career as a constable by doing it. She no longer cared. Finally, she had done something positive. Besides, the bureau-crats in Dun Hythe wouldn't know unless someone sent them a telegram and she had no plans to do that. She felt good for the first time since the aliens had kidnapped her.

# # #

The news appalled Luc Jehan. Arresting a robot? Was the female out of her mind? He charged out of his office and ran down to the front of the town hall building. He burst into her office and screamed, "Are you trying to destroy the town?" He slammed a clenched fist on her desk.

"Are you referring to the robot I have in a cell?" Higgin-bottom stared at the mayor.

Luc hesitated. Everyone else in the town hall would have quailed in the face of his outburst, but the constable just sat there looking at him with a raised eyebrow. She looked like she was about to giggle. "Hrrmmph. I order you to re-lease it immediately."

"You don't have the authority to give me orders."

"Blast it! I'm the mayor and I won't let you jeopardize my town with your foolish actions."

"Actually, I protected *our* town by stopping the robot from destroying a wall in the church."

"I don't care what you stopped it from doing. You have to release it before the aliens come here to rescue it. Have you even thought of the consequences of your stupid actions?"

"The folks in town were about to lynch it. I saved it by arresting it."

"Hrrmmph. Between you arresting a robot and that other idiot MacDrakin declaring war on them, we'll have the aliens swarming over Skensfirth and destroying it."

"I protected the town."

"Are you going to do as I ordered and release the robot?"

"No."

"I warn you. I'll send a telegram to Dun Hythe demanding that you be replaced."

"Good. Perhaps that will wake those idiots up. Maybe, it'll tell them that things aren't going too well down here."

Luc worked his jaws but didn't say anything. He turned and stomped out of Higginbottom's office. The folks in Dun Hythe were fools to set up the constables independent of the local officials? What good was it to be the mayor if you weren't in charge of everything in town? Higginbottom's refusal to follow his orders could mean bad news for Skensfirth. He felt a disaster rolling towards his town. It was only a matter of days, perhaps even hours, before the aliens arrived in force to rescue the robot and to punish the town. He decided the wisest course of action was to pack up and to get ready to flee at a moment's notice. That way he'd survive the attack. Afterwards, he would return and resume his job as mayor. Under his plan, the town would have a leader available to take control after the aliens left a swath of destruction in town. After all, if he stayed and got killed or captured, the other survivors wouldn't have anyone to lead them.

# # #

The land below the *Black Carrion Flower* was almost in darkness while Yunta waited for a report explaining the events of the day. She sat in her command lounge on the flight deck pondering her fate and fiddling with her medallion. Something had gone disastrously wrong with the mining operation. Shortly after the machines began climbing the mountain, they lost contact with the mother ship. Was that warrior to blame? Did he suspect his land interested them? Did he spring a trap? These natives were much too clever and unbelievably treacherous. She wondered if Shtap had been taken in by the government officials? Did they outwit her negotiator? Did they agree to the treaty knowing they wouldn't honor it?

In any event, more irreplaceable time had been lost. Another day had passed and nothing had been accomplished. The ship remained empty, her expenses mounted and they were one day closer to leaving.

The image of Shtap appeared on an overhead monitor.

"Well?" Yunta snapped.

"We examined the video reports from the robots and we now know what happened earlier today, captain." Shtap appeared hesitant.

"I am waiting."

"It was same warrior. He was not alone as we assumed. There were at least four others with him. They appear to be the same type of natives that cooked Unit 32. From the video streams sent by the robots, the short warrior stood on the road as if tempting the machines to run him over. While the lead robot focused its attention on him, the other natives hid in the woods alongside the road and destroyed the robot. With the first machine stopped, the others could not advance because there was no room to go around the lead machine. Then the robot in the last machine was destroyed, effectively trapping the ones in the middle. The other drivers were disposed of soon after that."

Yunta cursed and pounded three tentacles together. Slime splattered the flight deck from the force of her actions.

Shtap coughed.

Yenta scowled. "What else?"

"It appears Unit 13 has been captured and is now held in a small room. It is tied up."

Yunta could hardly stay still on her lounge. Was there no end to the perfidy of these natives? She wanted to kill something. She regretted not loading a nuclear weapon or two. Destroying the capital city would be extremely satisfying right now. That would get the natives cowering and put a stop to their treachery. "Tell me."

"The unit travelled toward the assembly point and the straightest route went through the town. It transmitted pictures of the natives. They looked very hostile. On its way, it naturally searched for minerals and verified that the town has a rich deposit. In tracking one vein, it attempted to drill through a stone wall. A female native tied it up with ropes and dragged it into a building where she locked it up. Believe it or not, the female who did this is one of the natives we brought up here to learn their language."

"Is that relevant somehow?"

"I did not think it was necessary to indoctrinate those two natives, but I see now it was a mistake not to. This incident might not have happened if she had been programmed to stay in a friendly state of mind."

"You are right. You should have considered that." Yunta really didn't think it was Shtap's fault. No one on board had experience dealing with hostile native populations. Actually, she couldn't think of another ship captain who had such experience. Nevertheless, she had to blame someone for the monumental screw-ups that had occurred ever since they parked in orbit over this accursed planet and Shtap was the most convenient.

After a minute of gloomy silence, she said, "Do you have a plan to salvage today's disaster?"

"I guess we should start on the town."

Shtap's vague plan shocked Yunta. Usually his plans were precise and detailed. He was the most promising officer she had seen in a long time, but the constant setbacks seemed to sap his strength. As it did hers, but her position as captain meant she had to persevere and continue the mission.

"We do not have enough machines to do a proper job on the town," she said. "We have to recover the machines and finish the job we started. We will mine the mountain before moving to the town." Yunta pointed a tentacle at the engineer who monitored the communication equipment. "Get me Mivex. Put him on split screen."

An apprehensive Mivex appeared a few seconds later.

"You will lead a mission to the surface. Your job will be to recover the stranded machinery and mine the basnasite. You have one day to finish the mission. Recall the cargo pod from the mountain and load it with six robots and a dozen crew armed with laser rifles. Make that seven robots. Just in case you need a spare. You will leave as soon as the pod is loaded. Attack at dawn. Recover the machines and start mining."

Mivex stared at Yunta. Finally, he said, "None of the crew have been trained to use a laser rifle."

"What is there to learn? You point it and push the firing device."

"Since they are not trained soldiers, how are we supposed to defend ourselves if we are attacked?"

Yunta was pleased to note that Mivex appeared to be on the verge of hyperventilating. "The natives have no idea how to kill a zaftan, so the worst that can happen is you will have some battle scars to impress the females when we get home."

"The natives are barbarians. If they capture me they could hack me into small pieces. That would kill me."

"In that case, my report will recommend the Medal of Valor be awarded to you." She clicked her teeth. "Posthumously, of course."

She turned to Shtap. "You will load up the rest of the machines on a second pod and be prepared to land them close to town once Mivex finishes mining the mountain. Go down at night so the natives in town will not see the pod landing."

"When I land," Shtap said, "I will send a robot into town under cover of darkness. It will place a beacon at the point where the mineral deposits are densest. That will be the point where we will begin. The beacon will maximize our mining efficiency."

"Very well. Both of you get on with your assignments.

"It will be as you order, Captain," Shtap replied.

Yenta waved a tentacle dismissing the two officers.

Both slapped the sides of their heads with tentacles.

She leaned back. The situation looked more promising than it had a short time before. Her corporate tree had survived a bad case of mites and was recovering.

# # #

The First Skensfirth Militia lounged around the old stable. Each had a mug of ale and a pipe loaded with weed.

As a result, all felt mellow and non-aggressive towards their fellow militia comrades. Paddy Stuart meandered in and greeted the group. "The spy has retired to his room. I left a private to keep watch."

"Did he do anything exciting tonight?" a half-pint corporal asked.

"He followed the constable around for a while, but then went back to the tavern and ate his dinner."

"I think he has the hots for Higginbottom," an elf private opined.

"I don't think so," Abercombie replied, "but I'm sure his nefarious plan -- whatever that is -- includes Higginbottom in some way. It is apparent our project is becoming increasingly vital to the survival of Skensfirth. We must be prepared to protect the constable."

"He must be pretty tired if he went to his room so early. Riding all over the place can wear a body out," the corporal said.

"I wonder why he quit ridin' after he saw the Dupre place?" Stuart said. "You sure that's what he did, Biddle?"

"Yep." Biddle blew a smoke ring toward the roof. It rose intact until a draft from a hole shredded it. "He rode all over until he spotted Dupre's silo. He went inside for a couple minutes then came out and rode back to town. I watched the whole thing from a stand of oak trees not too far away." Josh Biddle had volunteered to follow the spy on foot after he saw how old the mule was. He just stayed back far enough to remain out of sight and followed the mule's hoof prints.

"Maybe he was lookin' for a place for him and Higginbottom to be alone so they can smooch," the elf private said.

"Will you give it up?" Abercombie snarled. "This has nothing to do with romance. It's spying, plain and simple. The silo and Higginbottom are part of the spy's plans."

CHAPTER THIRTEEN

The racket woke up MacDrakin. He had expected an attack to rescue the machines and now it was imminent. Not far away, trees cracked apart and splintered, the same sounds yesterday he had heard yesterday.

"Dey come back," Gorya said. All five of them slept in the open some distance from the hut and without a fire. They took turns standing guard through the night.

"They want the machines." MacDrakin yawned and looked at the sky. A waning quarter-moon was on the verge of slipping behind the trees. "Maybe two hours to dawn. That's when they'll attack."

"Us give dem a surprise," a warrior said.

"Not this time." MacDrakin shook his head. "We surprised them yesterday. Today they'll expect a fight and the robots will be protected."

"Dey not gonna like seein' dis." Gorya grabbed the triple crossbow laying alongside of him.

"They'll have weapons much more deadly than yours. I think we should leave the mountain. We'll go to the bottom and watch from there."

"How us do dat?" Gorya asked. "Road all blocked up and den us gotta go passed da thing dat just landed."

"There's a path down the other side of the mountain." He jerked a thumb over his shoulder. "Pack up and let's get out of here."

MacDrakin went into his hut and, feeling by hand, threw a change of clothes and some dried food into a knapsack then dug up his pouch of emeralds. He felt like he was betraying his father by leaving the land and not defending it, but he knew that to stay would be suicidal. He recalled finding his first emerald. How proud he was. He had sent it to his dad as a gift and a souvenir. That thought brought a lump in his throat. He chewed his lower lip while he pocketed the pouch of gems. The irony was that to protect and defend the land, he had to leave it. The aliens knew where he lived and they were certainly after him in retaliation for destroying their robots. He had to find another place to stay, somewhere away from his emerald mines.

Outside the hut, he fetched his pony and, with one hand holding the reins, led the way down a steep path that was nothing more than an animal trail. In the darkness, they stumbled and made noise, but they heard no response from the aliens. Along the way, MacDrakin struggled trying to make a decision. Where to go? That was the question. He needed a place where his presence wouldn't endanger innocent folks yet provided a base close enough to allow him to attack the aliens.

Near the bottom of the mountain, he came to a small clearing and paused. It was a quarter-mile east of the road to Skensfirth. He tied the pony to a tree and the five of them squatted while MacDrakin briefed them on his plan. "We wait here until we can see what's going on with the aliens. Their primary job will be to retrieve the machines, but they may have other orders. Like killing us to get even for yesterday." He frowned in the darkness. "And for busting up robots before yesterday. We'll see if we can do some more damage this morning without getting ourselves killed."

Dawn broke and disclosed the alien vehicle. This close, MacDrakin was amazed that anything that big could be built let alone moved. Squid-like aliens swarmed around the area.

"Dem real ugly," Gorya said after he saw them for the first time.

MacDrakin noted the accuracy of Higginbottom's description of the aliens.

Escorted by the squids, seven robots lined up on the road.

"You're gettin' old, Colonel MacDrakin," a low voice said from the trees behind MacDrakin's back.

MacDrakin jumped up in surprise and whirled around to face a new attack.

"You'd never let me sneak up this close when you was younger," the voice continued.

MacDrakin's grimace of battle concentration broke into a grin. He lowered his ax and held out a hand. "Sergeant-Major Richter." He embraced the grizzled old dwarf. Richter wore ancient leather armor that covered him from the shoulders to the knees. The leather had a few holes in it made by pointed weapons. Behind Richter's back, six more dwarfs stood smiling at MacDrakin. He shook hands with each of them, calling them by name and asking after their families. He turned to Gorya. "Remember these old comrades?" he whispered.

"Yep." Gorya embraced the sergeant-major and greeted each of the other six dwarfs with backslaps and head rubs.

"I hope you brought your helmets," MacDrakin said.

"Of course we did." Richter slid his backpack onto the ground and opened it. He took out a metal helmet with a heavy leather chin strap. In his other hand he held a two-foot-long steel spike with screw threads on the bottom. He

held them out for MacDrakin's inspection. "And we got our
armor too." A second dwarf held up metal plates for the
shoulders and another plate that fitted over the spine.

"Good work," MacDrakin said. "Thanks for coming."

A sharp hiss from one of the yuks interrupted his conversation. MacDrakin crouched down and looked towards the
aliens. A squid lumbered towards them, its eye stalks twist-
ing in every direction. It carried a long thin stick that
MacDrakin assumed was a weapon even though it didn't
look very deadly. The alien had a bronze medallion hanging
from its neck.

Gorya crept close to MacDrakin. "Me never kill anythin'
like dat. Me claim right of first shot."

MacDrakin nodded. Gorya raised his triple crossbow,
sighted down the top bolt and fired.

The squid reeled backward making loud gargling
sounds. He had a bolt in what must be his head, another a
few inches lower while the third bolt had shot away an eye
stalk.

Two squids near the ship responded to the sounds from
the first. They pointed their sticks and fired. Orange light
beams sliced through trees and hit rocks. The rocks smoked
from the heat generated by the beam.

"Time to leave," MacDrakin said. "We go east towards
the river. Follow me." He had thought of a place to hide
out. The islands in the middle of the Skensfirth River
offered a perfect spot. He grabbed the pony's reins and
pulled it along.

# # #

Mivex, apprehensive about being on the ground with hostile natives, strode about shouting orders and snapping criticisms at the twelve zaftans under his command. He demanded instant obedience, not just to show his authority, but to provide a high level of protection for himself. He didn't want to get injured or captured because his soldiers were slow to obey an order.

He realized that, for the first time in his life, he couldn't blame a failure on others. He was on his own on a strange planet and he didn't like the idea of so much responsibility. Of course, Yunta showed her incompetence by sending him on this mission. Drek or Shtap should have gotten the assignment. Both of them were much more expendable in his view. After all, he had to control and maintain the propulsion plants on the ship.

With the robots lined up on the road and his soldiers ready to escort them to the machines, the pressure of command and the fear of the natives finally made itself felt. He had an immediate need to defecate. He couldn't return to the cargo pod since that might be interpreted as an act of cowardice by the crew. "Attention!" he barked. "Stand by while I investigate the woods to make sure it is safe to leave the cargo pod."

He slithered through the trees, his eye stalks sweeping around. A few hundred feet into the woods, he found an appropriate spot where he could do his business in private, but then he heard sounds like someone speaking. His eye stalks swiveled at hight speed searching in every direction. If he wasn't alone, he had to be in the presence of the natives. Possibly, armed ones. Possibly, even the one who had destroyed so many robots. He forgot about defecating and concentrated on getting out of there. He forced his body, semi-paralyzed by terror, to move. As he started to turn around, he spotted a green-skinned native pointing something at him. An instant later, intense pain filled his body. His main processing unit and all the ancillary ones short-circuited. He felt himself falling and then everything went black.

# # #

Andre Deville, a reporter for the *Gundarland Times* stood outside the Presidential Palace with his good friend Leonard Tibbs, who worked for the *Dun Hythe News*. Both reporters started the day hoping for a story that didn't include someone protesting against the pollution in town. DeVille was a half-pint and Tibbs a six-foot tall human. Consequently, they made quite a contrast when they stood together. Deville's head reached only to Tibbs' waist. DeVille wore a custom-fitted three piece suit, a white shirt and a striped tie; Tibbs, an ill-fitting suit, a stained, once-white shirt and no tie. DeVille didn't have shoes, but his toe hairs were curled and waxed; Tibbs wore scruffy boots. DeVille had dark brown hair and was clean-shaven; Tibbs had blonde hair, a droopy handlebar mustache and stubble.

"Look." Tibbs pointed to a large coach approaching the palace gates. "I wonder where that's going?"

DeVille stepped back as the coach, pulled by two horses, sped trough the gates. "It's got the president's crest on the door."

"I saw Sfiore and Crumlish in it. I couldn't make out who the other two were."

"Crumlish and Sfiore hate each other," DeVille replied. "They'd never go anywhere together."

The two reporters, close friends since journalism school, looked at each other and smiled. "A story!" they said in unison, and despite their height difference, exchanged high fives.

Tibbs stepped into the street and hailed a horse-drawn cab. He jumped into a passenger's seat and roared at the driver, "Follow that coach!" He reached down and hauled up DeVille just as the driver lashed the horse.

# # #

Mivex's undamaged processors rebooted and noted their inability to communicate with the main processor. They also noted the presence of a foreign substance in the main processor and another location. After four failed attempts to reestablish the linkage with the main processor, they initiated a chemical process to flood the bloodstream with enzymes and chemicals. Within minutes, a layer of skin covered the spot where the eye stalk had been. After another zaftan had pulled the bolts from his body, those wounds started to repair themselves.

With the foreign substance removed from the central processor, another ancillary processor operation began to repair the damaged tissues and restore them to their original state. By the time Mivex's inert body reached the mother ship in the cargo pod, the distributed processors began restoring the central processor's information banks. First, all stored information in the main processor was wiped clean to eliminate any data that might have been corrupted by the injury. Then the distributed processors uploaded stored copies of memories, accumulated information and lessons learned from experience.

By the end of the day, Mivex was resting comfortably in his own quarters and writing a report on his mission. He clicked his teeth as he realized his report was really a work of fiction. For instance, according to his report, he had charged into a group of natives and scattered them before they could launch an attack on the cargo pod. His brave actions saved the cargo pod and the crew from destruction. And there was no witness to contradict him.

#

It was early evening when Rodrigs finally made it to Skensfirth after the longest day of his life. Being tortured in a dungeon could not be more painful than spending an entire day cooped up in a train compartment with Crumlish and Sfiore. When the two weren't hissing and arguing, the hostile atmosphere produced a suffocating gloom. Even Boudreau, usually cheerful, had an angry attitude caused by traveling with those two insufferable bores.

Rodrigs had rarely left Dun Hythe and had never been this far south. He had been born and raised in the city's elfin quarter. His magical talent became apparent when, without any training, he developed defensive spells to protect himself from the gangs of school-age elves who terrorized any child who didn't belong to their gang. Soon, he had also developed retaliatory spells. On one memorable occasion, he routed a vicious branch of one gang while a wizard observed the confrontation. The next day, he found himself enrolled in preparatory school for wizards. Eventually, he graduated from the Wizardry and Liberal Arts College and got a job working on Webley's campaign for the Senate.

He never should have left Webley unsupervised, Rodrigs thought, while he picked at a fingernail. He should have insisted on staying behind in Dun Hythe. No one could predict what the man would do if an unexpected situation arose. In that event, Rodrigs was certain Webley would exacerbate the problem, not solve it.

He missed Pinky. His pet dragon rode in the baggage car along with Crumlish's warrior-wizards. Much of the hostility in the compartment came about because of these soldiers. Crumlish was furious that he didn't command those soldiers. Sfiore was furious for the same reason, and Boudreau was furious that he did command the soldiers. Rodrigs viewed the whole affair as an exercise in executive mismanagement. If he took enough notes on this journey, he could write a paper and have it published in a management journal.

Besides the train ride problems, the summer heat took a toll on them all. Everyone's clothes stuck to their bodies. Rodrigs's red-and-white striped bow tie had wilted. Crumlish, red-faced and sweat-covered, wore his usual military uniform. Boudreau wore a light pullover and tan breeches. He seemed to be the most comfortable of the group, but his toe hairs were tangled and damp from sweat. Sfiore, who hated bugs and insects, wore an ankle length black dress embroidered with pictures of bug-eating birds. Rodrigs could feel the anti-bug wards that surrounded the garment.

In late afternoon, the train pulled into the station at Ashton with a screech of brakes and puffs of dense smoke the color of burnt toast. They got off and milled about the station platform. It felt wonderful to move about and stretch his long legs. He, Crumlish and Boudreau each carried a single overnight bag, but Sfiore had two very large trunks that had to be fetched from the baggage car. While they waited for the trunks to get unloaded, he rented a carriage to take them to Skensfirth. It could easily hold four people without excessive luggage. With Sfiore's trunks, the ride to Skensfirth was even more uncomfortable than the train ride. At one point, he toyed with the idea of jumping off the carriage and marching with the ten warrior-wizards and the sergeant in command. Fortunately, he recalled that he had neglected to wear walking shoes. His glorified palace boots would never stand up to a ten-mile stroll over dirt roads.

Pinky rode on his lap in the carriage and had a marvelous time barking and snarling at cows and horses. For some reason, Pinky wagged her tail and whined whenever they passed a herd of sheep.

At the inn, he approached the desk clerk and inquired about rooms.

"Only got two rooms left," a female elf said at the desk of Kate's Inn. Rodrigs groaned. He would have to share a room with the other two males while Sfiore got a room to herself.

The elf showed them to their rooms and said, "I'll have a dinner for ya in a half-hour. Ya can eat inna dinin' room or inna bar."

"We'll eat in the dining room, like respectable folk," Sfiore declared.

Crumlish glowered at her, but she ignored him. After all, he had glowered at her all day.

"Iffen you stay out late and the saloon is closed, the rear door is always open. Ya can get to yer rooms that way."

"Is there a place where a squad of soldiers can set up tents for the night?" Boudreau asked her.

"A competent commander would have thought about that before now," Crumlish said.

Boudreau payed no heed to Crumlish and looked at the elf who pulled a face as she considered the question.

"I guess they could camp inna market square. That's at the end of High Street." She pointed to the north.

Boudreau went outside to where the warrior-wizards lounged around ogling the passing females. "Up there," he told the sergeant. "That's where you can bivouac for the night."

The sergeant squinted and looked up the street. "Right lads," he shouted. "Get to it. We want to get there before the market closes up for the night. We can buy some grub if we step smartly."

The soldiers fell in and marched up the street.

Dinner at Kate's Inn was a tough boiled chicken and lumpy turnips. The food did not improve anyone's mood.

"First thing in the morning," Sfiore said in a tone of voice that dared anyone to challenge her, "I'll interview the constable and see why she let the situation get out of hand."

"We'll all meet with her," Rodrigs said, ignoring Sfiore's tone.

"Constables belong to the Interior Department. I'll do the interviewing."

"We're here to assess the situation and fix the problems. We'll all interview the constable."

Sfiore sniffed and turned away.

Rodrigs noticed a dwarf sitting in the corner. He had cruel eyes and a single red beard curl but was otherwise clean-shaven. The stranger glared at Crumlish's back and the look of anger that creased his face startled Rodrigs.

# # #

Drek stood on the top of the road and glanced at the sun'-s position in the sky. He estimated another hour of light. Below him a pit yawned, a hundred-fifty feet deep. The native warrior's mine tunnels, filled with mining debris, were now scars on the side of the mountain.

He looked at the trees and shook his head in wonderment. On Zaftan 31B, a perpetually cloud-covered planet, everything was gray, brown or black. Here, there was so many colors, so much to look at and admire. He had never seen such a multitude of shades of colors. The various greens of the grass and tree leaves, the vibrant hues of flowers, the blue of the sky as background for the white clouds. He wouldn't mind staying longer on the planet's surface.

So far, his sudden appointment as Mivex's replacement had gone well even though the operation was now behind schedule because of Mivex's wounds. Mivex had been transported to the *Black Carrion Flower* after his unconscious body had been dragged into the cargo pod. The pod returned with Drek now in charge of the mining mission. He breathed deeply of the air, filled with dust and vaporized rock. Even laden with the pollutants, the air smelled wonderful after such a long time breathing the recycled air on the ship. Getting away from the arrogant captain was another advantage of being on the surface. Whenever anything went wrong on the ship someone got blamed, but Yunta never accepted any responsibility for the problem. As if she wasn't in charge. Who would have thought a simple mining expedition could have turned into such an agonizing disaster?

So far, the cargo pod had made three trips to the mother ship. Each trip brought up tons of bastnasite from the mountain. He decided not to work through the night. The crew needed sleep. He grabbed his communicator and checked on the cargo pod. It was two-thirds full. He ordered it to deliver the load and to return immediately. He watched the pod lift off the surface and rise into the sky. A quarter-mile up, it fired its rockets and disappeared in a blaze of green fire.

While he waited for the pod to return, he practiced chaining his processors into different configurations. He hadn't tried impromptu linkages in years and, at first, he had difficulty setting the links into a working configuration.

Drek was accustomed to linking his processors to induce a coma and allow his mind to flow far beyond the bounds of the ship. He used a second linkage set to transport individuals and a third to generate a ward.

After several failures, he connected the processors in a way that allowed him to create fireballs. He imagined Yunta standing in front of a large rock twenty paces away and used the image as a target. On his third attempt, he hit the target in the center of her head. He clacked his teeth. Next, he wanted to develop a linkage to create an air hammer, a favorite of warrior shamans. Air hammers caused impressive amounts of damage and terror.

Perhaps he would get an opportunity to shoot a native or two. That tale would impress females once he returned home.

The cargo pod arrived back at dusk and Drek ordered the chief robot to bring the machines to the road. With the machines lined up, the crew formed a protective cordon around them and the convoy moved downhill to spend the night in the pod. He detailed three of the crew for the first watch and ordered the pod control processor to produce a meal for the rest of them. Meanwhile, the robots ran maintenance checks on themselves and the machines.

Drek sat on the command lounge. Overall, it had been a pleasant day, a wonderful change from the tedium of the ship. By tomorrow afternoon, the mineral deposit would be exhausted -- it was much larger than originally estimated. After that, his orders called for him to relocate the pod and the equipment to an assembly point north of the town where he could link up with Shtap who planned to land after dark. With Mivex getting himself shot up by the natives, Drek could look forward to more time on the surface.

# # #

Leonard Tibbs and Andre DeVille slouched into Kate's Inn at dusk. Both reporters were in cranky moods after spending the entire day sitting in a crowded coach car on the train. Many of their fellow travelers desperately needed baths and stank almost as much as their foul-tempered chickens and goats. In Ashton, they had to wait while the rent-a-mule office found two available mules. They hadn't eaten since breakfast and they were tired. Then, there was the problem of what to tell their editors. Both were sure the editors had no idea where Skensfirth was, but both agreed they followed the trail of a big story even if they didn't know what it was. No one had ever seen the four most powerful politicians in Gundarland travel together. Especially to such an out-of-the-way town as this place.

They approached the desk and the female elf who filed her nails. "Help ya?"

"We need rooms," Tibbs said. "We don't know how long we'll be staying."

"Should have got here an hour ago," the elf replied. "Just rented the last two rooms."

"Is there any other place in town to stay?" DeVille asked in an exasperated voice.

"Nope. You might try squatting in the stables. Lotsa folks do that, I hear."

"Let's get an ale and figure out what to do," Tibbs said.

They want to the tavern and found two seats at the bar. "Two ales, please," DeVille said to the bartender, a half-pint who carried a wood crate around to stand on to reach the patrons.

With mug in hand, Tibbs said, "I don't fancy sleeping with the mules we rented in Ashton, but that may be our only option."

DeVille turned to the male elf drinking alongside him. "We just got into town. Anything exciting happening around here?" Both reporters had yet to develop a logical reason for the politicians to come here.

"Just those machines that fell outta the sky and ruined a lotta property." The elf seemed nonplussed by the question. "See more and more of them runnin' around of late."

"Can you explain what you're talking about?" DeVille asked, while holding his excitement in check. He beckoned for the bartender to refill the elf's mug. The refill brought a half-dozen other locals to their barstools. All had theories and information to trade for mugs of ale.

After ten minutes of conversation, the reporters knew they had hit the mother-lode of all news stories.

"I'd love to see one of these machines," Tibbs replied to an old half-pint who had described MacDrakin's destruction of a machine. "A firsthand description of them would really kick up interest in the story."

The half-pint chuckled. "Guess ya gotta talk to the constable then. She arrested one the other day. Still has it inna jail cell, I believe."

DeVille and Tibbs gawked at each other. "A scoop," they said in unison.

DeVille took out a large bill from his wallet and threw it on the bar. "Keep the change."

The reporters bolted out the door. "I'll find the constable," Tibbs said. "You find the telegraph office and keep the operator from going home until we file stories."

# # #

Alix returned to the police station after working overtime. It was dusk and the city shadows grew darker and more dangerous. She didn't look forward to talking to the cops. She was sure they had ignored her report, but she refused to give up. She planned to nag them until they took action. She paid taxes and the police were paid from those taxes. That made the police her employees and she would demand they earn their pay.

The desk sergeant gave her a huge grin when she walked through the door. "Well, look who's here? What can I do for you today, Missy?"

"I want to know what's going on about my kidnapping. Have you found the ones who did it to me?"

Several other police officers moved closer to hear the exchange.

"Well, you see, we can't find anyone matchin' yer description. There ain't too many of these giant squids runnin' around. At least not in Dun Hythe. You know what I mean?" He winked at the other cops.

"You don't believe me, do you? Did you send a telegram to Skensfirth? The constable down there can confirm my story."

"I'm sure the constable down where-ever is tied up with constabulary business. Here in Dun Hythe we like to do things ourselves. You have to understand there's a lotta other folks bringin' problems to us. So you'll just have to be patient while we work on yer case."

Alix scowled at the sergeant. He smiled back.

"Anyways, we got yer address. When we find some of these squids and we arrest 'em, we'll contact ya. Now iffen ya excuse me, I gotta go eat me dinner." The sergeant pushed his gut away from the desk and stood up. He walked away with two other police officers.

Alix heard them laughing.

# # #

MacDrakin dropped his knapsack on the ground, rolled his shoulders and arched his back. He had waited for full darkness before he and his mates reached the island in the middle of the Skensfirth River. Only a half-hour's march from his home, he elected to take a roundabout route to approach the river from the side opposite the town. The longer route meant fewer people would observe them. His pony had been lent to a farmer to use until MacDrakin needed it again.

The island, a few acres in extent and thick with five-foot-high weeds, sheltered them from the prying eyes of robots and aliens. With the river only knee-deep at this time of the year, they could rapidly reach either bank. It wasn't an ideal place to stay for a long time. Swarms of insects buzzed around their heads. Lighting a fire at night would be seen from the banks so food would have to be cooked during the daylight hours. Fishermen might also be a problem because the river provided good sport for them. Nevertheless, the island was situated close to town and MacDrakin felt he wouldn't need the camp for more than a few days. He sensed that events were coming to a head and the crisis was about to crash down on him.

He stood among the weeds and tried to ignore his loneliness and sadness. His home had been destroyed, Higginbottom wasn't talking to him and he didn't know what to do about her without compromising his principles. He picked a cattail and shredded it. He only knew that the situation with her wasn't going to change as long as the aliens infested the area around Skensfirth. Once he drove them out, possibly he could deal with Higginbottom. He threw the remnants of cattail on the ground and went to help set up the camp.

In the center of the island, the others stomped down the cattails and weeds and dropped their sleeping blankets. They squatted in a circle and shared whatever dried food they carried. Gorya and the Nut-busters swapped old stories and lies and caught up on their lives. Only Gorya's three warriors didn't know all the others, but those three were accepted into the band without a second thought.

MacDrakin smiled. He had liked being a battalion commander and only resigned his commission to take over from his father at the mines. Here he was again, in charge of troops. Not exactly a battalion, but a small group of experienced warriors who would stand shoulder-to-shoulder under the most adverse conditions. Given an opportunity, they would teach the aliens a few lessons.

#

Yunta worked out in the gym to relieve some of her tension. This voyage consisted of nothing but aggravation and problems. Every time she made an advance, a setback occurred. Today, that idiot Mivex got himself shot by the natives, causing a delay in the mining operations. Did any of the crew on the surface have the initiative to start the mining? Of course not. They stood around and wasted hours that could have been used productively. Drek had finally arrived on the surface and took charge. Now mining of the town had to be delayed another day. That left her with no time margin.

On the plus side, the mineral deposit on the mountain was bigger than expected. By the time Drek finished excavating it tomorrow, the ship would be filled to twenty-two percent of capacity. Using more machines and two cargo pods on the next deposit, the ship would be filled before they had to leave.

She reviewed the latest plan. After Drek finished mining the mountain tomorrow, he would move to the assembly point north of the town. Once there, he would supervise the maintenance of the machines to ensure they were in good condition. Mining minerals stressed the machines and wore them down: drill bits needed replacing, engines needed tune ups, linkages needed lubrication. Drek could also program the returning robots with language and weapons instructions. Tomorrow night, Shtap would take down another cargo pod with more machines and more of the crew.

Early the next morning, the final mining operation would begin. With no time left for delays or problems, any natives who got in the way would be crushed.

CHAPTER FOURTEEN

Within minutes of their arrival yesterday evening, all of Skensfirth knew that a bunch of haughty folks were staying at Kate's Inn. Suspecting that the visitors were connected with the plague of aliens, many folks asked Higginbottom for an explanation. She shrugged and didn't answer. She assumed these strangers were from Dun Hythe and she expected to be summoned to appear before them this morning. An elf lad who worked in the Kate's kitchen washing dishes delivered the message at nine o'clock.

The lad knocked on her office door. "Beggin' pardon, Constable, but those people who showed up yesterday wanna talk with you."

"All right. What are they like?"

"Grumpy. I don't think they like each other."

Higginbottom took a deep breath and left the town hall. She glanced at the mountain and wondered what had happened to MacDrakin. She worried about him, even though she wasn't talking to him. Had there been a battle there yesterday? Muted sounds of machinery occasionally made it to town, so she knew the aliens had taken control of his land, but she had heard nothing about him. Was he wounded? Was he taken prisoner? Did he get away? If so, where did he go?

She forced her thoughts back to her own problems. When she heard of their arrival, it dawned on her that she had hoped to talk to someone from the capital. She needed to hear from them why they had given her such strange and contradictory orders. She hoped they would explain what was going on so she could understand it. Of course, these four must be minor officials just sniffing around for their masters who remained in Dun Hythe. They probably wouldn't tell her a thing.

She entered Kate's and wrinkled her nose against the stench of old ale and pipeweed smoke. She looked at the messenger and raised an eyebrow. He pointed through the dining room and said, "The meetin' room on the left."

Higginbottom adjusted her sword belt, pulled on her shirt to straighten it a bit, glanced at herself in the mirror and moved her cap to make it less jaunty. She made a determined decision about her attitude. She would not cower in front of these minor bureaucrats. She was proud of the job she had done and she could have done it much better if Dun Hythe had stayed out of it.

She entered a small room with a half-dozen chairs spread around. An elf wearing a ridiculous dark blue bow-tie with white polka dots motioned her to close the door. To her amazement, a small, pink dragon ran up and sniffed her boots.

"My name is Francesco Rodrigs," bow-tie said. "I'm the Chief-of-Staff for President Webley. This is Kincaid Crumlish, the Minister of Defense. Alongside him is Benoit Boudreau, the Treasurer and finally, Meria Sfiore who you may know since she is the Secretary of the Interior."

Higginbottom gasped and almost panicked. Instead of minor officials, she stood in front of the elite of Dun Hythe's bureaucrats. Her determination not to cower wavered for a moment, but she recovered and held firm. She observed the lad had correctly described them. These folks didn't like each other. Hostility hung in the air like a noxious fog.

"We are here," Rodrigs continued, "to assess the situation and see what has to be done. To that end, we need to talk to you. Secretary Sfiore has some questions for you. Please have a seat, Constable. And don't worry about Pinky. She only bites me."

Higginbottom sat down and placed her hands on the hilt of the sword and the butt of her baton. In the back of her mind, a warning sounded that her body language was hostile, but she didn't care.

Pinky curled up at her feet.

"Constable Higginbottom." Sfiore's voice dripped with sarcasm. "What we want to know is how you let the situation get so out of control. Please explain your actions, or rather, your lack of actions. We also are most interested in knowing why so many robots have been destroyed and by whom. Enlighten us."

Higginbottom's heart pounded in her chest. Her skin grew clammy. These lackeys weren't looking for answer. They looked for someone to blame. They wanted her to take the fall for their incompetence. She jumped up, knocking over her chair.

Pinky yelped and skittered out of her way.

Hands still on her weapons, she glared at Sfiore, whose head snapped back in alarm. "How dare you come here and accuse me of letting the situation get out of control. It's all your fault. My job is to protect the folks in Skensfirth and their property. First, you send me a telegram ordering me not to interfere with the robots and saying these robots won't destroy property. But they did. A farmer named Dupree lost his entire farm. It's now under many feet of dirt. His house was knocked down and there is huge hole in the middle of his land. How is he supposed to earn a living? How is he supposed to feed his wife and children?"

Higginbottom advanced on Sfiore until she stood in front of her. "Then you send me another telegram ordering me to protect the robots and to arrest anyone who damages one of them. Most of the robots that were destroyed were trespassing on people's private property."

"Please calm down, Constable," Rodrigs said. "I'm sure Secretary Sfiore didn't imply you were to blame for the situation."

Higginbottom glanced at the other two males. Crumlish looked like he was desperately trying not to laugh. Boudreau looked bemused. Sfiore on the other hand, had turned pale and she gulped air. "Sfiore asked me to explain how I let things get out of control. That means she intends to blame everything on me. The real culprit is who ever sent out those telegrams." She stared at Sfiore. "Was that you?"

Sfiore glared at Boudreau. "I was ordered to send the second one," she said finally.

Boudreau stared at his toe hairs.

"Do you know anyone who has destroyed a robot?" Crumlish asked.

"One of the folks has a mine up on the mountain and he's killed three of them that I know about."

"What?" Sfiore, recovered somewhat, glared at Higginbottom. "What have you done about it?"

"Nothing. MacDrakin killed the first two because they trespassed on his property and wouldn't leave."

"MacDrakin?" Crumlish said. "Why does that name sound familiar?"

"He's named after a famous ancestor," Higginbottom replied.

"Ah, that must be it. Tells us about the third one."

Higginbottom pulled a face. "This happened four days ago. MacDrakin was in town talking to me when a robot showed up on High Street. I was in its way and it pushed me aside, almost knocking me down. MacDrakin took out his battle ax and killed it."

"If this was four days ago," Sfiore said, "you had the telegram that ordered you to arrest anyone who damaged a robot. I assume you arrested this MacDrakin?" Her voice had retuned to its original icy tone.

"No, I didn't." Higginbottom crossed her arms and stared into Sfiore's eyes. "MacDrakin protected me from an assault by a robot." Higginbottom smirked at Sfiore. "Besides, plenty of folks saw MacDrakin do it and they cheered him. If I arrested him, the folks in town would have rioted. And the riot would have been your fault, because of your stupid telegrams."

Crumlish cleared his throat. "I believe the constable cannot be blamed for this situation. It is clear the aliens lied to us. They never had any intention of protecting property. I also think the constable is to be credited with fast thinking for preventing a riot."

Higginbottom was surprised by the look of hatred Sfiore shot at Crumlish.

"I agree," Boudreau said. "Secretary Sfiore has no cause to blame Constable Higginbottom."

Sfiore's hands tightened into fists. Her upper lip trembled. She stared at the far wall.

"What are you going to do if the situation gets worse?" Higginbottom asked. "Somebody better come up with a plan."

No one replied and none of them would meet her stare. Finally, Rodrigs said, "I'd really like to get a look at a robot."

"If you want to see one, I've got one in a jail cell. I arrested it."

Crumlish laughed out loud.

"Let me get this straight," an astonished Sfiore said. "You let this MacDrakin get away with destroying a robot, and then you arrested one of robots?"

"It tried to knock a hole in the wall of our church and the folks in town were about to attack it." Higginbottom glared at Sfiore. "Every male in town carries a weapon these days. Pitchforks, shovels, short swords. Anyway, to keep the folks from attacking it, I tied it up and threw it in a jail cell. Protective custody, I think you'd call it."

"We'll all go over and look at it later," Rodrigs said. "I'm concerned about the state of mind of the local folks. From what you've said, they are on the verge of taking the law into their own hands and attacking the robots. Is this correct?"

"It is."

"I think the problem is much worse than we imagined." Rodrigs looked at the others. "We have to rethink our assumptions about the aliens and their robots."

"We should start protecting the people and their property instead of assuming the aliens will keep their word," Boudreau said.

"I think you should know that MacDrakin declared war on them and vowed to destroy all the robots and the aliens."

"Oh dear." Rodrigs chewed his lip. "That sounds serious. Fortunately, one male can't do much damage."

"He isn't by himself anymore."

"What does that mean?" Boudreau raised an eyebrow.

"MacDrakin was in the military with the yuk who is now the chieftain right across the border. The chief and three warriors came over the join MacDrakin."

"MacDrakin was in the military?" Crumlish asked. "That's why his name was familiar. He was the battalion commander of the Nut-busters, one of my elite units."

"So there's five of them," Sfiore said. "Not exactly an army."

"He also sent a telegram to his old sergeant-major who lives in Ashton. I've heard that the sergeant and six other soldiers have arrived to join MacDrakin."

"This is getting serious," Rodrigs said. "If this MacDrakin starts a war, there could be some very serious consequences."

"Perhaps, I should send for more troops since Sfiore's forces obviously need assistance." Crumlish grinned at Sfiore.

Higginbottom wondered what was behind the enmity of Crumlish and Sfiore.

"Maybe we should meet with this MacDrakin," Rodrigs said.

"Maybe we should arrest him before he causes real trouble," Sfiore said.

# # #

President Webley sat behind his desk and wondered what he should do today. Usually, Rodrigs filled him in on the problems of the day, then Rodrigs went ahead and fixed those problems. He now realized that his Chief-of-Staff really ran Gundarland while he, the president, didn't do anything. Actually, he did a few things. Mostly he went out to dine so the Dun Hythe folks could see their President. Often, he was the guest of a corporate executive who generously paid the bill. The next morning, he would mention to Rodrigs a problem the executive brought up during dinner. Webley thought it only proper manners to try the fix the problem as a way of repaying the meal. He thought about that for a time and decided it was the way of the world. After all, he was the President and what good was it to be the President if he couldn't take care of the problems of the voters?

A secretary entered the office carrying the two principal newspapers in Dun Hythe, the *Gundarland Times* and the *Dun Hythe News*. She put them on his desk and left. He frowned. Without Rodrigs's assistance, was he supposed to read the papers? He didn't think it proper to ask the secretary to read them and give him a briefing. Besides, he couldn't recall her name. He tapped his fingers on the desk and pondered the situation. Finally, he made another decision, the first in days. He would have to pitch in and read the papers himself.

He unfolded the *Times* and gasped. The lead headline read: *Unknown creatures land in southwestern Gundarland*." How dastardly of the paper to put the issue right out in the open. He unfolded the *News* and groaned aloud. The headline read: *Boogeymen land*.

After the shock subsided a bit, he chewed on his lip and wondered if the situation required him to do anything. He hoped the answer would be negative, but it didn't come out that way. In the end, he realized as President -- and in Rodrigs's absence -- the situation demanded that he do something. Unfortunately, that something was an unknown quantity. All his adult life, he always had a staff around him that took care of things. That left him free to concentrate on important issues in case one of them arose. But the staff always took care of those problems also. Now, when he really needed them, his staff had gone absent.

He put his arms on the desk and placed his head on them. "Rodrigs! When are you coming back?"

# # #

MacDrakin left the island and waded to the west bank of the river on his way into town to buy supplies for his small army using a pair of emeralds. Before he did that, he found a tall, easily climbed tree and hoisted himself so he could get a better view of his land. The scar of newly overturned dirt made his heart plummet. From his vantage point, there didn't appear to be anything left of his inheritance. The machines still worked on the mountain this morning and it looked like the tunnels were now plugged. His spirits sagged. He didn't think he had the ambition to reopen the tunnels. It would be like starting over with a piece of virgin land.

He jumped down and continued to town. Along the way, he saw Busby Abercombie sitting in an old chair by the dilapidated stables the militia used for meetings. The old man waved a hand for him to stop and chat. MacDrakin walked over and squatted down on his haunches. "Morning, Busby."

"MacDrakin. I have news. I know you're sweet on the Constable--"

"Who told you that?" MacDrakin raised an eyebrow.

"Everyone in town knows that. We're not blind you know." Abercombie paused to spit a gob of phlegm. "But that isn't what I wanted to talk to you about. There's a stranger in town and I think he's a nasty piece of work. A spy he is. I'm convinced of it. He wears a single red beard-curl. Looks silly if you ask me."

"A spy? How odd. Why would anyone spy on Skens-firth?"

"That's for the spy to know, not us ordinary folk. Whatever he's up to, it involves Constable Higginbottom, that I can tell you."

"Really? How do you know that?"

"I knew him for a spy when I spotted him for the first time." Abercombie tapped his nose with an index finger. "I have an instinct for these matters. Consequently, the militia started an operation to thwart him and we have monitored the bugger's every move. He follows the Constable around where ever she goes. We've also caught him watching her house at night."

The information astonished MacDrakin. He had no reason to doubt the old man. The militia was eccentric, everyone knew that, but that didn't mean they hallucinated. Why would a stranger follow Higginbottom around? That didn't make any sense. Unless the stranger had a crush on her. The thought of another male courting Higginbottom brought up an unfamiliar pang of jealousy. He tried to rationalize that the feeling was unjustified, especially since she was mad at him. The two of them really didn't have a romance going. At least not yet. Maybe they never would. She disagreed with his decision to go to war and she wasn't likely to change her mind about that. His arguments didn't lessen the pang of jealousy.

Abercombie kept talking, but MacDrakin didn't hear him, absorbed as he was with his thoughts. He almost fell over when Abercombie gave him a shove. "Are you listening to me?"

"Sorry. What did you say?"

"I asked you what the militia should do? You're the only one doing any fighting so we'll take orders from you. We're all too old for battle, but we can gather intelligence."

MacDrakin doodled in the dirt with a finger. "Knowing what's going on in town would be good. As long it's not gossip. I'd appreciate it if you would keep an eye on this stranger and let me know what he's up to."

Abercombie cackled and winked. "I thought you would ask that. Know that the militia is a hundred percent behind you. We won't let you down."

MacDrakin stood up, nodded to Abercombie and continued on his way to town. He mulled over the information from the man. Could the spy, if that's what the stranger was, be an agent for the aliens? Possibly, the spy was charged with locating pockets of resistance. As far-fetched as that seemed, he decided to take precautions.

Inside Aterrano's general store, a few males had gathered near the front to share the latest rumors and gossip. "Mornin', MacDrakin," a half-pint said. "Sorry to hear about your land."

"Thanks." MacDrakin nodded to the group and looked around to find Aterrano.

"Kill any robots today?" an elf asked. The group chuckled.

MacDrakin grinned and spotted Aterrano checking his inventory in the rear of the store.

Aterrano greeted MacDrakin and expressed condolences on his mine.

"I'm running out of supplies and I hope you're up to bartering again."

"Tell me what you need. Where do you want it delivered?"

"Leave them behind the store before you close up. Someone will pick them up."

Aterrano raised an eyebrow.

"I trust you, but if you know too much you may be in danger. It's better not to know where I'm staying."

"Ahh." Aterrano gave MacDrakin a wink. "Right you are. Give me your list."

MacDrakin handed over a list of supplies. While he read it, Aterrano asked, "So what's the latest on your mine? We know you've been fighting the aliens. And they landed machines near your mine yesterday."

"I left there. It looked like a death trap if I stayed. So likely, my property is a goner. Nothing but a deep pit."

"Well, you aren't fighting alone, you know. The constable arrested a robot who was trying to cut a hole in the side of the church." Aterrano chuckled. "Quite a gal. She still has it in a jail cell."

MacDrakin scrunched up his face. Could Higginbottom be coming around to his viewpoint? Was she now ignoring the stupid orders from Dun Hythe? He had to talk to her. If for no other reason than to see if she mentioned this stranger. He fished an emerald from his pocket and held it out to Geno.

Aterrano shook his head. "This time, it's on me. I can't join your group to fight, but I can support your effort by furnishing supplies."

MacDrakin choked up from the unexpected support and could only smile and nod in appreciation.

"Don't forget," Geno continued, "if you need cash, my cousin can arrange a loan to finance your work. He has very competitive rates."

MacDrakin left the store and walked towards the town hall. To his surprise, Higginbottom came out of Kate's Inn just as he reached it. She looked angry. She saw him and stopped. "I suppose you're going to give me a hard time too." She crossed her arms and glared at him. From her body language, he knew she had just been through a nasty experience.

"No hard time. I wanted to see if you're all right. You look upset. Is there something I can do?"

She paused and stared at him. Finally, she sighed and said, "A bunch of big-shots came all the way from Dun Hythe. How's your land and mines?"

"I don't think I have mines anymore. It looks like the aliens dug up the whole mountain. Why are these people from Dun Hythe here?"

"One of them is trying to blame me for all the troubles we're having." She pulled a face. "I have to take them to the town hall to see a robot I arrested."

"Aterrano told me about that. Taking on a robot by yourself was a brave thing to do." MacDrakin looked past her shoulder to the doorway of Kate's Inn. "That's Crumlish. Is he the one who's trying to blame you?"

"No, it's the elf bitch. Her name's Sfiore and she's my big boss."

"MacDrakin!" Crumlish called out as he bounced down the wooden steps. "The Constable tells us you've started a war."

"I didn't start it. The robots did. One of them fired a weapon at me. That's what started the war. No one shoots at me and gets away with it."

Rodrigs introduced himself and said, "Look, we don't want trouble with the aliens, so please call it off. Or at least don't cause any more trouble."

MacDrakin's nostrils flared as if he smelled spoiled meat. "It's too late." He pointed to his mountain. "The aliens destroyed my land. In fact, they're still digging it up. I intend to make them pay. Not in money, but in other ways."

"Bah!" Crumlish said. "You always were a hothead. You never were one to follow orders."

"I didn't follow useless or stupid orders that endangered my soldiers."

Crumlish's head shot back as if he had been punched.

Sfiore giggled.

"My name's Boudreau. I'm the Treasurer. Do you know what the aliens will do next?"

"No, but I'm willing to bet they destroy more property."

"How many troops do you lead now?" Crumlish asked.

MacDrakin stared at him and didn't respond.

"Listen, MacDrakin," Boudreau said. "We have ten warrior-wizards and a sergeant camping in the market square. They're here as a precaution. If the aliens destroy more property, the situation could get out of hand. If it comes down to protecting Skensfirth from the aliens, would you be willing to join them with your troops?"

The request surprised MacDrakin. These Dun Hythe big-shots must be rattled to make such a unusual request. He thought about the question before answering. "I'll do it, but I have a single condition that must be met."

"What is it?" Boudreau asked.

"I'm in complete command. None of you interfere with what I do or how I do it."

"I'm the Defense Minister," Crumlish sputtered. "I oversee all military operations."

"You're the reason I made that condition. You always were a pompous and arrogant jerk. I'm not in the military anymore, and I won't listen to or obey your orders." He looked at Boudreau. "I don't care whether you accept or reject my condition. That's up to you, but I won't change the demand."

"I think we'll have to talk more about this," Rodrigs said. "Where can we reach you?"

MacDrakin didn't intend to let Crumlish know where his camp was. He didn't trust the minister. He had heard too many rumors of assassinations while he was in the army. "I'll be around."

"Let's see this robot," Sfiore said. The four ministers walked towards the town hall.

Higginbottom gave him a curt nod and turned to follow the ministers.

MacDrakin wanted to say something to make things easier between them. Before he could think of anything to say, he spotted a dwarf with a single red beard curl standing in the crowd. The dwarf stared at Higginbottom. "Who's that stranger?" he asked her.

Higginbottom stopped walking and looked at the crowd. "His name is Bauer. I see him everywhere I go. He's creeping me out." She resumed following the ministers.

MacDrakin realized he was holding his breath. He let it out in a whoosh.

# # #

Sergeant-Major Franz Richter led his squad of six Nut-busters through the woods on the east side of the Skensfirth River. It was mid-afternoon and hot, even in the shade of the trees. Sweat ran down Richter's face and, under his armor, his shirt stuck to his damp back. His body itched from the heavy armor, especially under the piece that covered his back and neck. It was iron worn over a quilted pad. While it had saved him from wounds several times, it was agonizing to wear in the summer.

He had organized the patrol to get his charges and himself back in shape. All had been out of the army for years and the civilian life had left them all with paunches and shortness of breath. A walk in the woods would re-hone their skills and work off some excess weight. One of their atrophied skills was walking through wooded areas without getting the two-foot-long helmet spike caught on branches. From the constant grousing of the men, he knew he was having success with his conditioning plan. They had moved north and east for an hour, practicing stealth movement. He had ordered the Nut-busters to move from a single file to a wedge formation and back until they got the maneuver perfect. Slowly, the old skills reemerged and Richter felt he had accomplished something.

He heard a clanking noise close by. He froze and held up a hand to stop the patrol. Another hand signal had the dwarf warriors squatting behind bracken and trees. Richter moved a branch aside and saw two robots moving northwest. He grinned. This was an ideal situation for an attack. He tapped three Nut-busters on the shoulder and pointed to the rear robot. They nodded. He placed a finger across his lips:

no war cries. He tapped the other three and pointed to the lead machine. They acknowledged the assignment.

Richter held up a hand for the troops to wait. When the robots had moved past them into a more favorable attack position, he made a fist and wagged it at the first group. The three Nut-busters stood up, stepped in front of the bracken, lowered their heads until the helmet spike was parallel to the ground and charged. When these dwarfs were halfway to the target, Richter indicated the second group and they charged the lead robot.

The trailing robot turned at the last second, saw the dwarfs and beeped a signal just as three helmet spikes crashed into its body. Before the spikes lifted it off the ground, the robot slammed a metal fist onto the back of one dwarf. The fist rebounded with a metallic clank. That dwarf cackled as the formation drove the robot back ten feet before they all crashed to the ground in a heap of metal and flesh. The dwarfs opened their chin straps, pulled their heads out of the helmets, placed a foot on the robot and yanked their helmets and spikes free.

The second group attacked in the same manner and three spikes punctured the robot's torso. The spike from the middle warrior hit a transformer and sparks shot up the length of pointed metal rod. The dwarf yelped. His entire body shook from electric shocks.

Richter followed behind to observe and take notes on how to improve the next attack. He saw the twitching body of his Nut-buster, dropped his notebook, grabbed the dwarf's hips and pulled. The spike came free and Richter ended up on his backside with the dwarf sitting on his lap.

"Get off me," Richter growled as the dwarf unstrapped and removed his helmet.

"Look at this, Sarge," the dwarf replied without moving. He pointed to the tip of the spike. Molten steel dribbled down the spike. "Bloody Hell. It's an inch or two shorter than it was. I gotta sharpen a new point on it."

"If you don't get off me, I'm gonna jam the spike up your butt."

The dwarf stood up and offered a hand to Richter.

"Well done." Richter looked at his squad. "That felt good, didn't it?"

"Been a long time, Sarge," a Nut-buster said, "but it comes right back to you."

"You gonna find us some more robots?" and other asked.

"Naw. These two was just luck. But MacDrakin? He's gonna find us a whole mess of targets."

# # #

Dagger sat on the bed in his room. Ever since he had spotted Crumlish yesterday evening, his mind swirled with confusing and contradictory thoughts while his gut felt like he had swallowed a large rock. Why was Crumlish in Skensfirth? For a minister of his stature and importance to visit a rural place like this meant something extraordinary was afoot. Did it involve himself? Was Crumlish out to get the secret on his own? If so, did that mean Crumlish wouldn't pay him?

He paced his room, desperate to figure out the true nature of Crumlish's appearance. After a while, his fevered brain cooled off and he could reason with himself. He had gone on any number of missions for Crumlish, all of them secret and each would cause a scandal if it was exposed.

The uproar from the disclosure would topple Crumlish from power.

Another horrible thought crept into his mind. Perhaps Crumlish wanted to eliminate him to limit his future risk of exposure. Possibly Crumlish would terminate their association when the minister got the alien secret. Could the secret be so explosive that Crumlish couldn't take a chance that anyone else knew about it?

Dagger cursed aloud. All this heavy thinking gave him a headache. Well, Crumlish wasn't the only one who could play games. The first thing he had to do was get his hands on the secret. He had to do it fast, before Crumlish got oriented about Skensfirth and acted on his own. Once he pried the secret from Higginbottom, he could assess its impact. Only then would he make a decision on how to deal with Crumlish. If the secret was as important as Crumlish hinted it was, maybe he should go into business for himself. He could offer to sell it to the highest bidder.

# # #

Yunta lounged in her cabin late at night awaiting Shtap's report. She was tired, worn out by the never-ending struggles with the treacherous natives. Fortunately, she could see the successful end of the voyage. Soon, the ship's holds would be filled with valuable minerals and she could return to Zaftan 31B.

The wall monitor blinked. "Answer."

Shtap's image filled the screen. "We are ready, Captain. Drek has overhauled the machines. Most of the robots have assembled here and have been reprogrammed with language and weapons. We are still missing some of the robots, but I am sure they will arrive shortly."

"Very good, Shtap. I look forward to more reports in the morning."

"We will start at dawn. Meanwhile, I have dispatched a robot to place a beacon at the densest part of the mineral deposit. The natives are in for a big shock tomorrow."

"Until then. Good night, Shtap."

Yenta shook two pills out of a bottle and swallowed them. Within minutes they took hold and her mood brightened. She chuckled as she pondered the future. The profitability of the mission, she reasoned, would be less than expected and she needed a good story to explain away the shortfall. The hostility of the natives offered the best possibility. She could claim the profits, as small as they were, represented a major victory seeing as how they were snatched from treacherous, nasty natives who fought tooth and nail to protect their land. Unfortunately, for that scenario to work she couldn't strand Mivex on the surface. She would have to bring him back. Even worse, she would have to make him into a warrior-hero, badly wounded in the stalwart defense of a cargo pod that was attacked by the natives. She would simply have to put up with him for the rest of the trip.

Oh well, she thought. It was a small price to pay for her own advancement to fleet admiral. With a cover story out of the way, she turned to more pleasant work: making new lists. To advance beyond fleet admiral called for more than simple talent. She needed an organized campaign aimed at influencing important zaftans, hence the new lists. With the promotion to fleet admiral, her old lists would became obsolete. The first new list contained names she would have to suck up to. A second list was names of powerful zaftans she would

have to bribe. Assassination candidates filled the third list.
This liquidation list was a time-honored tradition for all corporate, military and political leaders on Zaftan 31B. It was
the quickest way to eliminate competition and potential em-
barrassments. Mivex and Drek headed this third list. They
know too much about what really happened on the voyage.
She was unsure about Shtap. She trusted him, but the future
was filled with so much uncertainty. She tapped a tentacle
on the deck. After a moment's reflection, she left Shtap off
the list. For now anyway.

# # #

The First Skensfirth Militia concluded its business for
the night when the last drop of ale was squeezed out of the
keg and the last shred of pipeweed smoked. Tonight's meeting was called at the last minute to celebrate Josh Biddle's
inheriting a sum of money from his brother. Josh sprang for
the barrel of ale and two pounds of pipeweed. It was past
midnight and a sliver of moon provided the only light as the
militia stumbled up the dirt road leading from their meeting
house. With some difficulty, they managed to negotiate the
slight rise from the river bank to the center of town.

"Uh-oh," a dwarf private groaned. "I drank too much.
I'm seein' lights inna middle of High Street."

"Hey!" a half-pint corporal said. "I see them too."

"Stop! All of you!" Abercombie threw out his arms, almost poking Biddle in the eye. "I suspect spy-craft. We
must use caution."

With a great deal of guffawing and snickering and using
each other as props, the militia sneaked up on the strange
device in High Street, near the corner of the church. They

examined it closely, mostly by squinting or closing one eye to focus better. It was a short metal rod with a blue light on top. The light flashed off and on periodically.

"Someone must test this device to see if it is dangerous." Abercombie spoke in a whisper. "Which of you brave males will volunteer?"

"Why don't you do it, Abercombie?" Biddle said. "You're always trying to get one of us to do the dirty work."

"I would gladly volunteer, but my keen powers of observation might be compromised by touching it. I need to see the impact on someone else so I can assess the danger."

Several members snorted.

Finally, two dwarfs made a bet and one of them reached out and touched the pole with a fingertip. He snapped his hand back, groaned, fell to the ground and rolled around in pain while squeezing his finger.

"What happened to you?" Abercombie asked. "This is vital information. Quickly, tell me before you expire."

"Nothin' happened." The dwarf sat up and chuckled. "I just felt like rollin' in the dirt."

"Your sense of humor is appalling," Abercombie sniffed.

"Think the spy put this here?" Stuart asked the group at large.

"That could be why it is here," Abercombie replied.

"Why would he put a metal stick in High Street?" an elf private asked.

"Obviously, it is a signal beacon." Abercombie wagged a finger at the group. "He must be expecting reinforcements. Notice it's just across the street from where he is staying. He must be signaling the others where he can be found."

"That's pretty far-fetched even for you, Abercombie," Biddle said.

"What's your alternative theory?"

"Don't got one. Whatever this is here for, it ain't good. Let's take it and throw it inna river." Biddle looked around for support.

"Wait!" a dwarf private said. "Why don't we move it to an island inna river. That should screw up whatever the plan is."

"Excellent idea," Abercombie said. He could picture the militia getting a citation for this night's work. Maybe even a write-up in a newspaper.

"We can use my boat," the private added. "I got it tied up by the town stables."

# # #

MacDrakin woke up because someone shook his shoulder. He rolled over and looked at the night sky. The moon was directly overhead so it had to be the middle of the night. He squinted to see who stood over him. It was one of the Nut-busters.

"Someone's inna river, sir. Over at the next island."

MacDrakin snapped awake and sat up. He cocked his head and heard splashing, whispered orders, cursing and giggling.

"Who ever it is don't know the meanin' of silent maneuvers," the Nut-buster said.

Gorya and Richter moved alongside MacDrakin as he stood up. "Me think us gotta problem."

"All the troops are awake and armed," Richter said, "and taking up defensive positions."

"I don't think it's a threat," MacDrakin grinned in the dark. "I think it's the militia. Sounds like they had a meeting." He tugged off his boots, rolled up the legs of his breeches and waded into the river. As he approached the island a hundred feet to the north, he heard, "Someone's comin'." The slurry voice sounded like a stage whisper.

"H . . . halt. Who goes there?" another voice said.

"Abercombie? It's me, MacDrakin. What you guys up to?"

"We're confounding the enemy," Abercombie said from somewhere in the darkness. "That's what we're doing."

MacDrakin stepped onto the marshy island and found the militia leader standing by a row boat. "What are you talking about?"

"MacDrakin!" Abercombie grasped his arm. "There's a yuk sneaking up behind you."

"That would be Gorya. He's an old friend. Now, what are you doing in the river in the middle of the night?"

"We made a last sweep of the town before going off duty and found this planted on High Street." Abercombie held out a metal rod with a blinking blue light. "Our intelligence assessment is that it is an enemy artifact placed to indicate an assembly point. We decided to move it out here onto an island and watch who approaches it. We are convinced it was placed by the spy I told you about."

MacDrakin took the rod and examined it as best he could in dark. It had a cool, smooth surface. He had never seen or heard of a blue light. "I think this was placed by the aliens. Whatever it means it isn't good news for Skensfirth."

Richter approached and looked at the rod. "Could it be a signal lamp? Remember, we used signal lamps so the troops could find their starting position in the dark before an attack." He tapped the rod. "Only we used lanterns covered up on three sides."

"You're right, Sergeant-Major." A chill swept over MacDrakin. Whatever the aliens planned, it would certainly endanger Higginbottom. He realized that his war against the aliens was about to turn nasty and would reach a crescendo of violence very soon. "This is a great idea, Abercombie, moving the beacon. But who ever comes to find it, will be very, very angry."

"I believe we are approaching a nexus in this campaign. I have an instinct about these matters, you know."

"I think you're right. Tomorrow will be an interesting day." MacDrakin tapped Richter in the chest with one knuckle. "I want everyone up and ready to fight at dawn."

"Attention! All members of the First Skensfirth Militia. The crisis is upon us. Henceforth, we will abstain from ale drinking and pipeweed smoking so that we are ready to do our duty. The cit--"

"Bloody hell. What are you talkin' about, Abercombie?"

"No ale? I put it on my cereal. How am I supposed to eat breakfast?

"--izens of Skensfirth rely on us."

"I rely on ale. Ain't safe to drink the water, you know."

"Silence. We must be alert, the better to protect Skensfirth. We will patrol the town in pairs from now on. One will be the eyes and the other will be a messenger to report all intelligence to the militia meeting house. That is where I will set up my command post."

"I'll leave you to it, Abercombie," MacDrakin said. "If you pick up anything important, make sure you get it to me."

"You can count on us, MacDrakin."

MacDrakin waded back to the camp in a deep thought. If he was right and the beacon brought a swarm of aliens and machines, his small force could be overwhelmed. He had better be prepared to retreat in the morning. Higginbottom and warrior-wizards had to be alerted. It was too late right now, but he had better get up early and spread the word. Possibly, he could do that and still get back in time to watch what happened at the beacon.

He realized he now truly followed in the footsteps of his ancestor, but he wondered what numbers would come up on his dice roll.

CHAPTER FIFTEEN

Before dawn broke, MacDrakin waded across the Skens-firth River and headed towards Higginbottom's home. He had much work to do along with some fast talking if he wanted to defend the town from an invasion by the machines. Moving the beacon wouldn't confuse the aliens very long. Then they would get back on track and head into town.

When he left, his troops were awake and ready for whatever happened. They would probably have to abandon the camp once the machines swarmed all over the adjacent island. No doubt the machines would be escorted by the squids armed with the weapons that shot light beams. He didn't want his small force to fight a battle. He wanted them to slow down the machines by causing damage and havoc. After that, they were to retreat to defend the town. His job was to get help for them.

He reached Higginbottom's house. No lights shown. He took a deep breath before he pounded on the door. "Constable. Get up. Quick."

No response. His throat turned dry. What if she wasn't home? He needed her to help convince the Dun Hythe visitors of the danger. They could issue orders that would get a defensive line set up.

He chewed on a lip while he rapped on the door a second time.

"Who is it? What's the matter? MacDrakin, is that you?"

"Yeah, it's me. I need your help and we don't have much time. The aliens plan to invade the town."

She opened the door wearing a robe. "What do you want?" she demanded.

Her response wasn't what he had hoped for. In a strained voice, he told her about the beacon and the militia. She returned to the bedroom to get dressed. He shouted through the door and told her what he believed the aliens were going to do.

She came out of her bedroom in her constable uniform. "But what can you do? You can't stop them."

"My troops will reach town later this morning. We have to convince the Dun Hythe politicians to get their soldiers to help us fight off the machines."

"Oh dear. I don't think they like to make decisions. Especially serious ones like this."

"That's why I thought you could help. I don't think they will listen to me alone."

They walked towards Kate's Inn.

"How have you been?" he asked. "I haven't seen you much lately."

"I'm fine." Her voice was strident.

"Have the Dun Hythe folks hassled you any more."

"No."

MacDrakin realized it was useless to try to talk to her. Their budding friendship was at an end.

At Kate's Inn, MacDrakin rattled the locked front door. Eventually, a sleepy female serving dwarf showed up, unlocked the door and scowled at them. "What do ya want?"

MacDrakin and Higginbottom pushed past her into the saloon.

"Wake up the ministers," Higginbottom said.

"I can't wake 'em! They don't get up 'til eight o'clock. It'll be my job."

"Where are they? What rooms? I'll do it." MacDrakin took a step towards the stairs behind the dining room.

"Please, sir? Have a care. I need this job."

"You won't be blamed. I'll see to that," Higginbottom said. "Now please go and wake them up. I think it'll look better if you did it rather than MacDrakin."

The serving dwarf looked dubious, but walked away to do Higginbottom's bidding.

"Tell them it's an emergency," MacDrakin said to her back.

A few minutes later, Rodrigs and Boudreau came down the stairs. Pinky hopped down behind them. Both wore robes and suppressed yawns. Crumlish showed up, scowling to telegraph his foul mood. He wore a pajamas that looked like a military uniform and had a gold star embroidered on each shoulder. Sfiore took another five minutes to appear. She wore night clothes, but her make-up had been applied.

"Now what is this about?" Rodrigs said once they were in the conference room with the door shut. He sat down and Pinky jumped on his lap.

"Skensfirth is about to be invaded by the alien machines." MacDrakin was pleased to see the shock on their faces. "I think they plan to dig it up the way they dug up my mountain. My troops will buy us some time, thanks to the militia, but we have to alert your soldiers and get them ready to help my force when it arrives here. Together we might be able to defend the town."

"I'll let your ragtag amateurs join my warrior-wizards, but only under my command." Crumlish crossed his arms and glared at MacDrakin.

MacDrakin stared at Crumlish before replying, "This isn't the time to let your exalted position get in way of what of has to be done. I have combat experience, you don't. I've fought the aliens, their robots and their machines, you haven't. My troops have fought them and yours haven't."

Crumlish stood unmoving.

"MacDrakin is correct, Crumlish," Rodrigs said. "He's the only one who can defend the town."

"If he refuses to obey my orders, he'll not be in command of my forces."

MacDrakin waved a hand in disgust.

"Stop being so stubborn, you stupid man." Higginbottom stamped her foot.

Sfiore laughed out loud.

Crumlish remained impassive under the verbal attacks.

"All right," Boudreau said. "If that's the way you want to play it, Crumlish. I'm the senior minister in the cabinet and I have the authority to give you orders. I order that the warrior-wizards be placed under the independent command of MacDrakin. Since the aliens promised us they would respect property rights and since they have broken that promise, I order MacDrakin to protect the town of Skensfirth and its people from damage by the aliens, their robots and their machines."

"You'll regret this," Crumlish growled.

"I think you're the one who will have regrets, Crumlish," Rodrigs said. "I plan to make a full report to President Webley when I return to Dun Hythe."

"Can you write down an order for me to give the sergeant?" MacDrakin asked Boudreau. "Just to avoid any confusion."

"Right away. And after I get dressed, I'll go up there to make sure they understand what is going on."

MacDrakin breathed easier. It hadn't been as hard as he anticipated it would be. Of course, if Boudreau hadn't been here, he probably wouldn't have succeeded Perhaps, not all politicians were worthless.

# # #

Shtap stood in the early morning sunlight and watched the robot drivers mount the dozen machines. The massive dirt movers coughed into life and idled while they warmed up. Drek slithered up to him followed by the crew. The original twelve crew members had been supplemented by an additional eight leaving Yunta and the *Black Carrion Flower* quite shorthanded with only a few crew and assistant shamans left onboard to operate the critical systems.

Shtap's camp had been set up in a meadow north of Skensfirth, halfway between the town and the warrior's mountain. The road to town ran through the center of the meadow. Beyond the meadow and to the right of the road stood a thick grove of tall plants.

Shtap's anxiety level was higher than at any time in his life. Higher even than when he awaited his final grade for his thesis on the best ways to conceal false negotiating positions. Involuntarily, several tentacles entwined themselves making it difficult for him to slither around. Whenever he got in a state like this, his slime dried up and the skin itched. He wanted everything to go well this morning so they could get off the cursed planet quickly. Before more trouble occurred. Mivex getting wounded was not a good sign.

"The crew is in a foul mood," Drek said. "They want to go back on the ship."

"I noticed. However, I do not think they will mutiny. If they do, they will never get back home. We will strand them on this miserable planet."

"Nasty." Drek chuckled. "Stranded with all these treacherous natives. I do not think they would survive very long."

"Machines are prepared and ready," the lead robot squawked to Shtap. All the robots in camp had been pro-grammed with the native language and armed with stun pis-tols. Shtap wondered what happened to the ones who hadn't arrived back at the assembly point. He had lost track of how many robots still remained, but he knew two more had stopped reporting yesterday.

"Form up the crew to escort the machines," he told Drek. "Do not lead. I do not want you wounded like Mivex be-cause I need you to help me run the operations. Stay safe. Find the beacon and start mining."

"Do not worry. I will command the convoy from the rear. That way I can see if the natives have any tricks to play on us."

"Issue the command, then." Shtap raised a tentacle and patted Drek on the back.

"Move out," Drek yelled. "Head for the beacon." Be-sides the blue visual signal for the zaftans, the beacon sent out electronic pulses at two-second intervals for the robot drivers. "I'll be digging minerals in less than an hour," he called back to Shtap.

The lead machine, a ponderous backhoe with a plow on the front to deflect native missiles moved down the road a short distance and then veered to the southeast crushing the vegetation in its path.

Shtap frowned. According to the report from the robot, the beacon had been placed due south of their position. Why were the machines not staying on the road?

# # #

Gorya lay behind a screen of cattails with Richter at his side. The rank smell of decayed vegetation emanated from the river mud. Insects buzzed everywhere. Mist rose from the river and evaporated as the sun climbed higher and warmed the air. From his position, Gorya could see and hear the machines converging on the river in two lines. The closest machine had a thick metal sheet in front of it and a large bucket in the back. He wondered what the machine could be used for. Behind the first two, five more pairs of machines moved in a convoy with squids sliding alongside. He watched as the first two plunged down a small embankment and enter the river accompanied by huge splashes that drenched the machines and their drivers. After moving a few feet further into the river their engines coughed and stopped. The next two pulled out of line and went around the first two. They did no better. They stopped after traveling about ten feet from the river bank. The rest of the machines halted, blocked by the four in front. The squids slithered back and forth and yelled in their strange language, a mixture of squeaks and yelps.

Gorya and Richter looked at each and grinned. "Want some target practice?" Richter asked. Richter's soldiers didn't have any missile weapons; consequently, only Gorya and his warriors could attack the robot drivers from a distance.

"Dat a good idea. Me get me guys." Gorya slid backwards and crawled to the center of the island where his warriors and the Nut-busters awaited orders.

Gorya and his three yuks crawled back to the edge of the river. "Me get one onna closest machine." He touched the yuk next to him. "You get da one alongside." He gave targets to the other two and they poked their crossbows through the cattails. "Got yer target?" Gorya whispered. All three murmured affirmatively.

"Shoot when me say 'shoot'." Gorya sighted again along the top bolt of his weapon. "Shoot!" He pulled the triggers and three bolts shot out of the crossbow. He heard the twangs of the other weapons firing.

Gorya's robot, hit with two of the three bolts, flew off the machine and fell into the river with a loud splash and a sizzle. The other robots remained on the machines with bolts sticking out of them. One burst into flames. The other two slumped and emitted puffs of bluish-green smoke.

"Reload," Gorya ordered. "Dis time aim at da squids. Shoot when yer ready."

The zaftan escorts reacted like they were disoriented; unsure of why the machines stopped, and not knowing where the silent bolts came from. Two escorts fired their laser rifles at the far bank of the river. One of aliens screeched in pain when a bolt hit him in a tentacle. His partner looked at the bolt and deduced its flight path. He fired a shot at the island just as two of Gorya's bolts struck him in the torso. He dropped his rifle and writhed in pain while the third bolt clanked off a machine. Another arrow plowed into the dirt at the tentacles of a different zaftan. The escorts quick-slithered behind the machines and fired at the island.

"Dese guys are bad shots," Gorya said as beams of orange light hissed far overhead or bounced off the water not far from the bank where the aliens were. Steam rose from the water where the beams touched the river.

"Still, it's time to go, old buddy," Richter said to Gorya. "Let's get out of here before they get the range and do us some damage. We'll cross to the far side of the river, go downstream and cross back over. Let's hope MacDrakin got some reinforcements waiting for us 'cause these squids are really pissed."

# # #

Shtap, already confused by the direction the machines took, became further confused by the yells and screams in the distance. It had to be the natives. He decided that staying alone in his camp was a bad idea -- protection-wise -- so he slithered along the track made by the machines. As he went forward, the sounds grew louder. From the tone of the voices, he knew the day's operation was in trouble. Native mischief had to be the cause. How he was supposed to complete the mission when the natives expended so much energy and initiative breaking the treaty he had negotiated? Could the natives have been trained in deceptive negotiating classes like he had? That would explain their actions. Indeed, he thought, he could learn a lot from the natives.

When he reached the machines, the confusion and carnage bewildered him. Several robots lay inert on the ground. Four silent machines sat in the water. The crew and remaining robots milled about aimlessly. He found Drek in a foul mood as he ministered to two wounded crew members.

"What happened?" Shtap demanded.

Drek looked up at Shtap, ignored him and continued to tend to the wounded. Finally, he stood up and replied. "The natives lead us into an ambush."

"Why did you not go to the town? That is where the beacon was placed."

Drek didn't respond immediately. Instead he slid over to the closest machine and took the beacon out of the driver's area. "The beacon was not in the town. It was on an island in the river."

The news stunned Shtap. The treachery of these natives was the stuff of legends. If he wrote a paper on their conduct, it would become a classic textbook case. If it was believed, it would be taught for centuries and he would become famous as the author. Unfortunately, before he could write the paper, he had to survive and get off the planet.

"For some reason, our machines become disabled when they go into water." Drek hurled the beacon to the ground.

"Did you kill any natives?"

"I doubt it. They were clever. They hid on a different island and waited for us. After we started shooting back, they fled. Then I waded out to the island and found the beacon. So all we have for our efforts this morning is a pair of wounded crew, four destroyed robots and four inoperative machines."

"What is the problem with the machines? Why did they stall?"

"I have no idea." Drek shrugged. "That is a question to ask Mivex's engineers."

Shtap used his communicator to call the ship and it took the lone engineer remaining on board almost an hour to get back to him. "Well?" he said when his communicator buzzed.

"I uncovered the reason for the machines' erratic behavior. All of our previous mining operations were conducted on asteroids, moons or planets without liquid water. We have never come across conditions such as this planet has."

"This engineering blather is tedious. Why did the machines stop?"

"They are not waterproof."

Shtap cursed. Nothing seemed to go right on this wretched planet. "How can they not be waterproof? What kind of incompetent design is that?"

"Waterproofing is expensive and the probability of coming across liquid water is almost zero. Any water we encountered in previous operations was always in a solid state. Conditions such as we have on this planet are rare."

Shtap wondered how he would explain this to Yunta. He suddenly felt homesick. He wanted to go home and forget about this place and its double-dealing natives. "Why did the robots not avoid the liquid water?"

"Their normal programming does not mention liquid water. I guess Mivex did not bother to update the program."

"Can the machines be repaired?

"They should work again after they dry out. Perhaps you can try again later or tomorrow. By the way, liquid water explains why we twice lost contact with all the robots."

Shtap had a feeling he didn't want to hear about it.

"Under certain atmospheric conditions, liquid water can fall from the sky. The robots get wet and shut down until they dried out."

"How do I protect the machines and the robots if this happens again?"

"Keep them dry. That is all I can tell you."

Shtap disconnected and looked around at the failed expedition.

"Now what do we do?" Drek asked. "I really want to find a few natives and kill them."

"I think you will get a chance to do that. For now we must protect our assets. Tow the wet machines back to camp. We will wait there until they dry out."

Drek tapped a tentacle end on the ground. "Let me take the rest of the machines into town. I can start on the mining. And I can kill a few natives. Those actions may placate Yunta a bit."

Shtap pondered the proposal for a few seconds. He shook his eye stalks. "You will have great difficulty opening up the deposits without all the machines. Besides, it is too dangerous to split our meager forces. We must stay together."

As they slid back to camp, Shtap said, "I guess I better tell the captain we have to postpone operations until the machines dry out. I do not think we will mine the town until tomorrow."

"It could be worse." Drek patted him on the back. "At least you don't have tell her beak to beak."

# # #

Higginbottom didn't get back to her house until well after dark. She was exhausted from both the late hour and the emotional ups and downs of the day. It started before dawn with MacDrakin and anxiety about what the aliens were up to. She was hard-pressed to stay mad at him. After all, he was the only one defending the town, but he still hadn't apologized for his boorish behavior so their relationship remained businesslike. Finally, there was the constant fear of an alien attack as well as not knowing what would happen after that.

She had spent much of the day calming the fears of the residents and assuring them that MacDrakin and his troops were determined to defend the town. The mayor had shocked her by leaving town with his family and a wagon-load of furniture. He claimed he was going to visit a sick relative.

All during the day, where ever she went, she saw that creepy Bauer staring at her with his cruel eyes. The bizarre thing was that two of the militia always stood near Bauer. Those old fools in the militia were up to something, but she didn't have time to investigate it. She hoped whatever they were doing was harmless.

She changed into her nightclothes, fell into bed and listen to the soft gurgle of the Skensfirth River. She was asleep in seconds.

A pounding on the door jerked her out a deep sleep. She yawned and stayed in bed, convinced the noise was part of a dream. The pounding started again. A voice called out, "Constable! I have a message from MacDrakin."

She leaped out of bed. The alien attack must have started, she thought. She unlatched the door and opened it. Bauer stood there holding a long dagger. He pushed her into the room and shut the door. "Don't make any noise." He waved the blade in front of her face.

Higginbottom reacted with rage. This was the last straw! It was bad enough she had taken a ton of grief from the Dun Hythe politicians and had to protect robots, and now this stranger invaded her home! She backpedaled away from the door, grabbed a flower vase from a shelf and hurled it at Bauer. It hit his forehead, rebounded and shattered against the door jamb. Her assailant had a cut on his forehead, and blood ran down the side of his face. He roared and charged her. She retreated until she backed into a wall. Bauer slammed into her, knocking the breath out of her. She head-butted him and saw blood flow from his nose. He took a step back and punched her. Stars filled her vision and the room swirled around. She felt rather than saw him slap her. Her upper lip split open. When her vision cleared, she could only see through one eye. Bauer's bloody face was inches from hers. The point of the dagger pressed against the bottom of her chin. "You'll pay for this. Oh, yes, you will."

Terror constricted her throat so she couldn't make a sound even if she wanted to.

"Don't move." Bauer put the knife in his teeth, took a knotted rope from his pocket and looped it around her right wrist. He pulled it tight and tied it to her other wrist. He used a towel from the kitchen to gag her. Through one tear-filled eye, she watched him stanch his bleeding wounds with another towel.

He pushed her through the door.

"Get on the mule," he said. "Quick." He climbed behind her and set the mule moving on a route that avoided the town.

The fear of alien invasion she felt earlier in the day was as a child's fear of a scolding. The danger from the aliens now seemed minor. She sat on the mule and trembled. As bad as the aliens were, she knew Bauer was much worse. Everyone who could help her was exhausted and sleeping or else stood watch in the market square. She was alone with this maniac.

# # #

Three candles and two lanterns illuminated the command center for the First Skensfirth Militia. Abercombie sensed the ghosts of former meetings in the smell of old ale and smoke. He paced back and forth casting spooky shadows on the walls of the old stable. He awaited the arrival of the few members who hadn't returned after they were recalled from their patrols. He seethed with anxiety. Time was of the essence, he thought, and still they didn't act. This was a golden opportunity to test the mettle of the First Skensfirth Militia and to demonstrate its value to the town.

Finally, the last three members arrived. Two had been on patrol and the third had been sent to fetch them.

"They was patrollin' under a couple of trees. Hard to find them," the messenger explained.

"That was so no one could see us watchin'," one of the patrollers explained.

"Good thing they was snorin' or I never would have found them."

"Never mind that," Abercombie said. "We have important matters to discuss and a decision to make."

"Bloody hell. I hate makin' decisions," a half-pint private groused. "That's wot officers and sergeants are for."

"Sergeant Stuart," Abercombie continued. "Please report on what you saw a short time ago."

"That danged spy kidnapped Constable Higginbottom. Got her to open the door and pulled a knife on her. Couple of minutes later, they came out, got on his mule and rode off. She was tied and gagged."

"Why didn't ya rescue her, ya buffoon?" an elf private asked.

"Our orders said we are to watch and report back to the command center." Stuart gave the private his angry sergeant's stare. "That's why."

"Now you see the wisdom of my sobriety order. If we were drinking ale, we wouldn't be able to mount a rescue mission."

"Ya sure we want to rescue her?" Joe Biddle asked. As head of the refreshment committee his words were considered extra weighty. "Maybe this Bauer character is courtin' the constable."

"With a knife and a kidnapping?" Stuart scoffed. "I don't think so."

"He's a dwarf, ain't he?" Biddle countered. "We all know how weird dwarf courtship rites are."

"Here, here," Abercombie said in a stern voice. "We waste time in idle wrangling. We must begin the rescue."

"Stuart didn't tell us where they went," a half-pint corporal said. "How can rescue her iffen we don't know where they are?"

"They went to Dupre's silo," Abercombie replied. "Remember we had a report about him scouting it." He banged his empty ale mug on a table. "We have no more time to waste. Stuart, unlock the weapons rack. Fetch your gear and let's be on our way."

The First Skensfirth Militia grabbed their arms from the rack -- weapons were locked up during the meetings for obvious reasons -- and fell into a marching formation with Sergeant Stuart in the lead.

"Forward, march" Abercombie yelled.

"This reminds me of the time I was in a raid onna yuk bandit camp," an elf corporal said to the dwarf on his right. "Did I ever tell you about that action?"

"Only a hundred times or more," the dwarf snapped.

"Silence in the ranks," Stuart roared.

# # #

Under the moonlight, MacDrakin surveyed the sad fortifications his troops had constructed during the day. They straddled the road into Skensfirth from the north and consisted of a few firing pits and trenches to slow the machines. Several large tree trunks blocked the road. Everything he could think of had been done. His troops were exhausted from the efforts and most of them slept. He kept two sentries on guard, but he didn't think an attack would occur until morning. One of the few pleasant surprises of the day was the absence of an attack. He believed the aliens were waiting until the four stalled machines were repaired. Who would have ever thought the actions of the militia had saved Skensfirth. At least for one day.

He pulled a face. In the morning, he would find out if his dice roll came up with a winning or a losing number. This time he had no tricks to confuse the squids or to slow them down.

He thought of Higginbottom. He had urged her not to go home. Her house was isolated and too far from the market square where the warrior-wizards had their camp. He pleaded with her to stay closer, but she refused, saying she needed to sleep in her own bed. He hoped she would be safe, even if she was still mad at him.

He reviewed what he believed the aliens would do in the morning. Their machines, driven by robots and escorted by armed squids and still more robots, would charge into town to dig up the streets for minerals. All that stood between the monstrous machines and the town were eleven wizard-warriors, four yuks, seven Nut-busters and himself. In addition, a group of useless politicians would cheer the troops and offer stupid advice.

If the warrior-wizards didn't have success with their spell casting, he couldn't stop or even slow down the machines. In that case, Skensfirth would sustain much damage and possibly even be destroyed.

He balled his hands. How did the situation get so out of hand? Why didn't the aliens request permission to dig and work out a deal with the property owners? Why didn't the politicians force the aliens to follow some simple rules? Why wasn't something intelligent worked out in advance? If that had happened, he wouldn't be standing here awaiting an attack by a group of vicious squids. He wondered if all wars and fights started over a problem that could have been fixed by talking about the situation. Even now, if the politicians talked to the squids, a peaceful solution might be worked out.

He eased his mind by rationalizing that the damage to the town could be repaired over time. The folks would be unharmed and all they had to do was fill in a big hole and build new homes.

# # #

Inside Dupre's silo, Dagger pushed Higginbottom against a wall. "Sit." He lit a candle that he took from the mule's saddlebags, placed it on the ground and squatted alongside her. A trickle of blood still leaked from his nose. He grinned at her. "Are you ready to talk now?" He jumped up and skipped around in anticipation of her answer. He could almost taste and feel the riches that awaited him after he pried the secret from her. Dagger relished the look of terror on her face. He ripped off her gag and threw the towel away. "We won't be needin' that anymore. There's no one within miles of this place. Scream as loud as you want. Scream as long as you want. Scream until I get tired of hearin' it."

"Please? Let me go? I'll make believe this never happened."

Dagger chuckled. "So naive."

He took out his long dagger and held it front of her eyes. "This is my persuader." He stuck it into the dirt. "Now, let's begin. Tell me the secret you learned from the aliens."

Higginbottom's lower lip quivered. "I . . . I didn't learn any secrets."

"That's not what my patron said. He's got a lotta resources and he'd never hire me to find out somethin' that wasn't true."

"I don't know any secrets. Why won't you believe me?"

"You'll tell me the secret before the night is over. If you tell me right now, I'll slit your throat and it'll all be over pretty quick. If you don't tell me, you'll still die, but not 'til I've done a lotta painful carvin'. Painful for you, but fun for me."

"I can't tell you something I don't know."

"I was hopin' you'd be stubborn. I ain't cut anyone up inna couple months and it pays to stay in practice." He grinned at her. "This is the last time I ask nicely. What's the secret?"

Higginbottom sobbed and placed her tied hands in front of her face.

"Tsk, tsk. Now I have to work to force the secret outta you. Thanks for that." He picked up the dagger and wiped the dirt off on his pants. "We don't want dirt gettin' inna cut, do we? After all, it could get infected." He laughed out loud. He grabbed her hands and pried her left pinky away from her fist. "We'll start with this one and work our way up the hand before we start on the other one."

"Wait," she sobbed. Higginbottom suddenly remembered MacDrakin's weapon. "I know someone who has an alien weapon."

"That's more like it." Dagger released her hands. "Who is he and where does he live?"

"MacDrakin and I don't know where he stays now. The alien machines destroyed his home."

Dagger pondered the implications of what he had learned. Crumlish's information had been correct; the constable did indeed know an alien secret. He'd have to kill her know so she couldn't warn this MacDrakin. He moved the knife to her throat.

Dagger froze, cocked his head and listened. He stood up and tiptoed to the doorway. Footsteps! More than one set of them. Could Crumlish have set him up for an ambush? He peeked out and saw an old dwarf moving quietly towards the silo. He saw several other figures outlined in the moonlight.

"There he is," the old dwarf shouted. The dwarf pulled a cutlass and charged the door.

Dagger fell back, shocked at Crumlish's betrayal. He looked around for the rear door he knew was somewhere in the darkness. He turned back just in time to use his dagger to block a sword slash. The power of the blow radiated up his arm from wrist to shoulder. It tingled and he had trouble holding onto the knife. He jabbed it at his assailant. The dwarf jumped backward and Dagger ran into the darkness.

Higginbottom saw Dagger running past and shifted her weight. She thrust out a foot and hit his boot. He fell flat on his stomach and skidded several feet, jumped up and ran into the darkness.

"I found her," the cutlass-armed dwarf said. "Over here."

Higginbottom, to her amazement, saw her rescuer was one of the militia, but she couldn't remember his name. Her surprise continued when several more of the militia entered the silo, including the leader, Abercombie. She didn't know these old guys had weapons let alone knew how to use them. Even stranger, she realized they were all sober.

"You, you and you." Abercombie pointed to three of the militia. "After the wretch. Track him down and bring him back." The three selected ones ran off into the darkness. "How are you, my dear? Did he hurt you? Stuart, where are your manners? Untie the lass."

Stuart leaned over and sliced through the ropes with his cutlass.

"Thank you." Higginbottom rubbed her wrists to get the blood circulating. "How did you ever find me?"

"We have had that cretin under watch ever since he showed up in town," Abercombie replied. "I knew he was no good the first time I spotted him in Kate's Inn. I have a talent for this, you know." He tapped his nose. "When I heard the report of your kidnapping, I knew he would bring you here. One of my militia followed him when he scouted out this silo a few days ago."

Higginbottom stood up, but her knees started to give out. Stuart grabbed her elbow and steadied her. She gave him a smile. She felt guilty about misjudging the militia so badly. She thought they were useless old drunks and all the time they were protecting her.

"What I propose, Constable, is this," Abercombie said. "You ride the mule and we'll escort you to your home. Then we'll set up a guard to make sure that the contemptible being doesn't bother you again."

She nodded in agreement. "I can't tell you how grateful I am for your help."

"Nonsense." Abercombie waved a hand dismissively. "Events like tonight was why the First Skensfirth Militia was formed. To aid the town and its citizens."

The three militia pursuers returned. "Can't find him. He disappeared inna woods and it's pitch black under the trees."

"We'll find him back in town," Abercombie said.

Higginbottom walked outside and mounted the mule. The dozen members of the militia formed up around her with Stuart in the lead. She forced her mind to think about Bauer. Who was he? Bauer can't be his name. It must be an alias. Who was the patron that hired him to pursue the nonexistent secret? She felt ashamed about telling on MacDrakin. She would warn him in the morning. Just what he needed with all his other problems, a maniac dwarf searching for alien secrets.

# # #

Yunta strode around the empty storage hold trying to work off some of her anger. Her outrage over the beacon movement had forced the remaining crew members to avoid her until she calmed down a bit. The treachery of the natives was stunning. No trick was too low for them to use. Placing the beacon on an island so the machines would have to enter the river was a brilliant strategy; even in her fury, she had to admit that. How did they know the machines and robots weren't waterproof? Could they have observed a robot after it got wet from rain? The answers were irrelevant now. Despite another screwup by Mivex, she had to concentrate on the mission and revenge. Before she left this benighted planet, the natives would regret their lack of cooperation.

Meanwhile her corporate tree struggled to survive the unhealthy soil it was potted in.

Her communicator beeped. "Yes, Shtap?"

"Captain, I have been thinking. These natives are quite resourceful and I am sure they have more surprises in store for us in the morning. While our superior civilization will win in the end, their activities will further delay the mining operation. I think I can end these obstacles by negotiating with their leader. I can meet with him in morning and work out a deal to allow us work without interference."

"Out of the question. I do not want cooperation. I want the minerals and I want the operation to lay waste to the area. Early in the morning, I will dispatch the last cargo pod with a few more reinforcements. I will leave only a skeleton crew up here. The pod will have seven assistant shamans along with Mivex."

"But Mivex was wounded."

"I will kick the slacker out of sickbay. He is milking his injuries to avoid work. Use the shamans and Mivex to throw combat spells on the native warriors. That should disperse them."

"Yes, that will help us smash our way into town." He wondered what sort of combat spells the shamans knew.

"When you get to town, destroy every building in it while you are mining the minerals. That will be my revenge on these natives. And do not worry about whether the buildings are empty or not."

# # #

Dagger was exhausted by the time he reached Kate's Inn. Sweat drenched his clothing. He had run all the way from the silo, pausing on occasion to catch his breath and to listen for pursuit. His fury at Crumlish's betrayal fueled an adrenaline surge that kept him moving. Along the way, he dissected the night's fiasco. Only treachery explained the facts. How would that group of old thugs knew he planned the kidnapping? They must have watched his movements and followed him. Why would they do that? Crumlish must have hired the gang for that purpose, knowing no one would suspect them. Nothing else made sense.

He opened the rear door to the Inn, the one that was always unlocked. He listened for sounds of movement, but heard only muffled snoring coming from the upstairs rooms. He tiptoed through the hallway and up the stairs to his room. He unlocked the door, slipped inside and lit a candle. Using the dim light from it, he pulled his travel bag out from under the bed. He opened it and took out another dagger. With a second dagger on his hip, he felt a little better, a bit more secure. He threw a few loose items into the bag and locked it. He needed to get out of his room before Crumlish's minions got back to town with the constable. He slipped down the stairs and out the door. At the head of the alley that opened onto High Street, he paused and scanned the town. Nothing moved. He crossed the street and entered the church, another place always unlocked. The folks in Skensfirth were awfully trusting, he thought. No one in their right mind would leave a door unlocked in Dun Hythe.

He sat in a pew. The interior of the church was almost as dark as it was on the street. Only a single candle in the front broke up the darkness. He opened his bag and, working by touch, took out his black, three-curled beard. He pulled off the red one and dropped it in the bag. Changing beards without a mirror and a light was tricky but he accomplished it. At least he thought he did. He wouldn't really know how it looked until the morning when he could see his reflection. Next, he changed out of his sweaty clothes. Instead of his usual black pants and white shirt, he donned tan pants and a brown shirt. He covered the shirt with a lightweight maroon sweater. Now, no one in town would ever recognize him.

With the change in disguise taken care of, he pondered the future. He regretted losing Crumlish as a client; the Minister paid well. Dagger could think of only a single reason for the treachery; he knew too much about Crumlish's dirty tricks. After all, he, Dagger, had been hired to do most of them. So Crumlish wanted to clean up his resume, but now Crumlish had a big problem. Dagger couldn't ignore the attempt to kill him. His reputation, indeed his honor, demanded retribution.

He smiled in the darkness. All he had to do now was figure out how to murder Crumlish. He had to do it while the Minister was still in Skensfirth. Once he returned to Dun

Hythe, Crumlish's assassination became much harder. The longer it took him to get Crumlish, the more opportunity Crumlish had to organize another attempt against him. No, he thought, he had to get Crumlish now, before he left Skensfirth. Slitting his throat tonight while he slept was too dangerous. The other politicians in the room might see him.

Before or after he killed Crumlish, he had to find this MacDrakin and get the alien weapon. He smiled while debating whether to keep it or sell it to the highest bidder.

PART FOUR:

CONVOLUTION

INTERLUDE THREE: DUN HYTHE

Dun Hythe had always been a unique city. In the days when dukes controlled the provinces, Dun Hythe remained an open city governed by an elected mayor. This open status came about because of the city's seaport. It was the only one in the northeast part of Gundarland and it was the largest port in the whole country. Imports were unloaded from the ships and sent along the Trade Road to all parts of the land. Similarly, the Trade Road carried products to Dun Hythe for shipment throughout the known world. These imports and exports benefitted the economy of all the provinces, hence the dukes' interest in keeping Dun Hythe a free city. Their greatest nightmare was that one of them would gain control of the city by violent means and use its revenues for all-out warfare against the others.

Within the city walls, two broad boulevards separate the old city into four quarters. Traditionally, one race dominated each quarter, so the four districts were named the Human, the Elfin, the Half-pint and the Dwarfen Quarters. Over time, these distinct groups melded together, and the four districts evolved into one semi-homogeneous population.

Other changes occurred slowly. One of the most troublesome was the separation of the classes. The middle class and the wealthy moved outside the city walls to new suburbs while the working classes -- always poor -- stayed in the tenements that lined the streets in the old city.

After the government of Gundarland replaced the rule of the dukes, unemployed warrior dwarfs flocked to the city

swelling the already teeming population and added a dangerous new element; trained soldiers.

Inside the city walls, the workers sweated and sickened
in the many factories built in each quarter. The dirt streets
were filled with mud puddles and dung from horses, mules,
pigs, chickens and goats. The housing consisted of ancient
tenements without running water. Their water came from
fountains located on street corners. The only entertainment
for these workers occurred in the cafes and bistros that occupied almost every street corner. Here, the inhabitants of the
city's inner districts drank ale or rot-gut wine, ate a cheap
meal, played dominoes and engaged in their favorite intellec-
tual activity: plotting revolt. These cafes also formed the
centers of the many labor movements that organized the
workers with varying success. A favorite weekend activity
was football games between the labor organizations. The
games draw great crowds and always end with a tension-re-
lieving melee no matter which team won.

With their tradition of independence from the dukes, the
inner city inhabitants hated the Gundarlandian government.
These citizens resented the government's intrusion into their
lives. Taxes, restrictive laws and interfering bureaucrats
angered all the city's inhabitants inside and outside the walls,
but the workers carried the hatred to a blood sport they
called 'Going to the Barricades'. Police officials dreaded the
barricades. Lately, the favorite reason for going to barricades was the pollution emitted by the factories.

A few labor leaders feared the citizenry was getting lax.
Sometimes a month passed without a demonstration or a barricade. Some leaders blamed the absence of demonstrations
on the summer heat. Still others believed the folks were
waiting for a really good cause.

CHAPTER SIXTEEN

Shtap twisted three tentacles together while he watched the dark mass of the cargo pod settle on the grass. The dying camp fires provided a few shreds of illumination in the pre-dawn darkness. A door slid open and a bright shaft of light exploded out of the pod. He raised two tentacles to shield his eyes so he could examine his reinforcements.

Mivex charged out of the craft and almost collided with him. Scowling, he bunched a tentacle under Shtap's beak. "That female exceeds her authority. I should be in sickbay, not on the planet. I will write a report and send it to the CEO. How dare she treat me like this, after I saved a cargo pod the other day."

Shtap patted Mivex on the torso to try to calm him down. "You will have plenty of time to write your report on the return voyage. Meanwhile, we have a mining operation to worry about. I can use your help."

"Since I am still recovering from wounds, I will not be much help. Perhaps I can guard the camp while you go do your mining."

Yunta was right, Shtap thought, Mivex was a slacker as well as a complainer. "We do not need camp guards. We need protection for the machines. You will march with the others." He turned away from Mivex and faced the assistant shamans.

One assistant, a female and obviously the group's leader, stood in front of the other six. She oozed with hostile body language while the others seemed hesitant. She crossed two tentacles and glared at Shtap who asked, "Where are your rifles?"

"All the rifles are down here. There are no more on the ship."

Shtap sighed. More rifles would have increased his firepower by a considerable margin. "You will all work with Drek to keep the natives occupied with your shamanistic talents."

"You will not get anything out of this lot," Mivex said. "They took a strike vote on the way down."

Shtap groaned aloud. Dawn was about to break. It was time to launch his attack and he had to deal with a group of junior members of the crew.

"We demand that we be returned to the *Black Carrion Flower* immediately," the strike leader said. "We are not warriors."

"You are employees of *Furstanker Inc.* and you took an oath of loyalty to the corporation. Your new assignment is to help us protect the machines while they dig out an important mineral deposit."

"We are on strike against the dictatorial orders of Captain Yunta. We demand that her orders be rescinded."

Shtap looked toward the machines and the crew who awaited his order to mount up. He didn't have time to use his negotiating skill to defuse the situation. He had to get the machines moving and he needed these assistants to provide another layer of protection for them. "I am ordering the attack on the native town to begin immediately. If you chose to stay here on strike, you will continue to stay here when we leave the planet for the return voyage. Choose! Follow my commands or be exiled on this wretched planet."

With a great deal of reluctance, the assistant shamans took another vote then slithered off to join Drek.

Shtap ordered the cargo pod to lift off and return to the mother ship. As a safety precaution, corporate policy didn't allow the full complement of the pods from a ship to remain on the ground longer than necessary.

# # #

Sergeant-major Richter and the Nut-busters, surrounded by darkness, lay in the grove of trees and watched the squid camp. Nothing much had happened during the last few hours and the camp fires slowly died down. To his amazement, a silent, dark shape descended from the sky and settled on the ground. He saw more zaftans emerge and join the others. Great, he thought, reinforcements. Just what we need. Even the handful that just landed could turn the battle against MacDrakin.

He dismissed the new development and reviewed his plan. One of his soldiers had scouted the area and found a squid sentry a short distance away. Richter planned to attack the squid when it grew light enough to see. The lookout tapped fingers on his helmet making a slight sound indicating danger. The dwarf pointed to the camp and Richter saw another squid moving towards the trees. "Must be the relief for the one we found," he whispered. "Let's get both of them." He pointed to each Nut-buster and assigned him to a squid; three Nut-busters per squid. With eight tentacles, a squid could injure the attackers despite the helmet wounds, so as a precaution, two Nut-busters would attack with their helmets while the third stood by ready to use his sword to protect the other two from a counterattack by the alien.

Richter moved them closer to the squid sentry. He sniffed the air. The alien stench nauseated him. He held his breath and continued closer.

When the relief alien came within ten feet of the trees, Richter roared, "Now!"

The teams of Nut-busters broke from concealment and charged in different directions while holding their noses.

The alien on sentry duty spun his eye stalks toward the sound and saw two large spikes coming at him at high speed. Before he could defend himself the spikes pierced his torso. He squealed in pain and lashed out with a tentacle to wrap up one enemy and crush him. To his shock, the tentacle was severed by a third assailant. He slithered backward and used more tentacles to try to push the assailants away.

The two dwarfs released their helmet straps and stepped back, leaving the helmet spikes embedded in the alien. Both of them threw up. The squid tripped over brush and fell backward. He squirmed in pain.

"I ain't goin' in there to get my helmet back," one dwarf announced after he stopped puking. "I'll get flayed alive with those tentacles wavin' around."

"Leave it." The dwarf with the sword held his nose. "We can get more helmets."

"Let's help the other team," the second one said.

The three Nut-busters ran out of the woods to find the second squid slithering at high speed with two helmets stuck in his torso.

A dwarf in the second team stopped throwing up long enough to hold up a long heavy stick-like object. "I got that one's weapon. I wonder how it works."

Richter grinned at his men. "Let's get out of here before the squids recover and do something nasty."

#

Cries of outrage, squeals of pain and roars of victory came from the trees. Now what? Shtap thought. Did something happen to his sentries? He couldn't wait around to find out. He had to get the operation under way before something else occurred to delay it. He wanted to get it finished and leave the planet; it was too unhealthy for zaftans.

"Start the engines and prepare to move out," he ordered. "Get the machines in a line. The crew and robots will form up to escort the machines. Shamans, you will form a reserve group and march behind the last machine. In case of trouble or interference from the natives, you will discourage them with whatever it is you can do. Once you disperse the natives, you will advance and keep them away from the convoy. I'll give further orders once we get near the town."

#

MacDrakin suffered from his usual pre-combat jitters. His mouth had turned bone-dry: his stomach felt like it had a lump of stone in it. Now that was light enough to see the entire area, he was sure the attack was only moments away.

A grove of walnut trees separated the two camps and prevented him from seeing the aliens, but he could hear them. A while ago, sounds of a commotion came from the trees. He had heard alien screams and yells of pain, so Richter must have done something. He hoped the Nutbusters were all right

A three-foot high stone wall ran alongside the tree line. It stretched from the well where he stood and almost reached the Skensfirth road. At one time, it must have served as a boundary marker. The well, also made of stone, was used by the cluster of houses on the northern edge of town. The inhabitants of these houses had fled yesterday, leaving them unoccupied.

The politicians from Dun Hythe idled around the well, but he ignored them.

The roar of the machinery moved closer to where his troops were concentrated near the road. He hoped the trenches would stop them, or at least slow them down, but he had no idea of the machines' capabilities. The things were so big and so powerful, that possibly the trenches wouldn't work. Nevertheless, he had to try something to stop them. He had to give his troops something to do so they believed they could win.

He looked at the sky. Angry, dark clouds moved in from the north turning the early morning light into semidarkness. He wondered how a rain storm would change the situation. It would make Gorya's crossbows inoperative until the strings dried out or were replaced. That would be bad news because Gorya's crossbows constituted a major portion of his offensive strength.

# # #

Shtap slithered alongside an auger machine as various units under his command moved toward the town. He reflected on the change in posture in his troops. A few minutes ago, the crew members were bored, but confident. Now that two sentries returned with hideous spikes sticking in their bodies, the crew fidgeted while checking their laser rifles. Their eye stalks never stopped revolving. Every zaftan on

the ground was now petrified about getting stuck with the
spikes the barbarous natives used. The assistant shamans
moved as a group with tentacles linked to each other. Shtap,
with all the confusion going on, had forgotten to ask them
what they could do to help defeat the natives. As a consequence, he didn't have any idea how to use them and he
was too proud to humble himself now by revealing his ignor-
ance. He also wasn't convinced the shamans would obey all
his commands.

Nearby, Drek bounced on his tentacle ends. He seemed
to be the only one looking forward to the battle. He wanted
to kill natives.

Shtap looked at the sky and wondered about the weather.
The rising sun no longer shone. It was hidden behind a thick
layer of gray clouds. Would the weather effect the battle?
He wished he knew.

He forced his mind to concentrate on the issue at hand.
He had to get the machines past the natives and into the
town. He deeply regretted Yunta's decision forbidding him
to negotiate. He was convinced the natives would have allowed the mining as an alternative to fighting a battle. Now
the success or failure of their voyage depended on the outcome of a combat operation. He knew the fierce warrior led
the native forces. Obviously, the warrior had battle experience while he, Shtap, had negotiating experience. But he
wasn't permitted to negotiate anymore, so how was he supposed to compensate for his lack of combat experience and
win a battle?

Shtap crossed two of his tentacles and hoped his decisions would accomplish something positive. One of his
decisions placed a second robot on each machine. That robot had an active stun weapon held ready and they were pro-

grammed to shoot at any native who approached the machines or blocked the way.

He hoped the natives would run away when they saw the strength of his command, but that solution seemed ridiculously easy and probably wasn't realistic. The natives hadn't backed down before and he didn't think they would now.

# # #

Higginbottom, accompanied by Abercombie and Danziger, staggered the last few steps to Drakin's command post, a stone well. Both of the old males looked exhausted. From an inspection in the mirror when she woke up, she knew she didn't look any better. Her face was haggard and battered with her black eye and split lip. She wondered what she would look like if the militia hadn't rescued her. She certainly had been wrong about them. Now it was obvious to her that the group of old soldiers drank because they had nothing better to do. When this crisis surfaced, they jumped into the fray and made a significant contribution. They had saved the town from a surprise attack yesterday morning and last night they saved her life. When this was over, she would buy them a keg of ale as a way to say 'thank you'.

She found MacDrakin and the politicians standing around the well discussing the imminent alien attack.

"What happened to you?" MacDrakin raise an eyebrow when he saw her. "Are you all right?"

"Just tired. I had an unusual night." She winced in pain from her split lip, removed her cap and ran a hand through her short brown hair.

"Did the aliens show up at your home?" MacDrakin looked alarmed.

"No aliens." She almost smiled at his concern. "A kidnapper. That dwarf stranger Braun kidnapped me and took me to Dupre's silo. He planned to torture me into telling him a secret I learned from the aliens." She gripped his forearm. "I panicked and told him about the weapon you took from a robot."

"He wanted my weapon?" MacDrakin asked, a look of surprise plastered on his face.

Higginbottom shrugged. "And I have no idea who told him I knew an alien secret. He said he worked for a powerful client. I wonder who that could be?" To her surprise, Sfiore looked shocked and she caught Crumlish giving Sfiore a furious look. Sfiore turned red and looked away. She wondered what that was about and if it had something to do with the kidnapping. Could one of those two be the patron Braun had mentioned? She promised herself to think about that aspect after she caught up on her sleep and could think straight.

"How did you escape?" Boudreau asked.

"The militia rescued me."

"But . . . how did they know you were kidnapped?" MacDrakin asked.

"Abercombie has been suspicious of Braun ever since he arrived in Skensfirth and he had the militia keep an eye on him. One of them saw Braun kidnap me and they all followed us to the silo. Unfortunately, Braun escaped."

Abercombie interrupted the conversation by laying a finger alongside his nose. "You see, I have a talent for uncovering matters like these."

"Braun." MacDrakin twirled some of his beard. The curls had long since come apart. "Doesn't he wear a single red beard curl? He shouldn't be to hard to find."

"If he's still around. I suspect he's far away from here by now." Higginbottom yawned. "I suppose I should check with Kate's staff to see if they know his whereabouts."

The roar of heavy machinery grew closer and drowned out her last few words.

"So it begins," Rodrigs muttered. "The Battle for Skensfirth."

Gorya marched up and slammed MacDrakin on the back. "Us gonna have a lotta fun today."

Higginbottom forgot about Kate's Inn and stayed to see what would happen.

# # #

Crumlish walked away from MacDrakin and Higginbottom so they wouldn't notice his anger and dismay. The constable's kidnapper could only be Dagger. And he had discovered a secret. Unfortunately, MacDrakin had it. Getting his hands on an alien weapon was the greatest thing that could possibly happen to him. It would give him enormous power. His wizards might even be able to replicate it. He could have battalions armed with new weapons. They would become invincible. No one would be capable of standing up to his troops. Sfiore would be the first to go. Followed by Webley and the rest of his ineffectual cabinet. He wouldn't have to go though the ridiculous ritual of wooing voters to become president. He could simply announce his decision to take over. If anyone objected, well, they wouldn't be around too long.

He frowned. MacDrakin had the weapon and that stubborn mule wouldn't simple hand it over. The weapon would have to be taken by force. He couldn't do it by himself. Perhaps, Dagger could do it. Unfortunately, he didn't know how to contact the assassin and change his orders.

He eyed Sfiore. She stared at the sky, in deep thought. He knew what she was thinking; she wanted the weapon as much as he did. It must be Sfiore's secret that his agent reported on. Why hadn't she gotten hold of it? Something wasn't right, but he'd worry about that later. Acquiring the weapon had taken on more urgency. It was now a race between him and the forces of evil to see who would acquire it first.

# # #

Sfiore turned away so the others wouldn't see her embarrassment and confusion. Something had gone horribly wrong. Apparently, that idiot Crumlish had taken reprehensible actions in response to her disinformation. He had overreacted to what was nothing more than a prank. It always surprised her that males could be such fools. She should have known better. She should have anticipated that he would make a hash of things. It took a powerfully deranged mind to go so far astray. She bit her lip. To hire an assassin and send him after the Constable? That was going too far, even for a male. Even for a dwarf. Even for a dwarf male. Apparently, there was no limit to Crumlish's depravity.

The odd thing was that her misinformation had been correct. The constable did indeed know of an alien secret, a weapon no less. The constable should have sent a telegram to her in Dun Hythe asking for instructions. That was what any responsible constable would have done. After this crisis, Higginbottom would have to be sacked for her gross incompetence.

Meanwhile, there was the issue of gaining control over the weapon. She was sure Crumlish lusted over it. If he gained possession of it, he would surely misuse it to increase his power. Perhaps even to secure the presidency. Her future now depended on who controlled the weapon. Once she had it, she could dictate to Crumlish who would be powerless to resist her. How to get it? Perhaps she could use Higginbottom. Her and MacDrakin appeared to be sweet on each other. In return for getting the weapon from MacDrakin, she could keep her job. That might work.

Once she had the weapon, life would be good. Until her Godmother found out about it. She would have to develop a plan to stall the old bat.

# # #

Boudreau tapped Rodrigs on the arm and with a gesture of his head, walked away from the well and the others. Rodrigs followed.

"Did you notice the reaction of Crumlish and Sfiore when the constable told us about her kidnapping?" Boudreau asked.

"I did. There is something fishy going on. I wouldn't be surprised if one or both of them had something to do with the kidnapping."

Boudreau examined his dusty, unkempt toe hairs while he pondered the situation. Those two ministers were always attacking one another. Most of the attacks took the nature of an attempt to stab the other in the back. He knew both had spies in the other's department. He had his own spies to spy on their spies. He considered that normal political activity. It was the only way to do business because he couldn't trust the reports either one gave him. Their reports were too self-serving to be believable.

"I think it's one of the usual stupid games they play, but this time something got out of control." Boudreau paused. "I'd love to be able to talk to this Bauer guy. He'd tell us lots of delicious stuff, I think."

"It's time we got those two out of the administration." Rodrigs adjusted his blue silk bow tie. "No matter how hard it is to persuade Webley to make the decision, I've got to do it. Gundarland can't afford ministers like those two."

"If we could get this Bauer, it would make that job a log easier."

"We have to get rid of those two with or without Bauer."

# # #

Gorya and his yuks crouched in a trench and waited for the lead machine to come closer. The machine clanged into view with others close behind. Gorya held up a hand to prevent anyone from shooting prematurely. He was surprised to see two robots on the machine. One of them held a small weapon like the one MacDrakin had captured. This robot looked around as if searching for targets. Gorya grinned. He'd kill two robots with one salvo. He hoisted his triple cross bow and sighted on the robots. He waited until the machine came within fifty feet of his position. "Now!" He pulled the triple triggers. His bolts shot forward, veered suddenly and flew over the machine. The bolts fired by his hunters bounced away and fell to the ground. He scowled at the machine and realized it was protected by some sort of magic thingee. He shook a fist at it. The second robot spotted him and fired a beam of orange light. He ducked into his firing pit and the beam flew close to his head with a buzzing sound. With a whole line of machines coming towards him, he and his hunters were trapped.

"Hey, Chief. Us gotta big problem," one of the hunters said. "Da robot things gonna get us if us move."

"MacDrakin da one wid a big problem," Gorya replied. "He gotta get us outta here. Us safe inna trench."

# # #

MacDrakin ground his teeth. Gorya's attack had no effect. He hadn't anticipated the squids using magical wards because he didn't know the aliens had magicians. Where did they come from? How many of them were there? He had assumed his warrior-wizards gave him a magical edge, but that advantage had just been neutralized. Enemy magicians made the battle much more complicated. A few magic spells could upset a battle plan and change the outcome of the combat. Right now, he had to do something to help Gorya. The yuk and his hunters were much too close to the road to stay there. He ran over to the warrior-wizard sergeant. "Throw something at the first machine. Let's see if the ward is effective against your magic. Maybe the spell will give Gorya a chance to pull back from the road."

The sergeant tapped a warrior-wizard on the shoulder. "Lightning spell. Aim at the lead vehicle." He squinted at the machine. "Elevation, zero. Azimuth, ten degrees left. Range, fifty yards. Power, six kilo-necromans.

The man nodded and pointed his M17C military wand at the machine. His lips moved silently. A bolt of jagged yellow light leaped from the tip of the wand and flew towards the first machine. It hit and broke apart with pieces flying in all directions. The machine continued to lumber along, unfazed.

MacDrakin chewed his lip and clutched his unbraided beard. He had nothing to stop the aliens. His offensive weapons were ineffective against the wards. He didn't want this to turn into close combat. It was too risky against machines and the huge squids, but he didn't see any other way of extracting Gorya.

Thunder boomed overhead and a drop of rain fell on his forehead. He glanced up just as the sky opened up and deluge of rain soaked him. He heard more claps of thunder. He grasped at a slim hope. What if the rain did to the machines what the river did to them? If so, he'd have a chance to get Gorya back to safety; relative safety.

As he watched, the roar of the machines slackened and then stopped.

A cheer went up from the warrior-wizards and Gorya's hunters who scrambled out of the trenches.

An idea came to him. He decided to test the alien ward to see just how strong it was. "Full barrage on the lead machine," he ordered the sergeant.

The sergeant and nine of his ten warrior-wizards in their camouflaged robes stood up and pointed their wands while the sergeant called out firing conditions. "On the count of three," the sergeant said in a command voice. He counted and flashes of lightning shot towards the machine. It exploded into flames.

"Sergeant, did you overwhelm the ward or did the rain wash it away?"

The sergeant scratched the stubble on his chin. "Wards don't wash away. We overwhelmed the bugger."

The rain stopped as fast as it had started and bright sunlight flooded the area. MacDrakin wondered how long the machines would be inoperative. A hot sun would dry them out fast. He didn't have much time to decide how to take advantage of the confused enemy.

Sergeant-major Richter and the Nut-busters emerged from the woods. "We got two squids and one of their weapons." He jerked a thumb over his shoulder. "They got a bunch of our helmets as souvenirs."

# # #

Shtap tensed as the lead machine continue to move forward and approached the native positions. At any moment, the battle would start. He flinched when he saw a flock of missiles fly at the lead robot driver, but the missiles caromed away harmlessly. Shtap almost clacked his teeth. Drek's method of protecting the robots worked; the machine lumbered on unimpeded.

A few minutes later, a lightning bolt hit the first machine. Shtap could only gawk as the bolt shattered and bits flew in all directions after it hit the machine's ward. The machine continued onward.

Shtap gasped. The natives had shamans? Where did they come from? How many did they have? Was his small group of shamans outnumbered? He didn't like this new development. In response to his increased tension, his slime started to itch.

A deep, booming sound in the sky surprised him. He glanced upward and frowned. Did the natives do that? Did they have a weapon he didn't know about? Were the machines riding into an ambush? There were so many questions he didn't know the answer to. There were so many questions he didn't know to ask.

A drop of water splashed on his left eye stalk. Puzzled, he looked up in time to see a jagged bolt of lightning streak across the sky followed by blast of noise that he could feel. Rain cascaded out of the sky. He was drenched in a few seconds. He groaned as he suddenly remembered the engineer saying the machines and robots weren't waterproofed. As evidence of that, the lead machine stopped. So did all the rest. The robots froze in place.

A cheer went up from the native positions.

Shtap pounded a tentacle on the ground. He hated this accursed planet. He hated the accursed natives.

His hatred increased when a barrage of a dozen lightning bolts overwhelmed the ward and set the lead machine on fire.

CHAPTER SEVENTEEN

Alix Cyr read the alien article in the *Dun Hythe News* and rejoiced.

Her mother had worked as a domestic for a rich elf family when she was a child and Alix accompanied their children when they were tutored. After the family moved to a suburb outside the city walls, the father dismissed her mother who died soon after leaving the young Alix on her own. Her lower-class status limited her to poor-paying jobs despite her ability to read and write.

She read the article again through tear-filled eyes. Finally, she was vindicated. Now the rest of the country knew about the aliens. Today's edition carried a follow-up article to the *Boogeyman Lands* story from two days ago. After that first story hit the street, she became a celebrity. No longer did folks scoff at her description of the kidnapping by the aliens. Prior to the paper publishing the story, no one listened to her. Friends avoided her rather than listen to her alien tales. Now, everything changed. She couldn't go into a cafe without ten folks demanding she have a drink on them.

She folded the newspaper and put it on the table in the factory break room. She worked as a stainer in a furniture factory and her fingers were temporarily colored dark yellow. She stood up and nodded to the male dwarf who was the President of the Furniture Workers of Dun Hythe Labor Movement. Alix served as its Treasurer and was its best public speaker.

"I'll introduce you and then you give your speech," he said.

"Fine." Alix experienced the usual stage fright she always felt before addressing a large crowd of her coworkers. She smoothed the house dress, but that did nothing to disguise her dumpy figure. Her bare feet displayed elegantly coifed toe hairs, her only vanity. Her brown hair was cut close and her brown eyes displayed fire. She was about to call the government to task for their dereliction of duty concerning the aliens. She followed the dwarf out of the room and onto the factory floor. He climbed on large lathe while she chose a planer to stand on.

"Attention, workers," the dwarf shouted over the machine noises. "Come here and listen. You all know Alix Cyr, one of our own. She has a demand that the government must meet if it wants to retain a shred of dignity. Pay close attention. When she's finished, we will vote on appropriate actions to take." He pointed to Alix and stepped down from the lathe.

"Workers!" Alix said. "Once again the government ignores the legitimate needs of the poor." She shook at fist in the direction of the Presidential Palace. Her strong voice carried across the factory floor and could be heard despite the sounds of the machines. "You've all heard that I was kidnapped by smelly aliens and held for several days with another innocent citizen. I filed a police report when I was released. Did the police do anything to apprehend these aliens? Of course not. Now we find out from the papers that the government and the aliens are in collusion. The aliens are allowed to kidnap citizens and hold them in a freezing cold room and nothing happens to the criminals. The aliens are destroying the private property in Skensfirth while the government looks the other way." Alix paused for a breath and to let the anger of the workers grow.

Alix recognized of the irony in her speech. She used desecration of private property to whip up the worker's ire, but none of the workers owned property nor did they have the slightest chance of ever owning property. Certainly Alix didn't, but that didn't matter. Every worker in Dun Hythe dreamed of someday owning a piece of land somewhere away from Dun Hythe. The government, by its refusal to act, threatened that dream. Since dreaming was tax-free, it was one of the few pleasures the workers could enjoy, and after a few mugs of ale in a cafe, they did enjoy the dreams. Alix's words pointed out that the government had taken away their hopes. Nothing could charge up the workers like a threat to their dreams.

The growls of the workers grew louder and angrier. Some shook fists. Others gave out shrill whistles.

Alix held up her arms for silence. When she got it, she continued her speech. "Some of you may not care that the government lies to us and cheats us, but I do. I will not allow it. The government must be punished for its refusal to act on our behalf. Are you with me?"

The workers howled their assent.

"Then to the barricades! We will stop all trade in and out of Dun Hythe." She turned to the dwarf leader. "Send a messenger to the docks. Have the stevedores join us."

Alix jumped down from the planer and waved her arm towards the factory door. "Follow me."

She had forgotten to take a vote.

# # #

Shtap reacted to the burning machine by turning to his shamans. "Drek! Do something to protect the machines. The rest of you work with him to increase the strength of the wards. We have to protect the machines from the native shamans."

"How can the natives establish linkages?" Drek spoke to no one in particular. He turned to Shtap. "You've met them. Do they have multiple processors?"

"Give us a few weeks to experiment and practice," the aborted strike leader whined, "then maybe we can figure out how to increase the strength of the wards."

"Well, at least shoot at the native positions. That may keep them occupied so they do not have time to destroy more machines."

"What are we supposed to shoot with?" the whiner replied. "We were never taught combat spells."

Shtap felt a vicious multiple headache gathering force involving at least four of his processors. Obviously, it never occurred to Yunta to check if the assistant shamans knew any useful spells before she dispatched them here.

"I can teach them some linkages," Drek said. "I practiced a few the other day while I mined the mountain. Watch."

Shtap was relieved when Drek launched a powerful, highly compressed volume of charged air. It tore through the grove of walnut trees, shredding branches and finally crashed into something on the other side. Sounds of destruction came from the native camp. He searched the area and saw Mivex idling against a large boulder. "Can you do that?"

Mivex sneered at him. "I am not a combat shaman."

"You shoot shamanistic energy into the propulsion system," Shtap replied. "Do that now. Perhaps it will be useful as a weapon."

Mivex lifted himself off the rock with a display of resignation. He closed his eyes and two-seconds later a reddish-brown blob of energy flew away from him. It landed twenty feet away and burned a hole in the ground. Mivex opened his eye stalks and smirked. "That is as far as I ever have to squirt to reach the sub-fusion pile."

Shtap glared at Mivex. With all his problems managing a battle, he had to be saddled with this uncooperative wretch. "Drek, teach these useless shamans how to launch an air hammer and a fireball. Mivex, got over there with them and learn. Any more insolence from you and you will lead the next attack. In front of the machines."

Mivex's reaction pleased Shtap. He turned to the shamans. "We need covering fire from you before we can move forward to the town. What I hope for is a continuous barrage to keep the natives occupied." He wagged a tentacle at them for emphasis. "You must learn how to help us and you do not have much time to learn."

Drek slithered over to the assistants and began instruction them. Mivex, dripping reluctance, joined them.

Meanwhile, Shtap noticed that a robot standing in the sunshine had regained mobility. Others, in shade, remained inoperative. He checked the machines. Steam rose from the surfaces of the ones exposed to the sun, and they showed signs of recovering from the water. Maybe he could restart his offensive in a short while.

At the sound of a burping noise, he turned in time to see a tiny, fizzling fireball land fifty feet away.

"Well done!" Drek pounded one of the young shamans on the back. "You almost have it. Next."

Another fire ball came to grief a short distance away.

Shtap didn't see anything to get enthusiastic about. Two of his tentacles entwined into a knot.

Drek encouraged his charges by firing another air hammer at the natives.

A machine's engine roared into operation.

# # #

Andre Deville and Leonard Tibbs showed up at the stone well. They arrived during a lull in the battle and tried for an interview. Unfortunately, the four Dun Hythe politicians ignored the reporters and continued to watch the developments in the battle. All of them had conjured up umbrellas during the rain storm and now held them for the sun to dry.

After shuffling from foot to foot several times without getting anyone's attention, Deville tried a direct approach. "Secretary Sfiore, are you satisfied with the way your constable handled the alien situation?"

Deville quailed from Sfiore's look. He was almost persuaded she was about to enspell him.

"And what about the kidnapping of your constable?" Tibbs threw out. "Are you concerned the kidnapper will strike again." He had talked to Abercombie earlier and learned of last night's event.

Sfiore turned towards the road and didn't respond to the question.

"How about you, sir?" Deville asked Crumlish. "Do you think your warrior-wizards can handle the stress of battle?"

Crumlish acted as if he didn't hear the question.

"Minister Boudreau," Deville tried again. "Do you think the aliens will pay compensation for any damage they do?"

"The next time I talk to an alien I'll ask him that question." Boudreau smiled at the reporter while tapping one foot against the well to dislodge mud from his toe hairs.

"Mister Rodrigs?" Tibbs had a pencil poised over a notebook. "Do you think the aliens can be stopped here?"

Something smashed through the grove of trees and everyone instinctively ducking. A nearby building collapsed.

"What was that?" Tibbs asked.

"It was an alien spell," Boudreau replied. He looked worried.

The two reporters gaped at each other. "Combat pay!" they said in unison as they exchanged low high-fives.

# # #

The sound of cracking tree limbs caught MacDrakin's attention. Something unseen smashed a path through the grove. His heart accelerated and he sucked in air. A whomp from behind made him duck his head. He turned in time to see one of the small cottages collapse into a pile of rubble. He stared at the destruction, unable to conceive of what caused it. "What was that?"

"That was a spell from the other guys," the sergeant said, "and I don't have any idea what kind it was."

MacDrakin chewed his lip. The squid magic presented him with a serious threat.

# # #

Higginbottom, water dripping from the bill of her cap, looked at the stalled machines. They sent her hopes shooting up. If the machines stayed inert, maybe the battle would end without anyone getting hurt.

She fought the urge to curl up somewhere warm and dry to take a nap. Sitting on the stone wall, she began to nod off. She snapped awake and hunched her shoulders as a blast of air whistled over her head. She turned her head in time to see an invisible hand smack the closest cottage. It collapsed into a pile of rubble and a cloud of dust.

While she gaped at the destroyed house, a dwarf emerged from behind a second cottage and strode towards the well. He hesitated a bit when he noticed her. The dwarf wore tan pants and a maroon sweater, had the usual three-curl beard and carried a thick notebook. She had never seen him before and decided another reporter had arrived in Skensfirth.

She looked back at the machines. They had all stopped and the front one burned. There was a lull in the fight.

Higginbottom glanced back at the stranger. He was much closer and headed for the well. Something about him struck her as familiar. She scrunched up her face while she studied him. The stranger threw a look in her direction and she noticed his unusual eyes. Then it hit her. The stranger's eyes were as cruel as Bauer's. No other dwarf could have eyes like that. It was her kidnapper! He had changed his disguise, but hadn't covered the cut on his forehead.

Bauer opened the notebook and took out a dagger. The book must be hollow, she thought. She drew her baton and ran towards him. He focused on Crumlish's back and didn't look toward her. A surge of anger flooded her mind. She had to repay Bauer for the nasty experience he had given her last night

Higginbottom reached Bauer as he raised the dagger to plunge it into Crumlish's back. She smashed his wrist with the baton. He roared in pain and dropped the knife. She followed up with a second blow. This one clobbered him in his forehead. His cut started to bleed as he sank to the ground, groaned, rolled over, and passed out.

"W. . . What happened?" Crumlish said turning around.

"This is the one who kidnapped me last night." Higginbottom reached down and yanked on Bauer's beard. It came away from his face. "He tried to stab you in the back." She glared at Crumlish. "I wonder why he did that?"

# # #

Crumlish looked at the inert form of Dagger. His stomach muscles clenched and his breathing became ragged. His career and reputation stood on the edge of a cliff and both were about to get pushed over it. The damned constable was responsible for his current problems. First, she had escaped from Dagger and told everybody about him. She knew about an alien weapon and blabbed it about instead of telling him alone. Finally, she dumped the body of Dagger at his feet. Even worse, Dagger was still alive. He had no doubt that Dagger would disclose secrets to save his own miserable skin and that would mean the end of Crumlish's career. He'd never get to be President -- or Dictator -- after this. He and Dagger would spend the rest of their lives in a jail somewhere. Sfiore would triumph. Jail was one thing, so was a wrecked career, but he refused to allow Sfiore a victory sneer. He had to salvage the situation and his career.

Crumlish pointed to Dagger and snarled, "This maniac tried to kill a cabinet minister." He bent down and snatched the knife Dagger had carried. "He must be executed immediately."

Before he could stab the assassin, Higginbottom smacked his wrist with her baton. A searing pain shot up Crumlish's arm. He dropped the knife and clutched his hand. "You broke my wrist. I'll have you cashiered for this."

"No one gets executed in my town without a trial." Higginbottom waved the baton in front of Crumlish's face. "I don't care how powerful you are, in Skensfirth you follow the laws."

"Well done, constable," Boudreau said. His angry eyes stared at Crumlish who couldn't return the look.

"Can you do me a favor?" Boudreau asked Higginbottom.

It took her a few seconds to gather her wits. She was shaken for the aftereffects of preventing a murder and then attacking a high-ranking minister from Dun Hythe. Finally, she nodded.

"Good. Can you lock up this fellow?" Boudreau nudged the assassin with a bare toe. "And put a guard on him? Don't let anyone talk to him or even get near him until Rodrigs and I can question him." He looked at Sfiore. "After that, we'll have a chat with Minister Crumlish and Secretary Sfiore."

"Of course," Higginbottom replied. She turned to Danziger who sat on the stone wall with Abercombie. "Can you take this one to the jail?"

"Sure thing, Constable," Danziger said. He grabbed the back of Dagger's collar and dragged him away.

Crumlish watched Dagger's boots leave two trails in the dirt and knew his world had just crumbled. Not only was he about to be disgraced, he was about to lose his freedom.

His best course of action would be to disappear during the confusion of battle.

# # #

MacDrakin seized on the opportunity to attack the disabled enemy. With the machines lying helpless on the road, they were prey to the warrior-wizards. He had to act before the aliens launched more spells. Any spell that could collapse a small house would be deadly to his troops. "Sergeant, launch another barrage at the next machine in line."

"Yes sir." The sergeant knuckled his forehead, but did nothing else.

"Well? What are you waiting for?"

"We used up our magical power in the last barrage. We're waiting for our reservoirs to refill."

MacDrakin ground his teeth. Time was the one thing he didn't have. "How long?"

"Most of us'll be ready in five, ten minutes. Some'll take longer."

MacDrakin felt a tendril of imminent defeat flit through his mind. Gorya's cross bows were ineffective against the alien wards and most of the Nut-busters no longer had helmets. He needed the warrior-wizards to launch frequent spells to destroy the machines and to keep the squids from attacking his positions. If the alien leader sensed his weakness, MacDrakin's small force would be overwhelmed by an attack.

To put an exclamation point on his worries, another one of the mysterious and powerful spells blasted into the grove of trees. A tall, stout walnut tree exploded and showered the area with splinters of hard wood, leaves and immature nuts.

A splinter grazed MacDrakin's left forearm and blood began dripping from the wound. The sergeant yelped as another splinter gashed his right cheek.

MacDrakin heard the roar of a machine coming back to life. The situation, not too good to begin with, turned worse.

CHAPTER EIGHTEEN

Drek used the rain-induced delay to teach the shamans about techniques and linkages needed to launch combat spells. For the final lesson, he had every one of them place a tentacle tip on his back while he fired off an air hammer. He set his tentacles, shifted his weight and focused on a spot beyond the walnut trees separating the combatants. He waited as his processors linked themselves in the correct configuration. With the linkages established, the space immediately surrounding him shimmered as reality was pushed aside. He briefly experienced pressure on his torso as reality pushed back. Once a measure of equilibrium had been established, he triggered the air hammer. He felt as if a great weight lifted from his body and he rocked backward from the force of the air hammer escaping from the volume of unreality. "Did you sense how I did that?" he asked his charges. "Did you understand how I manipulated unreality? How I shaped it? How I aimed it? How I launched it?"

Two of them nodded and the rest looked pensive.

"Let me try that," Mivex said. His body went rigid, his slime oozed more heavily, but in a few seconds, he launched an air hammer. Much smaller than Drek's, it flew past the grove of trees and hit something beyond with a satisfying crunch.

"Well done," Drek said. "Now you." He pointed to one of the shamans. "Try a fire ball."

The assistant adjusted his tentacles and took a stance. In a few seconds, a smallish ball of flame shot forward and made it to the grove where it set fire to the lower branches of a walnut tree.

"Excellent." Drek congratulated the zaftan.

Drek hadn't had this much fun in ages, not since he was a squidling. Navigating was so boring compared to this. Perhaps he should change careers. Instead of being a navigational shaman, he could become a security shaman in charge of protecting the machines at mining sites.

"Everything is operational again," Shtap said. "Mivex? I want you to command the escort. Take the crew and have them accompany the machines. Keep everyone on the side away from the native positions, but keep them shooting their rifles between the gaps in the machines. Drek? You will move behind the last machine with the assistant shamans. Your job will be to launch covering fire at the native positions so they cannot interfere with the convoy."

"That is a good plan, Shtap." Drek turned to the assistants. "Form a line with ten feet between each of you. You may use fireballs or air hammers, whichever one you are most comfortable with. You must keep up a consistent rate of fire. It will be very tiring, but the success of the voyage depends upon it." He adjusted the line by moving two of the shamans further apart, then swiveled to face Shtap. "We are ready. Give the command and we will begin our harassing fire."

# # #

The police ruined the demonstration.

An angry Alix Cyr scowled from the top of the wobbly barricade erected on Dun Hythe's main street to stop traffic to and from the docks. In her right hand she held a stick with the flag of Dun Hythe fluttering boldly in the breeze blowing in from the harbor. The barricade was made of paving blocks torn up from the street augmented with furniture, empty ale kegs and a few carts. From her elevation, she had a good view of the entire mass of demonstrators. Her fellow furniture workers were bored with throwing bricks and stones at the few police officers who had bothered to show their faces. Already some of them had left the barricades and now sat in a cafe having a morning ale break. Others took out decks of cards. A group of females had formed a sewing circle.

She muttered a string of curses at the police. The cops caused the demonstration to lose steam because they hadn't shown up in enough force to harass the workers. What was the point in demonstrating if no one noticed? Why bother if the other side didn't care?

The President of the Furniture Workers of Dun Hythe Labor Movement climbed up and stood besides her. "Our righteous protest against government policy is slipping away."

"I know," Alix replied. "You'd think the police would want to keep a main street like this open. This is a symptom of the trouble with our government. Here we are blocking trade and no one cares. No one takes notice. The Secretary of the Interior should drop whatever she's doing and order the police to break up our barricade."

"You're correct. What's the point of demonstrating if there is no one to demonstrate against. The workers know this and they're losing interest. It's so difficult to keep them motivated these days."

"I'm not giving up yet. If the police refuse to recognize our demonstration here, we'll move it someplace else where they'll have to respond."

"It's not easy to move a barricade. What do you have in mind?"

"We won't move the barricade." Alix chuckled. "We'll leave it for the police to take down. That'll give them something to do. Let's get the workers charged up again and then we'll march forward."

"Attention, workers," the president shouted. "Alix Cyr has a message for you."

The workers stopped their activities, looked at Alix and waited. Even the ones in cafes came out on the street holding their mugs of ale.

"Workers! Once again the government ignores our legitimate concerns. Once again, we voice our demands and no one listens to us. It's as if we are invisible to them. Look around us." She swept an outstretched arm in a circle. "We have blockaded the port of Dun Hythe. Does anyone notice? No! Does anyone care? No!"

The workers cheered and stamped their feet.

She shook a fist in the general direction of the closest police building. "I say we invisible people have to go to where the government can't ignore us. Where the bureaucrats can't say they didn't see us. Where the officials can't say they didn't hear us." She pointed her flag staff towards the Presidential Palace. "Let's move the demonstration to the Palace. Let's march to the center of the very government that ignores us. We'll teach them what workers can do when the government treats them as if they are invisible."

She jumped down form the barricade. With the flag staff still pointing to the Palace, she roared, "Forward, Workers!"

#

Half the morning had past and by now MacDrakin knew every machine had dried out and headed for Skensfirth. He had nothing to stop them. His only hope was the warrior-wizards, but they took too long to recharge their magical energy. He looked around and saw the politicians hunched behind the stone wall. He was surprised they weren't on their way back to Dun Hythe to get out of danger or responsibility. He jogged over to them and threw himself behind the wall as another of those destructive blasts hit a house and punched a hole in it. The house shook and a few roof tiles fell off, but the house didn't collapse like the first one.

"Maybe," Boudreau said pointing to the house, "they're getting tried. That one didn't have the power of the earlier ones."

"We need something more than maybe. The squids are about to try again and I have nothing to stop them. Aren't you all wizards? If you are, I need you to start throwing spells at the machines." He looked around. "Where's Crumlish? His warrior-wizards take so long between spells they are next to useless."

"Perhaps they need more drills," Rodrigs said. "I wonder where Crumlish went."

"It's too late to decide the soldiers need more drilling after the battle starts." MacDrakin paused to look at the trees where a fireball had set fire to one of them. So far the trees had served as a protective wall, but the alien spells had destroyed many of them leaving clear fields of fire. "So what can you wizards do? If I don't get any help, the aliens are going to drive right into Skensfirth."

"Hey!" Rodrigs snapped his fingers. "I mentioned this once before. The aliens use a strange form of magic. Did any of you study the 'Big Bang' in wizards college?"

"Don't be absurd," Sfiore replied. "The Big Bang is poppycock."

"No, it isn't." Rodrigs punched a finger in the air in Sfiore's direction. "It's advanced applied occultism and it works. In college we tried a small experiment on another frat house. They liked to fool around with black magic and they had set spells all over the house. My frat house used white magic, you see, so one night, when all the students in the other house were out at a party, two of my frat brothers and I tested the 'Big Bang'."

"What happened?" Sfiore asked.

"The whole bloody frat house disappeared. It was replaced by a fish pond with predatory gold fish. Not a splinter left behind from the house. Me and my frat brothers all got knocked on our butts and our eyebrows were burned off." He shook his head. "Good thing the school couldn't prove we did it or we would have all been kicked out."

"What are you talking about?" MacDrakin snapped. He didn't have time to listen to frat house stories.

"A way to disrupt the aliens," Rodrigs replied, "but it's potentially dangerous."

"Whatever it is," MacDrakin said, "you only have a few minutes to get it going."

"We'll need all the warrior-wizards over here with us," Boudreau said. "What do you want us to aim at?"

# # #

Albert Webley sat behind his enormous presidential desk and whisked dust motes from its empty surface. He still worried about the newspaper stories on the aliens. After much mental anguish, he had concluded that ignoring the stories and the entire alien situation would be the best strategy. At least until Rodrigs got back. By ignoring the newspaper accounts he would demonstrate to the people that he was not worried. That should calm the masses. After all, the people trusted the government to do what was in the people's best interest. Everyone knew that.

A strange noise permeated the office. He realized he'd been hearing it for some time now. It sounded like a celebra-tion. As he listened, the sounds became louder. Whoever made the racket must be moving closer to the Palace. He stood and walked to a window. To his surprise, what looked like an untidy parade marched towards him. He wondered what or who the marchers honored.

As they moved closer, he realized, to his shock, that the marchers were angry. In the lead was a female half-pint waving a Dun Hythe flag. On either side of her, others set fire to Gundarlandian flags. By the stars, he thought, this must be a worker's demonstration. He had heard rumors of them, but what could they possibly be upset about? They lived and worked in Dun Hythe, the richest and finest city in the world. Most people would love to live in the capital.

A sudden idea thrilled him and he adjusted his chartreuse cummerbund. He would go out and talk to the workers. They would be pleased to see and hear their president. They could tell their grandkids about it in years to come. He pondered his speech to them and made a few mental notes. He would describe the great strides the country was making. He would tell them how the stock market had climbed under his presidency. He would quote several industrialists on how much their profits had grown in the last few years. He was sure he would smooth over whatever petty complaints they had. Wouldn't Rodrigs be surprised when he returned?

He was about to step away from the window to go outside when a police carriage pulled up in front of the marchers. The workers pelted the carriage with bricks and large stones. Webley stared, bewildered. The police officers in the carriage jumped out the doors on the side opposite from the marchers and ran for cover. The driver leaped off his perch and disappeared down a side street. Webley watched in horror as the demonstrators freed the two horses then set fire to the carriage.

The mob continued to move closer to the Palace and he could now make out their chants.

"Down with the government," they shouted.

"No more pollution!"

"No more aliens!"

A stunned Webley realized they were angry at his administration. What ingrates! He shook his head in despair. After all he had done for them, they repaid him by marching against his administration. How dare they criticize his presidency. They had no idea how hard he slaved to satisfy his corporate friends. They hassled him all hours of the day. Even interrupting his naps sometimes. He couldn't have a meal in a topnotch restaurant without some executive or CEO sending over a bottle of expensive wine with a note attached asking for a favor.

Enough was enough! The ungrateful louts pushed him too far. He made a decision and felt as if a great weight lifted from his chest. He went to the door to the office. "Excuse me," he said to a secretary. "I need to send a telegram to Treasurer Boudreau. He's in Skensfirth, I think. Can you help me?"

# # #

Shtap watched as Drek commanded his small force. Individually, they launched fireballs and small air hammers that smashed the remains of the walnut trees and impacted in the area where the natives cowered. Drek, meanwhile, hurled giant air hammers over the grove. They sent up showers of dirt and rock when they landed. To Shtap's relief, even Mivex carried out his orders. The members of the crew kept the machines between them and the natives and peppered the enemy positions with blasts from their laser rifles. Any native who showed himself had a good chance of having his head blown off.

The fire-blackened lead machine had been pushed to one side and the others rolled past it. For the first time, Shtap had confidence that they would reach the town and begin mining. After they destroyed it.

This experience would greatly enhance his resume. Since he already was an accomplished negotiator, leading a combat team against hostile natives would indicate great resourcefulness and flexibility. Even Yunta would have to be impressed. An official battle report from her would cause a sensation in his negotiating school. He knew he was about to become famous. Maybe the school would name a new wing after him.

The only question he had concerned the native shamans. What were they up to? They hadn't done anything in some time. He supposed they were too busy trying to stay alive under the ferocious bombardment.

#

Boudreau glared at the sergeant who said for a second time, "I'm not telling my soldiers to commit suicide." They and Rodrigs huddled alongside the stone wall. It was the only structure that offered protection from the alien spells that fell all around them and the beams of light that laced the air.

"It's the only way to stop them" Boudreau argued. "We need to combine all of our magic into one large unspelled mass."

"It's a bunch of bull." The sergeant pounded a fist into the dirt. "It isn't going to do anything but drain us of magic and we need that to protect ourselves."

"Sergeant!" Boudreau growled. "If you refuse to do this, you'll spend the rest of your career in a military prison. Do you understand me?"

Something crashed into the ground and sent up a large gout of dirt and stone, showering them with debris. The sergeant received a new wound, this one on his forearm. Blood dripped from a gash on Boudreau's forehead.

"All right." The sergeant bit his lip. "But it's risky, you know. No one has ever tried this before."

"I did," Rodrigs responded. "On a much smaller scale."

"You'll want firing data?" the sergeant asked.

"No." Rodrigs shook his head. "That's not needed. We can't enspell our magic." He looked around at his two fellow bureaucrats and the ten human warrior-wizards and the sergeant. "You have to gather your magic into an unspelled bundle and we have to launch all our bundles together. Hurl your magic at the area where their spells are coming from.

That will be where the convoy is. If I'm correct, our magic will interact with the alien magic and both magics will be neutralized with a great deal of fireworks and commotion. The effects will be more than a bit bizarre, so be prepared. And duck! Otherwise, you may lose your eyebrows if not some other body parts."

Another spell, much smaller, skipped off the top of the wall, sending rock splinters flying through the area.

"As you may have noticed," Boudreau continued, "we don't have a much time to do this so let's start concentrating." He turned to Rodrigs. "You did this before. You run the show."

"All right," Rodrigs said. "Close your eyes until you have your magical reservoir bundled up. Then open your eyes as a signal to me. When everyone is ready, I'll give the word to launch. Got it? Good. Begin."

Boudreau mentally pushed his magical reservoir into a glob. It resisted. It squirmed and tried to seep through fissures in the boundaries. He continued to exert pressure and the magic became more compliant. He shaped it some more and finally had it under control, ready to be released. He sensed it was shaped like a ball. He opened his eyes and looked at the others. From the stress on their faces, they were also having trouble getting their reservoirs under control. Magic didn't like to be compressed into a mass with boundaries.

Sfiore had a sweaty brow by the time she opened her eyes. One by one, the warrior-wizards opened their eyes while Boudreau struggled to hold his magic glob together.

At last, everyone stared at Rodrigs. Boudreau noted that some faces showed fear and others were tense.

Rodrigs faced the aliens. The others followed his lead. "Release!"

Boudreau stood flabbergasted at the cloud of roiling un-spelled magic flying towards the convoy. It was immense and so dense it cast a shadow on the ground. Jagged spikes of various colors flashed inside the cloud like miniature lightning bolts. Two much smaller clouds flew behind the main glob of magic. Evidently, everyone hadn't released at the same instant. Trees in the path of the blob vanished. He covered his ears with his hands to block out the hideous sounds of demented music played by deranged musicians on damaged instruments.

"Get down!" Rodrigs yelled and dove behind the wall.

# # #

Shtap groaned and rolled over. His vision was fuzzy, as if it hadn't yet recovered from the blinding explosion. His eyeballs also had dirt on them. He wiped his eyes and eye stalks with a tentacle and looked at the debacle of his combat command. His despair was almost overwhelming. How could he explain this to Yunta?

The meadow grasses had changed color from green to blue and red. Two walnut trees stood upside down with their roots in the air. When a breeze rippled through the roots, clods of dirt fell to the ground with soft thumps. The robots looked like a berserk graffiti artist had spray-painted them. Stripes in shades of reds, greens and yellow bands covered most of their torsos. They moved in circles, as if they couldn't travel in a straight line. The shamans -- the con-scious ones -- quivered, groaned and rolled on the ground.

All of them had their slime burned to a powdery yellow ash. The crew members seemed dazed, but otherwise unhurt.

Shtap glanced over at the machines. Three had disappeared while a few others remained intact. He could only marvel at the rest. One was a colorful carousel, complete with horses, mythical beasts and a mechanical band. Another was a marble water fountain with a naked, bigger-than-life native female statue in the center. Water flowed from her nipples. A third was a bronze godlike statue. One cargo pod, however, had the most amazing transformation. It had changed into an elongated fish tank, complete with a load of bewildered fish. One of the mining machines, now a miniature, pumped out air bubbles from the bottom of the tank. Some distance away, the second cargo pod stood with its front third embedded in the turf.

With an effort, Shtap stood up and almost fell down again before stabilizing himself by spreading his tentacles. It took a few more seconds before the magnitude of the disaster sunk in. The mining operation was over because he no longer had enough mining machines or cargo pods. The voyage of the *Black Carrion Flower* would go down in corporate history as a failure, possible the only one.

He examined his options and decided his primary duty was to protect the crew. If the native shamans launched another blast like the last one, no one would survive. To protect his charges, he must make peace with the natives. He lurched towards the grove of destroyed trees holding two tentacles above his head in what he hoped was a sign of peaceful intent. He called out in loud voice, "Truce? I want a truce to discuss an end to this battle."

As he slithered forward, his anger surged. He recognized that his career had been severely damaged -- possibly even ruined -- by the voyage. His dream of pulling off a textbook negotiation scam was dust. The corporation took a very dim view of failure and he had certainly failed. In spectacular fashion. When his family found out, he was quite likely to be disowned.

It was all the fault of these treacherous natives. If they had observed the conditions of the agreement, none of these disastrous events would have occurred. Taking the long view, what was the value of their property damage? It was all trivial. Over time, the scars left by the mining operations would disappear. And because the zaftans violated a few properties, the natives went to war? Where was the sense of proportion of these beings?

By the time Shtap approached the two natives who stood waiting for him. He was in a towering rage, and he didn't care if his emotions interfered with the negotiations.

CHAPTER NINETEEN

Higginbottom heard an alien call out for a truce and started to grin, but a yawn interrupted the incipient smile. Her sleep-deprived brain struggled to identify what made the voice sound familiar to her, but she couldn't make the connection. She shrugged and wrinkled her nose at the acrid smell that lingered in the air after the wizards' spell casting. The entire area stank like the telegraph office when the machine sparked a lot. She poked her head over the stone wall to take a look. One of creatures lurched towards the grove of trees.

MacDrakin, his troops and the Dun Hythe politicians all stood up.

"He wants to talk," MacDrakin said. "The magic must have worked." Looking around, he pointed to the carousel. "Look at that. No wonder the aliens want to talk."

Higginbottom noticed the strange effects for the first time and she gawked in wonder at them. She hoped the spell would persuade the aliens to leave Skensfirth so everything could return to normal.

"I'll go talk to him," Rodrigs said. "I think it's the one who showed up in Dun Hythe several times."

"No, I'll go," MacDrakin said. "This is still a military operation and I'm in charge until we agree to a truce."

"All right. We'll both go, but we don't want more than two because it may be a trap.

"Gorya, cover us with your cross bows. Just in case."

"Me do dat." He finished changing the bow strings on his weapon then waved a huge paw at his yuks. "C'mon." They moved off to the right to get a clear line of sight.

"These creatures stink like dead fish," Rodrigs said. "I'll set wards around us so we don't get sick."

Higginbottom sat on the wall so she could observe the parley. Despite her exhaustion, she felt happy that the end appeared to be in sight. After it was all over, she planned to go home and jump into a hot tub. While she soaked, she would ponder what to do about MacDrakin. If the aliens left, the reason for their bickering disappeared. That meant matters might improve and that was good, but she couldn't assume a male would react rationally. He still could be angry with her because of his male ego or because of some stupid male mental deficiency.

The alien slithered closer. Sunlight glinted off a shiny medallion hanging around the creature's upper torso. She frowned. The medallion triggered another memory fragment. Why? Had she see it before? With a jolt like an electric shock, she recalled the alien who questioned her and Alix. Could it be the same one? How many aliens wore a silver medallion?

MacDrakin and Rodrigs approached the alien.

"This is close enough," MacDrakin said to Rodrigs. They stopped a good twenty feet away from the alien. "I don't trust the slimy bugger."

"He is the one who came to Webley's office," Rodrigs said. "I recognize the medallion. His name is Shtap."

"Whoa!" Shtap said. "You are an ugly sucker."

"A robot told me that," MacDrakin said, "and I destroyed it."

It took a few seconds before the connection clicked in Higginbottom's mind. Her jaw dropped open. She had used those words when she had first met an alien. It was the same voice! It was the same medallion! It must be the one who kidnapped her! She jumped up, drew her sword and charged towards the parley.

"Enough of this foolishness," Shtap said. "I have summoned another cargo pod. When it lands, we will board it and leave your perfidious planet."

# # #

To MacDrakin, the squid looked furious. He couldn't stand still. The alien bounced on the tips of his tentacles which quivered as if shaking with rage. Shtap looked like the slightest provocation would touch off more combat. He told the squid, "We will not harass you as long as the truce is observed."

"Wait a minute," Rodrigs said. "What happened to the pollution plan you promised us?"

"After all your treachery, you expect us to honor our end of the treaty?"

"You promised to respect property rights," Rodrigs said. "Then you destroyed many homes and farms."

"Not to mention my home and my mine, but this doesn't help anyone," MacDrakin said. "What's done is done."

Higginbottom, waving a sword, ran past them and screamed, "You are under arrest for multiple kidnappings."

"Don't!" Rodrigs yelled. "You'll break the truce!"

Higginbottom ignored him. She skidded to a halt in front of the alien and frowned in confusion. "Which ones are your arms?" she asked while pinching her nostrils with one hand. "Hold them out so I can tie them up."

The alien roared and moved forward, engulfing her in tentacles. "You will go back with me to show Zaftan 31B what treachery looks like."

MacDrakin watched the alien slide backward while smothering the squirming Higginbottom in his tentacles. Various scenarios flashed through his mind showing possible future lives, all of them without Higginbottom. He didn't like any of them. He forced them away and calculated potential attack angles instead.

"Do not move," Shtap commanded MacDrakin and Rodrigs, "or I will squeeze her until she bursts."

MacDrakin's mind whirled at high speed assessing the perils of his actions. Higginbottom was in danger, but an attack by him might put her in even more danger. If he didn't do anything, he'd never see her again, and she'd be doomed to some horrible fate with the aliens. He knew what his ancestor would do.

He reached behind his shoulder and grasped the handle of his ax. His feet moved before the ax came free, but he needed to get higher to attack Shtap without endangering Higginbottom. As he ran, he leaped at the stump of a destroyed tree. He hit the stump with his left foot and pushed off. He flew forward several feet above the ground. In midair, he swung the ax, aiming at the top of Shtap's torso. The blade sliced completely through the body and the large lump with the eyestalks fell to the side. MacDrakin's momentum slammed him into Shtap's body. He bounced off and regained his feet after a momentary stumble. The tentacles still held Higginbottom. Ignoring his stomach's churning, he shifted his hand up the ax handle for better control and cut away two tentacles. He grabbed Higginbottom's arm with his free hand and pulled. She came away covered with slime. Part of her clothes smoldered and she stank.

Both tumbled to the ground with Higginbottom on top. MacDrakin patted her clothes as best he could to stop the smoldering. She raised her head to look at Shtap just as he toppled over on his side. She gaped at the inert form, then turned back to MacDrakin and kissed him. She winced from her split lip, but held on to the kiss.

"Here comes the cargo pod," Rodrigs said. MacDrakin and Higginbottom, still on the ground, ignored him and continued kissing.

"You can come and get this body," Rodrigs yelled to the aliens. "We won't interfere with your leaving." He turned to smooching couple. "Hey, Constable. What about the robot that's in your jail? We should let it go before the aliens do something nasty about it."

Higginbottom and MacDrakin broke the kiss to get some air. "All right. Send someone to the jail and tell Danziger to let it out." She turned to MacDrakin. "Let's get out of here before something else happens." She stood and held out a hand for MacDrakin. She pulled him to his feet.

They walked back to the stone well holding hands.

# # #

When Rodrigs got back to the well, Boudreau looked like he was in shock. "What's the matter?"

Boudreau looked at him, blinked a few times and handed Rodrigs a telegram. "The operator delivered this a few minutes ago." Before Rodrigs could read it, Boudreau told him what it said. "There was a worker demonstration in Dun Hythe. They marched on the Palace and Webley abdicated."

Rodrigs's mouth dropped open. "T . . . then you're the interim president"

Boudreau nodded. "I wrote out a message to send to the Palace. It announces that I'm now president and I told the palace staff to paste the announcement all over the city."

"We're a long way from Dun Hythe." Rodrigs pulled a face. "A lot can happen before you get there. Especially if the city is rioting."

"There's nothing I can do about that, but I told the telegraph operator to send another message to Ashton and order the train for Dun Hythe held until we get there. I also told the operator to get a carriage over here to pick us up." He stared off at the alien camp for a while then snapped out of his reverie and frowned. 'Sergeant."

The sergeant ran over and saluted.

"After the aliens leave, find Crumlish and arrest him. He is no longer the Minister of Defense. Then take Crumlish and his would-be assassin and escort them to Dun Hythe. We'll be going on ahead so you'll have to get tomorrow's train." He jabbed a finger at the soldier. "Keep them apart and don't let them talk to each other. I don't want them concocting a story together."

To MacDrakin, he said, "Can I take your alien weapon back to Dun Hythe? Perhaps our scientists and engineers can learn something about their technology from it."

"Sure." MacDrakin replied and he handed over the small weapon he took from the robot. "I'll get the big one from Richter. You can have that one also. And we'll collect the dead robots."

"I'd appreciate it if you and your troops would protect the machines and those big flying things from looters and souvenir hunters. I'll send engineers down here to figure out how to move all the stuff to Dun Hythe so it can be studied." Boudreau smiled at MacDrakin. "In a few years or less, I bet we have massive scientific breakthroughs thanks to the squids."

Boudreau turned to Sfiore who chewed on her lip.

"After Rodrigs and I interview Crumlish and the assassin," Boudreau said, "I'm sure we'll have a lot to talk about with you." He turned to Rodrigs. "Let's go back to Kate's Inn and get our luggage and your dragon."

Along the way, Boudreau said, "I'm appointing you to Treasury in my place."

"No, you're not. I hate accounting."

"My assistant treasurer will take care of all that. You'll only have to sign some documents. You'll have access to all the undercover agents I put in place, so you'll know everything that's going on. Since the job is so easy, you can also be my chief-of-staff."

"Are you going to run for the Presidency?"

"Yes, and you're my campaign manager. Pinky can be the campaign mascot."

# # #

In mid-afternoon, reporters Andre Deville and Leonard Tibbs approached Abercombie to ask him for an interview. The journalists were giddy from their success. They were the only two reporters on the scene during Skensfirth's monumental events. They had enough material to write feature stories for months and even to put out a book or two. Of course, their editors would demand different approaches. Deville's latest story for the *Times* depicted how woefully unprepared the military was. Tibbs' story, sent to the *News*, described how a female constable was snatched by an alien who ended up getting beheaded during a heroic rescue.

Meanwhile, they couldn't get any new information. They anticipated a juicy story about Crumlish's disappearance, but the new president and the other bureaucrats couldn't talk to them because they hurried back to Dun Hythe. MacDrakin and the constable wouldn't talk to anyone except themselves. The warrior-wizards wouldn't let them interview the attempted murderer. Abercombie and the militia were the only ones available for an interview.

They met the First Skensfirth Militia in their meeting house. Both reporters were amazed that the structure hadn't caved in before now. Abercombie sat off to one side away from the others who were doing serious damage to the contents of a keg of ale.

"Thanks for talking to us," Tibbs said.

"Nonsense," the old elf replied. "It's essential that you reporters hear all sides of the events in town."

"So, what was your role in these events?" Deville asked.

"I don't want to take anything away from MacDrakin. After all, he did the dangerous part in fighting the aliens. Nevertheless, without the help of the militia, MacDrakin would have been hard pressed to put up the good fight."

The two reporters glanced at each other. They sensed another unanticipated story. "Could you explain that last statement?" Tibbs asked.

"Of course. Every successful military campaign relies upon accurate intelligence. Without that, the army leaders are blind as to the enemy's intentions. That's where we came

in. We were the intelligence arm for MacDrakin's troops.
We provided the information that he needed to properly de-
ploy his troops."

"Is that so? How extraordinary," Tibbs said. "How did
you know he needed intelligence?"

"Intelligence is a basic need of military leaders." Abercombie paused to spit on the ground. "Therefore,
MacDrakin needed our information, and I have a nose for
smelling it out."

"So you maintain that you were an important element in
MacDrakin's victory over the aliens?" Deville asked.

"Absolutely. The First Skensfirth Militia was a vital cog
in the victory."

The two reporters gaped at each other. "A sidebar story,"
they said in unison as they exchanged high-fives.

"If you stay in town for another day or two," Abercombie said, "you'll get to see our annual militia parade. We're
finishing up the planning details even as we speak. You'll
also be able to cover the election for a new mayor to fill out
the term of that coward Jehan. You may have heard he fled
the town with his family. Anyway, Higginbottom persuaded
me to run since I have a nose for politics, you see." Abercombie tapped a finger alongside his nose. "I'm sure I'll
make a wonderful mayor."

# # #

Alix sat on an ale keg eating a chunk of black bread.
Around her, the workers took their ease awaiting further developments. Their demonstration had caused an uproar in
the Palace, but they didn't know exactly what went on in
there. Right now, noise and commotion came from the

palace grounds indicating something big was happening. Perhaps they were organizing an attack on the demonstrators. That had happened before and another attack wouldn't come as a surprise. Certainly her comrades expected an attack. They were antsy and had collected bricks, poles and chamber pots to defend themselves with.

The ashes of the police carriage still smoldered and the smoke made her view of the palace walls hazy. The front gate partially opened and a dozen pages slipped through. Each carried an armful of papers. They nervously watched the demonstrators while dispersing down a number of side streets. One page pasted a paper on the wall before running off.

"Someone bring me that paper and I'll read it to all of you," Alix called out.

A dwarf ripped the paper from the wall and carried it to her. She glanced at it while she chewed a chunk of bread. After a few sentences, the bread dribbled out of her open mouth and fell on her lap.

She stood on the keg, brushed the crumbs off her lap and shouted for quiet. When she got it, she said, "I just read this here announcement. It says President Webley has abdicated and--"

"Wot does abdi-whatever mean?" a half-pint male asked.

"It means he quit," she replied.

"Why didn't they just say that?"

"They're bureaucrats. They have to use big words to make themselves feel important. Now, listen to this next part."

"So, who's gonna be the new president?" a female dwarf asked.

"If you'll all shut up, I'll tell you." Alix glared at the female for a few seconds then continued. "The new president will be Benoit Boudreau. He's the Treasurer right now and he's next one in line."

"Big whoop," someone called out. "Another politician. Nothing'll change."

"Yes, it will. This Boudreau character isn't in Dun Hythe right now because he's in Skensfirth fighting against the aliens. There's been a battle with them and he won. The aliens have left."

"Wot's an alien?"

"What the newspaper called Boogeymen. And the best part? Boudreau's a half-pint. We all know how great half-pints are, don't we?" She winked at the crowd.

The mob laughed and hooted at her.

"Let me tell you what this announcement says in plain language. It says: 'We won!'"

The crowd took several moments to absorb that news, then broke out into cheers and backslapping.

Alix yelled for quiet again. When the demonstrators settled down, she concluded her speech by saying, "Now let's get back to work. We all have families to support."

Alix Cyr jumped off the keg and forced her way to the back of the crowd. Still carrying the flag of Dun Hythe, she marched off towards the furniture factory.

CHAPTER TWENTY

MacDrakin held Higginbottom's hand. They stood on the lip of the excavation on his land. The place where his house once stood was at least a hundred feet above his head. His three mining tunnels were dirt-filled scars high up the side of the mountain. The woods alongside the path had been knocked down to make room for the mining detritus and the dirt piles exceed ten feet in places. A few branches stuck out in scattered places.

It was afternoon on the day following the battle for Skensfirth.

"I'm so sorry, MacDrakin." Higginbottom squeezed his hand and started to smile, but ended up wincing from the scab on her cut lip. "Can you ever mine those tunnels again?" The swelling around her left eye had subsided, but the skin around it was an ugly green-black.

"It'll take an enormous amount of work to construct steps up to them. They'll have to be carved into the side of the mountain. Even after that's done, the tunnels would still have to be dug out." He sighed. "I'm through with gem mining. It's a pretty boring job. And a very lonely one."

Higginbottom shook her head. "So your land is worthless. What a shame."

"That's not true." He grinned at her. "The squids did me a big favor."

"What are you talking about?"

"The black stuff." MacDrakin pointed down into the pit. Except where piles of dirt sat, the entire bottom was black.

"It's all coal. The Dun Hythe politicians are worried about pollution, well coal burns cleaner than the peat they use now, and I've got this huge coal field. This will be a lot easier than mining emeralds. At least you can stand up down there. I had to squat to work in the tunnels."

"Can you make as much money from the coal as you did from the emeralds?"

"Coal is usually hard to dig out and that makes it expensive. My deposit is easy to mine and so it will be cheap. A lot cheaper then importing peat. I have to go to Dun Hythe to sell my emeralds. While I'm there, I'll meet with Boudreau and Rodrigs. They owe me a favor or two. I'll ask them to award me a contract to deliver coal for all the trains. The contract will be worth a ton of money. "

Higginbottom's eye brows arched. "You can't do that all by yourself."

"I'll have to hire miners, maybe a half-dozen or so to start. I'll need more later on. Good thing there's plenty of unemployed dwarfs in Skensfirth."

"You have to build a shower, too." Higginbottom smirked at him. "I don't want you coming home all covered with black dust."

MacDrakin's heart skipped a beat. "Is that the offer I think it is?"

"I have no idea what you're talking about." She looked down at the coal field with a smile on her face. "I just made a statement that you may want to keep in mind for future reference."

MacDrakin weaved a hand through his beard. "Marry me and I'll build a shower here." He gave her a lewd wink.

"And if I say, 'no'?"

"I'll spend the rest of my life covered in coal dust."

"In that case, I better say,'yes'. All right, I'll marry you. I'll even help you build a shower."

MacDrakin bounced on his toes. His dice roll had come up with a winning number.

EPILOGUE

Yunta couldn't sit in her command lounge when the *Black Carrion Flower* left orbit. In such a murderous rage, she knew she would slaughter one or more of the crew if they made the slightest comment to her. Instead, she locked herself in her cabin to protect them.

This latest outrage perpetrated by the natives killed off her dream of becoming a fleet admiral. She'd be lucky if the corporation let her command a garbage scow. Her only hope lay in concocting a creditable story about the natives. Perhaps Shtap, once his head re-grew, would give her more insights into the surprising and devastating attack on the mining expedition. She had Drek's report, and while she had no reason to doubt his account, she wanted to hear what the field commander had to say. Who knew the natives could build linkages like zaftan shamans?

She had ordered the engineering section to prepare a documentary about the robot attacks using the video the robots uploaded. She planned to edit the videos to enhance the dangerous planetary conditions and emphasize her heroic efforts to make a profit despite the treacherous natives.

It was a long shot, she knew, but several factors would influence her survival. First, Shtap would have to take the majority of the blame. After all, he had been duped by the untrustworthy natives. It was a bit of a shame; she really did like him. Next, she would recommend a citation for Drek, the only one of her crew who accomplished anything on the surface. His rescue of the machines on the mountain and extracting the minerals despite the hostile natives would demonstrate the unusually harsh conditions on the planet.

A sudden idea came to her. She slithered around the cabin while she worked through the details and the dangers. Finally, she realized it represented her best -- and possibly her only -- hope for a promotion. Acting as a hero rather than a failure, she would trumpet the voyage as a testament to the courage and the resolve of the crew and officers under her leadership. She would boldly insist the corporation set up a new policy; never again would it attempt to mine a planet with intelligent life forms until the natives had been conquered and pacified. Instead of blaming Shtap, she would demand citations for bravery for Shtap, Drek and Mivex. Her report would state that their heroism was due to her inspiring leadership. She thought about demanding promotions for them also, but rejected that as too extreme

After more slithering and thinking, she decided this audacious approach could work.

She shifted her mind to another subjected. The yearly gathering of her clan would occur shortly after she returned. The meetings celebrated all treacherous doings since the last meeting. She would tell the family of her ordeals and the insults the natives had subjected her to. She would get the clan to take an oath that someday, one of them, even if it had to be a distant descendent, would avenge her.

ABOUT THE AUTHOR:

Award-winning author Hank Quense lives in Bergen-
field, NJ with his wife Pat. They have two daughters and
five grandchildren. He writes humorous fantasy and scifi
stories. On occasion, he also writes an article on fiction writing or book marketing but says that writing nonfiction is like
work while writing fiction is fun. He refuses to write serious
genre fiction saying there is enough of that on the front page
of any daily newspaper and on the evening TV news.

Hank's previous works include *Tales From Gundarland*,
a collection of fantasy stories. Readers Favorite awarded the
book a medal and EPIC designated it a finalist in its 2011
competition. His *Fool's Gold* is a retelling of the ancient
Rhinegold myth and *Tunnel Vision* is a collection of twenty
previously published short stories. *Build a Better Story* is a
book of advice for fiction writers. *Tales for the Troops* is a
collection of short stories that he makes available to our military without charge.

Altogether, Hank has over forty published short stories
and a number of non-fiction articles.

He is presently working on a novella combining the
plots and characters from Shakespeare's *Hamlet* and *Othello*
with the character Falstaff thrown in for good measure. He
is also working on a follow-up novel to *Zaftan Entrepreneurs* called *Zaftan Miscreants*. Look for it in early 2012.

Links? You want links? Here you go!

My main website is: http://hankquense.com
My blog is located at:
http://strangeworldsonlin.com/blog Here you can follow my
antics, rants and an occasional snippet of wisdom.
I'm on Twitter: http://twitter.com/hanque99
I'm on facebook: My fan pages are here:
http://www.facebook.com/pages/Hank-Quenses-Fiction-
Writing-Page/102293491907#!/pages/Hank-Quenses-
Fiction-Writing-Page/102293491907?v=wall

OTHER WORKS BY HANK QUENSE

Build a Better Story
Tales From Gundarland
Zaftan Miscreants
Brunnhilde's Quest
Mini-Collection
10 Great Fantasy Short Stories

ZAFTAN ENTREPRENEURS READING GROUP GUIDE

1: How do you think Zaftans have sex? Why do you think that? Have you discussed these fantasies with your shrink?

2: Do you think the Defense Minister and the Secretary of the Interior are secretly in love? What can you provide as evidence? Will they be happy?

3: Do you think toe hair is sexy? Do you have toe hair? Do you want toe hair?

4: Why doesn't MacDrakin get a new weapon to replace his old ax? Is he cheap? Is he behind on the technological curve? Is he one of those defenders of the status quo? Justify each of your answers.

5: Did the Zaftan mining mission deserve to fail because of its timid approach. What could the Zaftans have done to be more aggressive?

6: Do you think there is a future for warrior-wizard units? Is the Pentagon researching this possibility? How do you know they are or aren't? Do you think this is a wise use of our tax money?

7: Does Skensfirth need more constables. Who will pay for the increased salaries?

8: Do you think Webley would make a good ambassador to Zaftan 31B? Will he able to negotiate with the despicable aliens? Will Webley's odd way of thinking disorient the Zaftan's? Will they retaliate?

9: Does Congress have wizard-politicians? Can that explain Congressional stupidity?

10: What will happen to property values if a zaftan moved into your neighbor? Provide a detailed economic analysis to support your position.

11: Do you think Yunta's clan will follow up on her demand for revenge? Share any insider information you have on this issue

Continuing the adventures of the gundies
and the zaftans:

ZAFTAN MISCREANTS
Book Two of the Zaftan Trilogy

PROLOGUE

(250 years after the conclusion of Zaftan Entrepreneurs)
The battle cruiser and fleet flagship, *Red Death*, hung
motionless in space just under a third of a parsec from Ceti
Taul. The rest of the zaftan attack force deployed in battle
formation around it. All the ships had a cylindrical shape
with a blunt nose. Weapon and engine pods broke the otherwise smooth outer surface. Seen from a distance, the fleet
formation resembled a skeletal diamond.

In the *Red Death's* flight deck, the squid-like Commodore Gongeblazn lounged on his couch and looked for
something or someone to annoy him. Happy only when he
had something to carp about, he was annoyed that nothing
annoyed him. Like all noble-born zaftans, Gongeblazn stood
over seven feet tall and weighted more than four hundred
pounds; his bulk overcrowded the small flight deck. Atop
his small round head with its cruel beak-like mouth, a pair of
two-inch-long eye stalks ended in his eyes, black with red irises. His gray-black skin oozed green slime. One of his
eight tentacles held a gold-emblazoned lash, its leather
thongs tipped with metal. The lash symbolized his high rank

as did the gold-and-diamond-encrusted medallion hanging
from a gold chain around his neck

Two other zaftans, the navigational shaman and the engineer, lounged in front of control consoles while Captain
Fleigel sat to his right. The captain, a female, was shorter
and lighter than Gongeblazn.

Gongeblazn lifted a tentacle and fondled the medallion.
It signified that he was a fleet commander. He led the
strongest fleet ever to venture this close to Gundarland-con-
trolled space.

He rotated an eye stalk to peer at the navigator who
squirmed slightly. "Gevelt! You are back. Report!"

Gevelt remained immobile.

"Memzer!" Gongeblazon said to the engineer. "Wake up
Gevelt. Give him a shove."

Gevelt almost fell off his couch from the shove. He recovered and his eyestalks swept the area seeking danger.
They alighted on Gongeblazn. "Greetings, Commodore."

"How dare you return from your scouting mission and
not report to me."

"My journey was far and difficult. After I returned, I
paused to compose my report to you and fatigue overcame
me."

"You lie. Someday, I will catch you in a lie and then
your miserable life will be forfeited. What did you find
out?"

"I found no evidence of the Gundarlandian fleet. All I
saw was our magnificent frigates wreaking havoc on their
colonies."

"This is true, Commodore," Captain Fleigel said. "We
just received a new report from the frigate squadron. They

have destroyed almost every trading vessel within a half-parsec. Now they attack the colony bases."

"Why has this not brought out the Gundarlandian fleet, hmm? I do not like this." Gongeblazn's eyes swept the flight deck. "Where is my aide?"

"I am here, Commodore." A six-foot-tall zaftan ranker slithered across the deck and stood near Gongeblazn. "How may I serve you?"

"By standing still." Gongeblazn lashed the aide's torso with a vicious stroke of his whip.

The aide's skin quivered under the blow. Slime splattered the immediate area. "Thank you, Commodore. May I have another?"

"Fleigel!" Gongeblazn roared. "Get this carrion out of my presence. Take a note. Never allow him to be my aide again. Throw him in the brig. Or overboard. Then get me a new aide."

"Please instruct me." Fleigel cowered on her couch. "What has he done wrong?"

"He likes getting whipped. How can I enjoy his suffering when he likes it?"

"I will get you an aide who will howl in pain at the sight of your lash."

"Make it so. Now where are the Gundarlandian ships? How can I destroy them if I can't find them? Engineer! Send a message to the frigate squadron. I order them to move deeper into Gundarland's space. They must be more aggressive. They are to attack more colonies and shipping routes."

He had heard the rumors that the High Command contemplated a surprise attack on Gundarlandian systems. He knew they would want his assessment of the strength and aggressiveness of the enemy. His intelligence information would be vital in developing the attack strategy. Therefore, he had to find an enemy fleet and fight it.